RIMROCK

written and illustrated by
Peter Sandel

THE ILLUMINATION STONE

RIMROCK

written and illustrated by
PETER SANDEL

ISBN: 979-8-9855192-0-4 (e-book)

ISBN: 979-8-9855192-1-1 (paperback)

This series of books is dedicated to my mother, Lois. She is a lover of books and reading, as well as a talented actor and a gentle soul. She read the classics to me when I was very young and has provided me with unconditional love my entire life.

THE RIMROCK CANYON

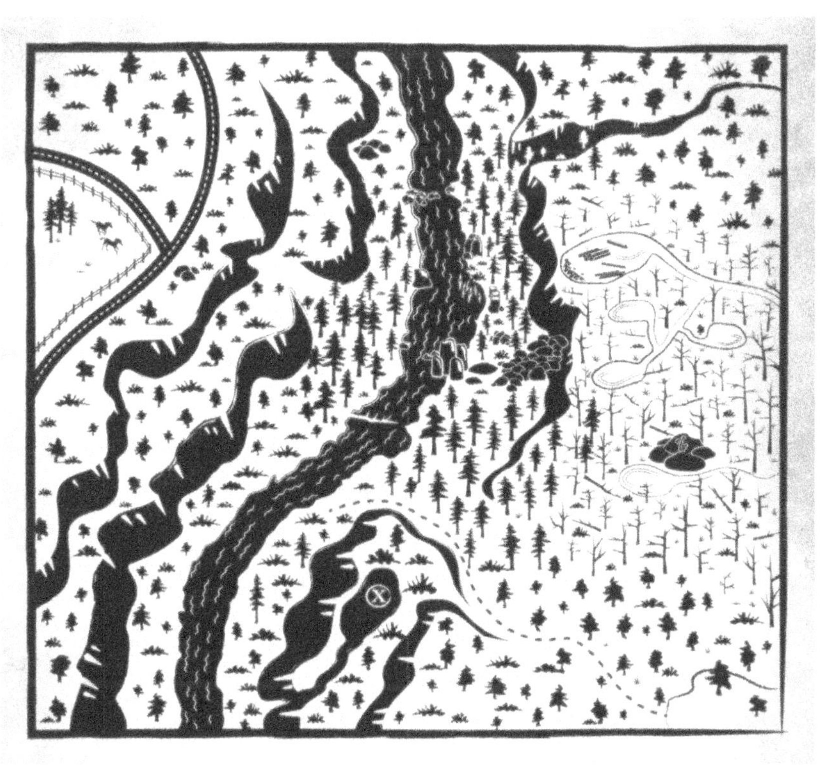

AUTHOR'S NOTE

In this first book of the trilogy, The Illumination Stone, you meet Teek, a brave young ground squirrel and leader of a small band of friends from the village of Rimrock, that go on a perilous mission to recover their stolen Illumination Stone, the talisman of colony culture, and the source of the colony's historical stories. With the help of a human named Walter Prudy, his granddaughter Sofia, and a raven named Kanti, they learn the secrets behind their origin.

Who are *you* on the inside? You may find out as you read The Rimrock Trilogy.

I hope you enjoy book 1.

– Peter

1

A NEW WORLD

The family station wagon wound its way up the narrow road. Its tires ground into the red lava asphalt as it spiraled precariously up to the top of an old volcanic cinder cone, one of many that dotted the landscape. Young Walter, positioned next to the right back-seat window, clenched the vinyl of the seat in front of him where his mother sat, watching her nervously stepping on imaginary brakes.

From Walter's unfortunate vantage point, it had quickly become apparent that the outside edge of the road had no guardrail and a very narrow shoulder. Thus, there was little room for error. The sheer drop-off presented the vast panoramic view—an ancient lava field stretching for miles, that had flowed from the very cinder cone that they were ascending.

He peered through the car window down to the outer edge of the road and beyond, his eyes wide with fright. It looked as though the car was perilously close to catching a tire on the shoulder, which would cause them to fall hundreds of feet and smash onto the blackened jagged landscape below. Miles of desolation stretched out from the base of the steep slope into the distance.

He shut his eyes, hoping that the terrifying drive to the top would soon be over. The car sped around the curves, and yet no one was being thrown to one side or the other as the entire extended family, including mother's parents from Pasadena, had squeezed together on the bench seats to share in what now appeared to be a high-risk adventure.

Walter was the youngest of three children. His brother, Bill, was the eldest, and Liz, his sister, was the middle child. Liz had the good fortune of being seated next to the left rear window, the uphill position. Although still alarmed, she was spared the view of the perilous steep drop-off.

Rounding another bend, the station wagon passed a car coming down the narrow road, causing the car to swerve even closer to the edge. In a rare moment of unity, the entire family shared a collective gasp. Everyone, that is, except the WWII hero, who was busy piloting the intrepid craft.

The colonel, Walter's father, had found just the right place to retire from the Air Force and raise children. He wanted to do what he felt was best for everyone, and so he and his wife, Ellen, had chosen clean and pristine Central Oregon as a place to start fresh. That morning, they had made sure everyone was up early, bathed, and properly attired for a special family outing. The colonel was proud of the location he had selected and was hoping for an enthusiastic endorsement from the entire family.

In honor of the visit from Ellen's parents, the colonel had decided that it would be a good day to explore one of the local tourist attractions, an interpretive center atop a well-known cinder cone.

The term "cinder cone" was used to refer to the many volcanic buttes in the surrounding area. They were remnants of small volcanoes that, in eons past, had exploded quite violently, blasting out massive amounts of lava, covering many square miles.

An old lookout structure stood at the summit, positioned to one side of the crater. It had been transformed into a natural history exhibit, complete with a full-time docent—a friendly, well-regarded older gentleman.

He was a retired columnist from the local newspaper and an author who had written a book about the area. He knew everything about everybody, and everybody knew about him. He looked somewhat official in his ranger shirt and badge, yet he donned a rather casual straw hat.

He had been expecting them. Treating the colonel like a VIP, he showed great pride in reciting his presentation, ushering the attentive family from one glass-encased diorama to another. Each presentation featured an indigenous animal, stuffed, and positioned in its final action pose. The last diorama contained a depiction of one of the most abundant of the local wild creatures, the Golden Mantled Ground Squirrel.

The docent's intention was to finish his presentation with a little humor, and so he added, "These little varmints can still be found running around everywhere."

The colonel and his family, having listened patiently and politely and having proceeded obediently through the displays, thanked him as genuinely as they could and headed for the exit.

As the family filed out of the interpretive center, the colonel noticed, to his displeasure, that his youngest son, Walter, had not been in attendance for the tour. Proceeding down the wooden stairs back to the parking lot, he thought– *For gosh sakes, can't that boy ever do what he's told?*

Walter had been enjoying his time outside seated on a lava stone wall overlooking the crater. His attention had been focused on a group of very alive and quite bold ground squirrels.

It was a beautifully bright and clear autumn morning. He felt the sun and the cool breeze on his face. He closed his eyes and breathed in the fragrance of the crisp mountain air.

Surely there must be nothing sweeter in the whole world, he thought.

He was intent on gaining the trust of the small reddish-brown critters as they darted around him. He fed them by hand with a few pine nuts that he had pulled from a cone and stuffed in his pocket.

The squirrels seemed to sense his gentle nature and his fondness for them. They sat up attentively, ready to scramble for each pine nut tossed their way.

Walter had just dropped his last pine nut in front of a particularly bold squirrel when suddenly he noticed that it had frozen still and was staring up at him with purposeful intent. As the squirrel's eyes locked onto his, Walter became transfixed.

He began to feel rather peculiar, as though some other presence had entered his mind. He had the distinct impression that he was being visited. His perception of the surroundings seemed to be expanding, as though a veil was being lifted or clouds were parting.

The squirrel stare-down continued. The rodent's deep liquid-black eyes were transfixed, studying him unblinkingly.

It was quite clear to Walter that he wasn't just being stared at—he was being altered. He was hearing, smelling, and seeing things he had not been aware of before. This was an altogether new form of communication, decidedly different than anything to which he had been accustomed.

Now as it happened, Walter was not the only family member at the lava wall. Behind him stood the original source of independent thinking in the family. Behind him was his grandmother.

"No… you can't bring him home," she chuckled.

Walter turned around to reply, but he found that she had already redirected her attention and her mood had shifted.

Examining the crater carefully, she studied the clear and vivid evidence of the volcano's blast zone, as though the event had recently happened. Then turning to look out over the landscape, she scanned the miles of lava surrounding the butte.

Walter observed the passing thoughts cross her face.

She peered out over the miles of black lava that had flowed across the land many thousands of years before. After all that time, only a few scattered ponderosa pines had managed to gain a foothold in an otherwise desolate landscape.

Her eyes returned to the crater. Shaking her head, she spoke to her grandson now squinting up at her with a face lit like porcelain in the bright sun.

"It looks like it's going to blow up any minute," she commented.

Young Walter's eyes widened as he began to ponder that possibility, and he thought, *it did look like it might all have just happened yesterday!*

In the actual context of geologic time, this event *had* only just happened yesterday. This was an ominous thought for a young boy in a strange country. There would be many more wondrous things to discover in this land, where history seemed to have stood still.

Recalling his strange encounter with the squirrel, he looked back down to where the squirrel had positioned itself, but it was no longer anywhere to be seen.

2

A RECONNECTION

Many years later, Walter S. Prudy was accomplished and hardworking. He had spent most of his life studying and practicing the law—more precisely, *employment law.*

His practice, he would tell himself and others, was the best way to make a comfortable living while helping other people.

He took his career and his responsibilities seriously. He was devoted, always punctual, well-groomed, and prepared to make a good impression. After all, it was his hallmark.

Walter had met and married Elisabeth Abbot while they were both still in college. Together they produced a child. They named her Helen. From the beginning and all through the years of their marriage, Walter's singular focus was his career. Given the choice between work and family, he continually marched down the pathway toward his next great achievement with relentless determination.

"If I just attend one more meeting or make one more phone call," he would tell himself, "Then I can pay more attention to Elisabeth and Helen."

But on he went as time went by.

He never seemed able to fit them into his busy schedule. Attention to his business consumed his time; evenings and weekends were no exception.

Then on one very disruptive and most inconvenient day, Elisabeth left him, taking with her their daughter, Helen, and headed east over the Cascades to live with her mother.

Walter was shocked. He felt most betrayed and extremely put out. It would take years for him to find peace with Elisabeth's decision to leave him. He just couldn't understand how some husbands made it all look so easy.

Did Elisabeth simply lack the character and temperament to make it all work?

Walter buried these frustrations deep down inside for many years. It seemed to him that whenever he tried to address these issues, it would only create more distance between himself and his family.

And so, Walter spent most of his life alone, married to his work, solely devoted to making himself and his practice successful.

Ultimately, life for Walter became complicated in ways he could not have imagined when he was a young boy.

Now, as he neared retirement, he began to wonder if he might possibly have chosen the wrong career, feeling less and less interested in the objectives that for so long had seemed important to him.

He realized that these values weren't who he really was, causing him to call into question the very principles that had guided him throughout his life. Walter became much less consumed with the success of his business and the practice of law, turning instead to those interests that he remembered as being important when he was young.

He found himself daydreaming about his childhood and of a time when he cared about other things—more beautiful things, the wonders of nature. They meant more to him then. He had found great joy in the small and delicate details of the plants and animals around him.

He thought back to a time when the beauty and purity of the natural world were the most important aspects of his life. Walter started to notice that he was once again hearing a quieter voice calling to him from the back of his mind—a voice that had whispered to him oh so quietly throughout his life, a voice that he had drowned out with the noise of ambition.

He was now elderly, somewhat thin and frail in frame. The years of working long hours had taken a toll, but those long years had also made him quite successful.

Walter's daughter, Helen, had spent most of her childhood quietly longing for a relationship with him; it was a time when she sought his approval.

But her mother, Elisabeth, went out of her way to keep Walter at a distance. She never accepted a gift, nor any financial support for herself or Helen. Eventually Helen had grown up without the benefit of her father's love and support.

The day eventually arrived when Helen thought she had found love, and so she married. Her marriage didn't last long, but it was long enough for them to have a daughter.

Helen named her Sofia. Sofia would spend most of her young life with her mother and grandmother in a small house in Redmond, Oregon.

Once Helen had managed to achieve some stability, she and Sofia moved into their own home, not far from her mother's. Helen now felt that it was a good time to place a long overdue phone call to her father, Walter.

And so, one late summer Sunday evening, Walter answered the phone to find Helen on the other end. This was a very welcome surprise and a moment for which he had hoped. The lines of communication were beginning to open, providing the chance to rekindle their overdue relationship.

"Why haven't you called? We never hear from you," Helen began.

She already knew the reasons why, yet those were the only words that she could think to say to him.

"Funny you should ask," he mused fondly. "I've been doing a lot of thinking about how to change that."

"Oh? What do you mean?" she managed to ask in an unassuming manner.

"Well, I think that it is about time I retired. And so..." There was a pause.

"Yes, what else?" she replied, breaking the silence.

"Well... what would you think about me moving closer to you and Sofia?"

There was more silence as Helen tried to hold back the emotion in her voice.

"Really, Dad? Move over here? Is that what you want?" She revealed her excitement.

"It is. In fact, I think this move is *way* overdue, don't you? And I also think that it's high time that I get to know my granddaughter. I thought I'd take a few days off and head over your way... Maybe next week... You know, to look around. Summer is almost over, and if I don't head over now, well, I might have to wait until spring, and that's just too long."

Walter waited patiently for Helen's next words. "Are you... All right?" she finally asked.

Because of the suddenness of his announcement, her suspicion was that her father may know something about his health that he wasn't telling her.

"I'm doing just fine. Look, I know this sounds sudden, but I've been doing a lot of thinking. I miss you. I think I should be closer."

"I... we miss you too, Dad," she replied.

There was more silence.

"I'd stay in a hotel, of course."

"Oh no, Dad, you're welcome to..." she began.

"No, no, it would be easier for you this way, and it'd be fun for me," he said. "It'd give me a place to sort of stay out of the way... You know how I kind of like that."

"Well, I know Sofia will be just thrilled, of course."

"I'm looking very much forward to seeing you too," he answered, translating her message. "It'll be really good to see both of you."

"Okay, Dad, I'll tell Sofia that you're coming," Helen added. "Look, I want the two of you to be able to spend as much time together as you want."

For Walter, the arrival of Sofia into the world, although some distance away from Portland, was a mysteriously powerful force reaching across miles of mountains, hillsides, fields, and towns to grab a hold of him and call to him. Their reunion would have a major impact in both of their lives.

From the beginning of her life, Sofia was one of those miraculous children born knowing exactly what she thought and wasting no time making that clear to her family.

It seemed somehow that she had been there before and was quite ready and well equipped to get on with doing whatever it was that she wanted to do. She was of strong mind and had equally strong opinions.

Sofia reminded her mother Helen very much of someone else in their family, someone who, at one time long ago, had meant so much to her—her father, Walter Prudy.

Walter was now aware that his granddaughter was roughly of the same age that he had been when he had spent most of his time immersed in the wonders of nature. He most certainly did not want her to miss that precious connection, so he thought of ways to reach out to her.

He wondered how little he knew about her, and if they would have anything in common. He would discover very soon that he was now the grandfather of a very special person.

⁂

The day arrived that found Walter making his way over the mountains toward his new life. He had decided to arrive a day early and alerted Helen and Sofia of his departure and destination—the canyon.

It was late morning and crispy cold in the high desert. Walter stood at the top of the rimrock near the edge of the cliff, gazing fondly at the glimmering ribbon of the Deschutes River far below, listening to its distant roar.

He was exhilarated by the vista that now stretched out before him.

It filled his senses and punctuated his life-changing decision. The canyon was a sharp contrast to the city from which he had just traveled, and yet it felt familiar.

He was outfitted for hiking, although to anyone else, he might have appeared overdressed, clad in apparel he had purchased from a proper gentleman's sport clothing purveyor.

Representing the finest traditions of quality, befitting the discriminating country sportsman—these were clothes of uncompromising standards, workmanship, and detail. They had hung neatly in a closet for many years, a purchase that represented one of those moments long ago, when Walter had somehow misinterpreted that quiet, natural voice that beckoned him from field, woodland, and stream.

There he stood prepared for the occasion, like a statue honoring a time gone by, when people dressed simply for the privilege of traveling. He wore a wool olive-green fedora, pleated wool pants, and a pressed cotton shirt with a tailored hunting jacket. His hiking boots, although lightweight, waterproof and stable, reflected a style born of traditional sensibilities and quality.

It felt good to once again have occasion to wear clothing crafted for a gentlemanly adventure. He felt quite comfortable in them. Still, something far more primal stirred deep at the center of his heart.

As he stopped to rediscover his favorite place on earth, he was being given a chance to rediscover his own true nature.

Behind him stretched a landscape of juniper and sage. Further than that were farmlands, roads, and once small quiet towns now bustling with new activity. Far beyond that lay a noisy bustling city and the life he was leaving. But the world that lay before him, cradled by the canyon walls, was quiet and serene.

As he stood, his mind drifted back to the time of his boyhood and to his carefree days spent exploring the banks of the river. His lifelong pursuit of success had taken him everywhere except back to this special place that had meant so much to him when he was young. It was a land that time had forgotten. Over the eons, the river had cut a deep canyon through a dry, semi-arid plateau on its journey northward.

As Walter navigated his descent, he stopped to glance back up toward the cliffs. He had known of this old path his entire life and was relieved to see that the trailhead had been turned into a public access point and not someone's private property. This location had always been one of the few places to descend into this tranquil strip of lush cool vegetation along the river.

Hardened by a summer of foot traffic, the trail's dry volcanic soil crunched under Walter's boots. He could feel his heart pound with excitement as he headed to a place as familiar to him as an old friend, to a place and time he had known when days were filled with wonder and adventure. The rimrock towered above him like the massive walls of some ancient megalithic city.

As he drew nearer to this place that he had experienced as a child, he thought he noticed an energy course through his body. Or was it simply excitement?

No!

He was certain. It was more than excitement. He felt as though he might be a little lighter on his feet, maybe even have a spring in his step.

Walter had always been a careful man. In fact, there were times when he was overly cautious. Today, however, he hadn't prepared his aging knees and ankles for the steep hike down into the canyon.

Quickly turning his attention back to navigation, he remembered the importance of placing his steps carefully.

I'd better stay focused on this trail, he thought, *or I'll end up at the bottom faster than I'd planned.*

The slope was steeper than he remembered and quite perilous. As Walter continued his descent, he felt as though time were receding with every step. He also realized that both he and the world were many years older.

The *ratchety–ratchet* call of a Kingfisher flying swiftly by the bank, searching for minnows, drew his attention away from the trail as it wove its way through the alder, willow, and cottonwood that hung over the water.

The river swirled under thickly clumped long-bladed grasses, shadowing undercut banks and dark subterranean hiding places. On the opposite bank of the river, willows and cattails bordered a meadow.

He sighed.

I have about as much chance of swimming across that current and reaching the meadow on the other side as I do in changing who I am now, he thought. *Then again, it might be worth a try.*

Thinking back on his life, he was reminded of all the hard lessons he had learned along the way, lessons that had made him exactly the kind of person he had become. And that, for now, was all right.

Stopping for a moment, he stood with his hands on his hips, breathing in the crisp mountain air. The scent filled his mind with memories.

He thought of fall in Oregon—was reminded of how it was always crispy cool in the shade and toasty warm in the sun. The chilly breeze whispered through the canyon walls and brushed his face. It was a pure, freshly scrubbed breeze that had stirred to life at the top of alpine fields of snow, remaining untouched by the exhaust of the world.

It swept through ponderosa and juniper forests and finally through meadows filled with sweet sage and grasses. It flowed like the river itself, through the canyon, delivering a familiar flavor, a flavor found nowhere else on earth.

Breathing it in was nourishing to him.

This air has calories, he thought.

The fresh high desert air was sweet and spicy with a slight wisp of drift smoke from the summer's still smoldering range fires. He was home.

Vacation days were over, and school was back in session.

The canyon was quieter now.

Throughout the summer, the rimrock walls had echoed with the sound of dogs barking and swimmers yelling and splashing about—the boundless noise of youth's energy. Vacationing visitors had finally left, and the canyon was much quieter now, and far from the minds of humans. It was, however, the most important time of the year for the indigenous creatures.

And so, an entirely new flurry of activity had begun again, activity that was possibly not as noticeable in the grand scheme of things but just as vital. It was time to prepare for the biting cold of the long winter to come. All those furry little creatures that would soon retire to the comfort of their burrows were busy gathering nuts, seeds, berries, grasshoppers, and salmon flies to stuff into their larders.

Walter was now halfway down the steep descent into the canyon and was afforded a completely unobstructed view of the river, still far below.

He couldn't help but think about how, over hundreds of thousands of years, the river had tirelessly chosen the humblest path, patiently etching its way through the hard lava bedrock. It tumbled over gravelly shallows, rolled by boulders, and spilled into deep pools, stretching out into its distant hazy journey of miles and miles in either direction.

As Walter gazed down upon this hidden primeval world, it seemed that life itself was on hold. The vastness of the panorama was so overwhelming it made him dizzy.

Losing his balance, he slipped, and reeled around stepping on a loose rock and uneven ground. Scrambling for sure footing, he found none.

Panic overtook him, and fate hit him like a bolt of lightning. Fractions of seconds seemed to slow down. Spinning around and stumbling to keep his balance, he realized that he was going to fall.

Down he went, sliding and rolling from one rock to another. At one point, he felt that there might be a chance to regain control, only to lose his grip and continue sliding and rolling farther down the hill.

He was keenly conscious of every impact, every scrape, and every gouge. His mind raced, quickly assessing his condition.

He thought, *how could I have been so careless? This is not my backyard. This isn't a walk in the park. I wonder if I will even make it out of here alive.*

Continuing to slide, he searched for answers.

Walter rolled and bounced for fifty feet or more on what felt like sandpaper-covered concrete.

And then he, and his racing thoughts, ground to an abrupt halt. The hard impact on the sandy slope tore his clothing and scuffed his knees and elbows. His head thwacked against the base of a sizable boulder. He groaned as he felt the nausea of shock well up in him.

3

NATURAL HISTORY

S hadowy images clouded Walter's mind. As he lay motionless on the rocky soil, the world around him began to change.

He held his head, wondering if the impact had altered his perception. Looking around, he noticed that his surroundings were now cast in a blurry silvery haze.

Was he conscious? Shadows began to slide quickly across the ground as if time itself were rapidly changing. Although Walter lay near the bottom of the canyon, he was also keenly aware of the entire surrounding countryside.

In this apparent altered state, he perceived the smallest detail, the smallest rock, as if it were as vast, as majestic, and as full of wonder as a grand vista or a massive mountain range. One was just as significant as the other.

How strange, he thought, trying to clear his head, *And yet, how completely natural.*

Time and distance now appeared immaterial.

Then from underneath the crust of the earth, there began a low rumbling sound—as much a vibration as a sound. It slowly built to a grinding and crackling roar.

The ground crumbled around him as the earth began to buckle and heave. Strangely, from where he lay, Walter didn't perceive himself to be in any danger, nor was he the least bit fearful.

He became aware as his surroundings began to spin and he lost all sense of direction. He found himself floating above the transforming landscape, peering down on the undulating earth below, struggling to comprehend what he now beheld.

It seemed to Walter as though he could "see" for millions of years. Geologic events simultaneously unfolded before him, and yet each event remained clearly distinguishable from the other. Colossal volcanic eruptions all along an expansive plateau stretched out for hundreds of miles; on a scale so vast and violent, it appeared that all the earth was exploding.

Could it be? he wondered. *It must be! The formation of the Cascade mountains!*

Walter called out the names of each peak he knew so well as they burst from the earth. Toward the west, rearing up like the backbone of some terrible dragon, the Three Sisters Mountains were forming. With deafening explosions, Mount Jefferson pushed upward to tower over the landscape, while Mount Hood lit the horizon with a hot fiery glow! Other volcanos reared up and then crumpled and fell beneath the remaining Cascade mountains.

"They *are* volcanoes! They are forming right before my eyes!"

The world around Walter churned and rolled violently. Immense eruptions producing millions of cubic tons of ash and lava poured over the land for hundreds of miles, elevating a high plain, ultimately creating the largest flow of volcanic basalt the world had ever seen.

Gases escaping from fumarole vents burst up everywhere. The bombardment of debris expelled from the Cascade volcano eruptions continued. A deep deposit of hot ash and raining rocks piled up along the western border of what now appeared to be a very young river.

The massive volcanic peaks made up of porous volcanic material allowed melting snow and rainwater to seep deep into the ground, finding its way back to the surface at lower elevations.

"I had heard how water percolates out from the base of the Cascades. Now I know it!"

The young river began to flow in a northerly direction. The river continued to swell while more lava flows pushed at its edge. All around, the land bubbled with volcanoes.

One of the eruptions began sending lava toward the newly-formed river flowing over its channel, creating a dam one hundred feet high, forming a lake.

Filling quickly, the lake, in turn, overflowed the lava dam and began eroding the plateau, gouging out a deep canyon as it went, draining in large thundering waterfalls. Disrupted and redirected by the lava flows, sediment-laden streams poured into the young river, carrying its detritus northward.

From the south, one of the largest explosions the world has ever seen sent massive lava flows into the deep canyons, once again disrupting the flow of the young river.

Far to the northeast, a vast inland sea was being created by impounded glacial ice. The ice dam burst open, and catastrophic floods scoured thousands of square miles, digging out a gorge so deep that in some places the walls stood four thousand feet high.

Walter clapped his hands and laughed. His hiker's geology books had never quite described the magnitude of the Missoula Floods. He never fully understood the enormity of the event until now.

How much time had passed? Hundreds of thousands...? No. Millions of years?

The land continued to move like the waves of the ocean, folding into wrinkles that confined the young river, locking it into its northerly flow. The eruptions continued. Lava covered five hundred cubic miles with basalt in a single flow, filling tens of thousands of cubic miles. A single wall of lava, at least a mile wide and two miles high, looked as though it could span the entire earth.

"I never imagined that there was such upheaval on such a scale. But all this is as it should be! As one thing is created, it affects everything else! Oh, how I feel it to be true! And when something is destroyed, it has far-reaching effects as well."

He was in the middle of this revelation and wondering if he had always believed this or if the bump on his head was the cause of it all when, as suddenly as it had started in a whirl and a whoosh, everything abruptly stopped.

Had he been unconscious?

A few small rocks rolled down the slope, crackling and popping as they went. Everything fell silent.

The rumbling sounds were replaced by the whisper of a light breeze, brushing Walter's face once again. He was back. He heard the gurgling of the river and the occasional distant chirping of songbirds.

4

THE AWAKENING

Choking and coughing, Walter felt as though he might gag on his own tongue. It seemed twice its normal size. His throat was bone-dry.

"Am I alive?" he muttered to himself. "I must be alive."

He struggled to gather his thoughts. He was shivering, but at the same time, sweat poured down his face. He was suffering from shock. He lay in that spot for some length of time, motionless. Moving his head from one side to the other brought back his nausea.

Walter moved his eyes enough to notice that there was a sizeable rock situated where a headstone would be. His vision still blurred, Walter wiped his eyes with his sleeve, attempting to clear them. An ever-so-quiet *"cheep-cheep"* sound softly echoed above his head. At first, it seemed far off, but soon the cheeps sounded closer, sharper, and more pronounced.

He squinted his eyes toward the bright sky above. The fog in his head began to clear until he could just make out a small face, which had suddenly appeared and was now looking down at him from the top of the *headstone* rock. The face was upside down. Frozen, it stared at him with unblinking black eyes.

Walter choked as he struggled to swallow. In a gravelly voice, he managed to croak the words, "Well, hello."

He fully expected the little face to disappear back into its hiding place, but to Walter's surprise, it didn't. The small dark eyes darted first left, then right, and then returned to peer down at him. It chirped again, only this time, to Walter's shock and amazement, the squeak was... intelligible! He could understand it!

"Teek! I'm Teek!" it said.

Walter's eyes grew wide as he struggled to come to grips with what he had just heard. Reaching into his shirt pocket, he pulled out his handkerchief to wipe his face. Still squinting, he mumbled to himself, "Whew, I did *not* just hear that squirrel introduce himself... did I?"

Walter failed to understand at that moment was that he had just unwittingly uttered words that have limited human perception for thousands of years. You see, squirrels happen to know that the very reason humans had lost their ability to understand the language of their fellow creatures was simply because over thousands of years, they had spent their lives telling themselves that it wasn't possible, and so they had come to believe it. This had always puzzled the other creatures.

"Why would anyone do that to themselves?" they wondered.

The squirrel waited, peering intently down at Walter, and then began again. "Hello, can you hear me? I am Teek. Are you injured? What is your name?"

The only thing Walter could think to do was to reply. "Uh, my name is Walter Prudy."

The squirrel sat motionless and then shifted its weight in less than a blink. "Two names?" It asked.

The small creature chirped the question so quickly that Walter thought for a few moments before he realized what he had heard.

"Uh, yeah...first and last," Walter replied.

"Hmm, two names, one name and then another name..." the squirrel concluded.

"Last name," corrected Walter.

The squirrel paused and then spoke again. "Well, there must be an awful lot of you if you need two names."

Walter chuckled and then winced in pain. "Yes, you could say that. Okay, so you... uh, you're some kind of squirrel?"

"Not just that!" came a rather curt reply. "I am what you humans call a *Kuggwi*."

This was a word from the native tongue of the Paiute people and so, meant nothing to Walter.

The squirrel seemed to ponder for a moment and then added "Or, let me see... ground squirrel?"

"Ah, yes," replied Walter. "I remember now. So... so... how is it that you're able to... well, to speak to me?"

The squirrel looked around again quickly and replied, "We are always speaking. How are you only now able to understand us?"

Walter paused, questioning his grasp of the world around him and this new twist of logic. "Hmm, don't know... good point." He was quite amused at hearing such a valid point from a squirrel.

"So, Walter Prudy," began the squirrel again.

"Just Walter is fine," interjected Walter.

"Oh. So, Walter, are you hurt? Can you move?"

Walter, now slowly sitting up, replied, "Not sure. I know I bumped my head—no doubt the reason I'm talking to you."

The squirrel leveled his gaze at Walter and concluded, "Well, I think that all human heads should be jostled a bit."

"Ha! Probably true... ooh!" Walter winced and then continued, "Whoa! I guess I'm still a little shaky."

"You had better stay still for now. I hope you are not lame!" exclaimed the squirrel. "If you are unable to ditch, then you are in real danger! You might get eaten," the squirrel added.

"Ditch?" asked Walter.

"You know... hide," replied the squirrel.

"Oh well, I'm too old and tough to be eaten anyway. I'm not very appetizing!"

The young squirrel tipped his head with puzzlement.

No sooner had they finished discussing danger and the need to *ditch* when, in a blink, the squirrel was gone. Walter looked all around but saw nothing.

As he sat wondering where the squirrel was, or if he had perhaps imagined the whole thing, he noticed a shadow glide over the sandy soil. Gazing up toward the sky, shielding his eyes from the morning sun, he caught a glimpse of a beautiful red-tailed hawk soaring just above the edge of the rimrock. Soon it passed by and disappeared behind the cliff. Walter returned his gaze to the ground around him. He found that the squirrel had returned and was now standing near one of his hands.

"Koos," the squirrel repeated. "When they fly, we hide, or we die. We call him a Koosagh Diaub, which means *Sky Devil*. He is a predator that flies."

"Oh, you mean that hawk up there?" asked Walter.

"It is most dangerous," was all it would say.

What a life it must be for these creatures, to have to switch so quickly from having a conversation to scrambling for their very lives to hide from a predator, Walter thought.

"You must need water. I can bring you some from the river," offered the squirrel.

"I can't drink river water," said Walter.

The squirrel stopped and stared, confused once again. "Why not?"

"Oh, among other things, Giardia," Walter replied.

"What is that?" inquired the squirrel.

"A parasite," Walter answered.

"A what?" the squirrel asked.

Walter stared down at the squirrel for a few moments. He was still reeling, possibly still in shock, and so he simply let the subject drop.

"You're right, I should drink water," he concluded.

"Then I shall return with it!" the squirrel declared, as he hopped over several large boulders, disappearing so quickly that Walter found it rather humorous.

As Teek bounded away, he called back in a high-pitched squeak, "If something happens, call out my name... Teek! Teek is my name!

"Teek!" Walter repeated to himself as he lay back down. "Okay, so I've been formally introduced to a ground squirrel! Great. Terrific. I've lost my marbles."

5

TEEK

Walter awoke. It appeared to be late morning. He could only assume that it was the same day. He opened his eyes to find himself surrounded. On every boulder and nearby ledge now sat a golden-mantled ground squirrel.

What appeared to him to be the entire local population of ground squirrels had gathered to see him. Some of them, farther away, were scurrying from boulder to boulder. But most of the attention appeared to be focused directly on Walter. Every few seconds one of them would turn to another, as if to share new information about their observations.

As Walter began to come to grips with the world around him, he noticed that he could understand an occasional word among the collective cheeps and peeps. At about the time that he had nearly convinced himself that his conversation with the squirrel had been the result of the bump on his head, he noticed the name *Teek* being bantered about.

"Everyone is anxious to experience what it is like to speak with a human, and they want to see if you are anything like the first human who came to us," said the squirrel named Teek.

Walter had just fallen in from a world that he felt had made some sort of sense to him most of the time. Now he found himself in a world in which he had more questions than answers.

"What do you mean? What other human?"

Teek did not answer; his attention was now directed toward the large number of squirrels that had gathered.

"All right, everyone, you are all going to have to stay hidden until we know that the Koos has finished hunting. The human will still be here, at least for a while," he called out.

Walter noticed that upon hearing Teek's words, everyone scurried away.

"A hawk?" asked Walter.

The squirrel was about to speak when his gaze was once again redirected, this time toward the river. Walter followed the squirrel's attention to the riverbank, and there, to his surprise, was a large river otter, soaking wet, right out of the water.

In the otter's mouth was the strap attached to Walter's small canteen of drinking water. The otter dropped the canteen and quickly slipped back down the hill into the water before Walter could utter a word.

"Well, look at that...," the squirrel exclaimed. "It looks like this object kept rolling down the hill. Our energetic friend, Fisk, found it and has brought it to you. He is a bit too much, that Fisk, but he is a nice, well-intentioned fellow. Most otters are. This *is* yours, yes?" asked the squirrel.

Walter replied by grabbing the strap of his canteen, unscrewing the cap, lifting it to his mouth, and gulping down what seemed to the squirrel to be enough water to drown in.

Half of the contents of the canteen spilled over Walter's mouth and down his front. The squirrel stood, mouth agape, in amazement. Walter then wiped his mouth with his sleeve and addressed the squirrel, "You must be some sort of an alpha male."

"A what?" the squirrel asked.

"A leader," explained Walter.

"Hardly," the squirrel replied.

Walter watched and took note, then added, "They all seem to do what you tell them. But you are sort of a young squirrel for that, aren't you?"

The squirrel thought for a moment and then said, "Yes. I guess you could say that. I am sort of, well, considered to be a bit... unusual."

Walter, still wondering how on earth it was that he understood what the squirrel was saying, looked over both shoulders to see if anybody was standing nearby observing him talk to himself.

Struggling to understand this new realm he found himself in, and the one he was used to, he became increasingly uncomfortable. Walter concluded that the most prudent thing to do would be to handle the situation in much the same way he had when encountering homeless people on the street.

"You know, this is all very interesting, but I'm just not sure what you need from me or what has happened. Perhaps..."

"You fell, that is what happened!" Teek interrupted. "Now I need you to listen to me!"

"But I...," Walter began.

"Let me look into your eyes once more!" the squirrel interrupted again.

Without another word, Walter tipped his head down and stared directly into the unblinking eyes of the unmoving squirrel. He had forgotten just how deep squirrel's eyes were, liquid black and very penetrating.

Walter could feel the effects of the squirrel's trance-like gaze. He realized, without a doubt, that he was not just being looked at but somehow being scanned or investigated. After what seemed like quite a while, the squirrel finally blinked.

"You do appear to have been awakened," concluded the squirrel. "It must have been a long time ago, but I am certain that one of us did awaken you. Were you stared at by a ground squirrel, just like me, when you were quite young?"

"Well, I'm not sure...," Walter answered. "I don't...well, now that you mention it, one might have when I was just a boy."

"Well, I have now looked into you, and I am pretty sure you were, and since you are here now, I suspect..." The squirrel looked around as if he were worried that he was being watched or that someone else might be listening.

He continued with a whisper, "Only one single human has ever seen what I am about to show you. But first I must ask you never to speak of this to anyone or show anyone else. Swear it! Swear it!"

"Uh, okay, I... I swear it," promised Walter, wondering to whom he would dare relate that he had ever conversed with a squirrel anyway.

"You see, we, that is, my colony, well, we need your help. Can you help us?"

"You need *my* help? What do you need? Do you need food? I can bring you food." Walter assumed that food was the only thing at the root of all creatures' needs.

"No, no! Something was stolen from us. I am asking you to help us try to get it back. You see, it is said that a long time ago the first human came to us, only *he* was searching for us. *You*, well, *you* sort of fell here. This first human, he was quite different from you. He was covered in different things—skins and beads, I have been told. *He* brought to us a great gift."

"What did he give you?" asked Walter.

The squirrel paused and then spoke again, taking great care to whisper directly to Walter.

"I am forbidden to speak of this outside the walls of the colony. But seeing as this most valuable object has already been stolen and is now probably known to others outside our walls, I shall whisper to you."

Walter bent down closer to the squirrel.

The squirrel cupped his mouth and whispered, "It was the Illumination Stone. It is what gave The Power of the Story to our elders and our colony. But now the Illumination Stone has been stolen."

Walter struggled to understand what the squirrel was telling him.

"I must say this again. You cannot tell anyone of what you are about to see."

Walter's brow furrowed "Yes. All right. I promise you I won't tell a soul." He looking around the immediate area nervously as he said these words, thinking, *who on earth would I want to tell this to?*

One very important fact that humans did not know at the time, and probably still don't, was that staring into the eyes of a ground squirrel has a power that travels in both directions. Walter had been affected by the stare of the squirrel's eyes, and the squirrel had also been affected by Walter's eyes, like a window between two worlds. Both had been given a new understanding of the other, as they would come to find out.

"Follow me, there is no other way for me to explain than to show you. Can you move?" asked the squirrel.

Walter thought for a moment and then asked, "Um, excuse me, are we going very far?"

The squirrel answered, "You are so close... in fact, it is just up this hill but so hidden you would not be able to find it unless I showed you."

Walter paused and stared up the slope, thinking, "I'm not sure that I'm ready to bushwhack through the underbrush."

The two new friends approached a thicket, and Walter gestured, saying, "After you."

He followed the squirrel, managing to push and shove his way through a tangle of brush and stinging nettles. He was nearly ready to turn back when the thicket opened to reveal the beginning of a small trail.

The squirrel was waiting for him in the middle of this trail on the other side of the thicket. It appeared to Walter that this tiny path had never been used, nor was it even known about by humans, or even deer for that matter.

Once the squirrel had made sure Walter was following, he bounded on ahead, calling back, "This way. Hurry! Just around this bend."

Rounding the bend brought Walter to a massive vertical wall of columnar basalt. He stopped and stood before the opening.

In all his days as a youth exploring the canyon, he had never seen this place before. It was almost as if it had just appeared from another dimension. It certainly could not be seen from the trail above the cliffs nor from down along the river.

He followed the squirrel through a narrow vertical opening in between two sheer cliff walls. Initially the crevasse was so narrow that even thin Walter had to squeeze through sideways.

The smooth gray stone walls of the passageway channeled gusts of cool air filled with the sweet pungent smell of lush vegetation. As Walter slid through, the crevasse widened, allowing him a few more feet of room.

Looking about, he noticed cracks and deep spaces between the massive columns of rock, in which clung small but incredibly old pine trees, sagebrush, and juniper. Their roots clung to the rock like gnarled old hands grasping for dear life.

Subterranean springs of cold fresh water streamed down the smooth walls of stone. He slid through the passageway. It jogged first left, then right, and then left again. Wildflowers of many colors blotted the stone surface throughout the crevasse, stuffed into the cracks and ledges. Bright orange and yellow lichens splattered the rock surface like paint.

Walter approached electric blue lizards that scampered in a flash around corners and into dark hidden places. Bright yellow clouds of butterflies fluttered just above his head.

As Walter gazed up at the butterflies, he could see the top of the rimrock and a narrow sliver of blue sky with billowy white clouds floating by. There was little doubt that this was no place a human had ever been, at least not in a very long time.

Walter stopped and turned to a particularly large and dark opening in the wall of the rock face. Peering into the blackness, he wondered just how deep and cavernous it was. He could hear his voice echo into what sounded like a sizable chamber.

Concluding that it was most likely empty, he looked away. Without warning and with sudden shocking speed, something lunged toward him. A hissing growl emanated from within with such suddenness and force that Walter jumped back, colliding with the opposite rock wall. The wind was knocked out of him, leaving him gasping for air and rendering him unable to speak.

He turned quickly to look for the squirrel, which was now sitting in the middle of the trail, waiting for him, saying, "Sorry, I should have warned you about that. You might want to stay clear of that one... He can be...*alarming*. You must admit, though, he does make a good guard, does he not? Please keep moving. We are almost there."

Turning, he scampered around a corner. Walter followed him through the narrow walls of the passage for some time until it opened wide and revealed a round open area, surrounded on all sides by tall basalt cliffs.

Over hundreds of thousands, possibly millions of years, the rimrock had split and caved in along this bend in the canyon. Portions of the rock walls had fallen into the base of this bowl-shaped open area, filling it with boulders. Sandy soil had filled in around the boulders, creating a sloping landscape. Rivulets of water streamed down the walls.

The only access in or out of this open space was the passage from where they had just come. But what magic forces had combined to create the scene that now lay before Walter in this little *hidden valley* was anyone's guess.

6

THE VILLAGE OF RIMROCK

At first glance, Walter noticed only the sloping sandy soil, large boulders, and an occasional small clump of sage surrounded by cliffs on all sides. But on closer examination, Walter began to discover mosses and beautiful green grassy areas that were interspersed between the boulders. With even closer examination, he could make out pathways and tiny fences.

The green grassy areas were groomed and bordered by the same beautiful clumps of wildflowers as he had seen stuffed into the cracks of the narrow passage. Then he spotted something truly unexpected. Tucked above, below, and between what had first looked like a rubble pile of boulders were small wooden dwellings, house facades with porches, front doors, and wooden slatted walkways connecting one door to another and then continuing down a series of pathways. Walter stood before a tiny village!

Off to one side, there were two particularly large boulders, and in the center of those two boulders, there was a set of very substantial double doors, substantial, at least, for the size of the village. This was apparently a place of great importance.

In front of these doors stood two older and rather portly ground squirrels deeply engrossed in conversation. One was holding a large nutshell from which he appeared to be drinking. The two squirrels in the middle of a rather urgent matter abruptly ended their discussion, stopping mid-sentence to turn and face a sudden and much more serious matter—the giant human peering at them from the entrance to the village.

One of the squirrels dropped his cup in alarm and astonishment. They quickly scurried through the double doors, slamming them shut behind them. Other squirrels that had been going about their daily routines heard the slamming door and now noticed the unexpected guest.

All activity came to a halt as Walter stepped out from around the corner of the passage. After briefly pausing to stare in amazement, they all vanished in a blink. Walter recalled that this sudden ability to find a place to vanish quickly was referred to as *ditching*.

Walter stood in silence. So completely unexpected was this scene he simply had difficulty registering what lay before him.

"There is no doubt about it, this has to be the strangest day of my life!" he concluded.

Continuing to gaze in wonder at his discovery, he determined that one of the green manicured areas of grass located in the middle of the village was a park or outdoor central meeting place. Contained in this little central park area were neatly groomed crisscrossing trails, one following along a tiny clear rippling brook. The water tumbled over smooth pebbles and collected in pools.

Glancing down at his feet, he identified the entrance to the village. Here he noticed what looked very much like spear points chipped out of black obsidian. There were three rows of them lined up across the entire entrance of the village, pointed outward. They had the appearance of offering some sort of defense, but it could only have been a defense against an intruder that crawled, or rather slithered, on the ground.

Walter refocused his attention to take note of some bowl-sized concave holes on a large flat stone at the other end of the village. They looked as though they had been ground out over an exceptionally long span of time. He spotted a grinding stone lying near them, giving credence to his suspicion that ancient humans had ground their grains and nuts in them.

The holes had been repurposed and clearly served the squirrel community as wells filled with the cold clear spring water from the rivulets running down the sheer rock walls. The first bowl was continually filled, spilling over into the bowl next to it, providing an unlimited source of fresh drinking water. The water then spilled from the second bowl and disappeared into a crack between two boulders, only to reappear as the babbling brook that ran through the green grassy central park area.

"Walter! Walter? Down here!"

Teek was the only squirrel left in sight. His cheeping, high-pitched voice interrupted Walter's transfixed amazement, recapturing his attention.

Teek continued, "This is where we live. This us. They say that he referred to himself as a shaman. He was an older human, like you, only he did not fall into our world. He searched for us and found us. Our story elders at the time reported that he told them that he was on what he referred to as a vision quest. From the story elders' description, we know that he covered himself quite differently than you. He wore animal skin and beads. He brought us the Illumination Stone, which held the power of our stories for our elders to reveal to our colony."

"What is an Illumination Stone?" asked Walter.

"Oh yes, thank you," continued Teek. "In the center of our Great Hall," he said, pointing to the large double doors where the two older portly squirrels had just disappeared, "was the most valuable and mysterious of all things, the Illumination Stone, brought to us by that first human. On certain nights during the great cycle, the bright light of day and the full cool light of night aligned with an opening in the ceiling of our Great Hall. During that time, a shaft of light would stream down and light the Illumination Stone. This occurrence made the entire Great Hall glow. When this happened, the stone would reveal events of our colony from our past to one of our story elders, who would then recite the story to the entire colony. This was always a time for the entire colony to be together, to eat special things, to celebrate, to remember our past, and to learn about our history. Many of these stories were of our great ancestral squirrels, those who came before us. The stone meant everything to us, and now we fear that without it, we might forget who we are! And you may be aware that there are many more humans encroaching on us than ever before. They ride giant metal monsters that destroy our homes and the homes of other creatures. These new humans have taken the land for their own use, and they have brought other creatures that are not so pleasant... those nasty, irritating rats!"

"Rats?" Walter wanted to make sure he heard correctly.

"Rats! I think they may now know where our colony is, and they intend to..."

Walter's sudden "Shhh" sounded like a hiss. The outburst made Teek jump back.

"Listen!" ordered Walter. "Listen!" he repeated abruptly.

The human's entire demeanor shifted, like the sudden chill one feels when the sun slips behind a cloud, or a cold wind suddenly whips up.

Teek watched Walter's attention become torn between two worlds. Holding up one finger, without another word, the human turned and disappeared back through the passage. Teek followed him back, but his hopes for gaining a helping hand and developing an alliance with a human now seemed to be slipping away the farther back through the passageway they went, back toward the human world. Back toward Walter's world.

"Daaaaad, Daaaaad?"

The voice was so faint at first that it might have passed for a distant call of a coyote or fox, but Walter could recognize a familiar human voice.

"Could that possibly be Helen? Helen is looking for me? Dear Sofia! I must go answer her!"

Walter crouched down to his knees and addressed Teek. "My dear new friend, I have to leave you for now. I have made a promise to you never to tell of the location of your colony. Please know that I will honor it. And I will promise you this, I will return to you. I will return and help you as soon as I am able, hopefully as soon as tomorrow."

Walter's heart pounded with excitement and joy at the sound of the voices of the family members from whom he had been disconnected for so long.

Arriving at the same spot that had stopped his fall earlier that morning, he craned his neck up toward the top of the canyon rim. He just managed to catch a glimpse of two small figures way up at the top of the trail. He waved his arms and shouted to them, "I'm down here!"

His granddaughter, Sofia, was the first to see him. "There he is!" she shouted.

Like most humans, Walter's focus quickly shifted and was now completely reconnected to the familiar. For now, he was leaving a new wondrous world behind, already beginning to question his experience.

In the excitement, he didn't happen to notice a small ground squirrel scurrying up from behind a boulder to watch him leave.

Teek watched Walter head back up the trail to meet his daughter and granddaughter. With a flip of his tail, he turned and disappeared back into the rimrock.

7

HISTORICAL STORIES

I f Teek had been able to fully explain to the human, the unfortunate series of events, he might have been able to convey just how important the Illumination Stone was to his colony.

Ground squirrels had no written language aside from the directional symbols or tiny signposts that humans passed by without noticing. Their language and their lore were passed down orally.

This does not mean that any information was lost in the retelling—oh no, these ground squirrels were sticklers for detail.

In fact, they had such an obsessive interest in, and attention to, the accuracy of small matters, that it was more of a problem keeping stories to a reasonable length. Many stories had to be continued for two or more days.

The longest story in history is said to have lasted so long that it had to be continued the next time the great cycle came back around. In other words, the story took two years to tell! And since most of the stories involved colony members or ancestors of colony members, there was never any fear of boredom. Interest level was always quite high.

In fact, listening to these stories was enjoyed in much the same way that human families enjoy their own family slides or home movies. So, as you might imagine, it was very important that the story elders took extra care not to offend anyone by passing down incomplete or inaccurate information.

And that is how Teek's colony understood the natural history of their place along the river and of their significance in the canyon.

For many, many years, the entire colony would look forward to being together, to hear the stories, to celebrate, and to eat good food. There were crunchy bugs, juicy grubs, berries, nuts, and seeds galore. There were also new shoots, fresh flowers, tender buds, and sometimes cherries, which were a rare delicacy.

The Great Hall was massive for ground squirrels. The burrow builders, those whose interests lay in doing most of the burrowing and construction, had chosen a location where the boulders were especially massive. The Great Hall was so large that it easily accommodated the entire colony.

Just off from this Great Hall, there were the food larders for storage and preparation. Another passageway off from the main hall led to the quarters for the story elders.

In the center of the ceiling of the hall, there was the opening to the sky above. Like the colony itself, it was impossible to distinguish this opening when viewed from the outside, but the opening *was* large enough to capture a shaft of light at a certain time of year from the bright light of day and then from the full cool light of night. The shafts of light shone down onto the Illumination Stone, which lit the hall with a bright glow.

Everyone, especially the young squirrels in the colony, looked very much forward to gathering and nibbling on the special treats that made up the storytelling feast. These were the happiest of times, with much laughter and affection.

Eechius and Seek were the story elders. Year after year, they would gaze into the Illumination Stone and recite the historical stories to the colony.

Everyone would gather in the Great Hall to hear them describe amazing feats of courage and fantastic events. They would all listen very closely to the wondrous tales of those who had gone before them.

Some of these accounts were quite old, but, by peering into the Illumination Stone, they knew every detail. The elders could even go back far enough to tell of a cold period when a giant ice dam had formed and then had given way quite suddenly. They told of ice flows that carried large boulders and carved-out deep gorges.

They even told of the origin of the sandy soil that coated their beloved canyon, which provided such a cool spot on a warm day. It was made up mostly of volcanic pumice, born from fiery magma below the crust. All these stories of brave ancestors, heroes, and loved ones were now at risk of being lost.

In the days leading up to the theft of the Illumination Stone, it was increasingly apparent that protecting and defending the colony of Rimrock was becoming more difficult. The world around them had begun to change dramatically due to the enormous increase in the numbers of new humans.

Consequently, there had also been an enormous increase in the population of rats.

Now rats weren't necessarily bad creatures per se, but unfortunately those rats that lived alongside humans (and they had the tendency to do so) were known to be carriers of disease and were quite pushy and more aggressive creatures than other rats.

They fed mostly on human garbage, ran around in packs, and seemed determined to harass, bully, and take over ground squirrel colonies.

So, this invasion of rats was neither respected nor tolerated by ground squirrels; knowing this made the rats quite angry and even more aggressive and resentful.

As the story goes, on one fateful day, two particularly large and conniving rats named Eek and Reek eavesdropped on a conversation that two young Rimrock ground squirrels (whom you will learn of soon) were having while out foraging near the river.

These two young squirrels unwittingly violated one of the most important rules of the colony by discussing the Great Hall and the Illumination Stone while outside the protective walls of Rimrock. They later confessed and were severely punished.

Unfortunately, the result of this indiscretion was that Eek and Reek learned where the opening in the ceiling of the Great Hall was and, of course, what lay within.

With vengeful intent, the two rats then told a particularly large gopher snake named Ish, a dreaded enemy of all ground squirrels, that by stealing the stone, he could cause all sorts of squirrels to search the area, giving him ample opportunity to strike.

Ish listened intently to the two rats describe the location of the opening in the ceiling of the Great Hall, and then he swallowed Reek.

Eek managed to escape, returning to the rat encampment, where he reported the full story to Sleg, the old alpha rat. He fully expected that this would elevate his position in the eyes of Sleg and put him in good standing. And for a while it seemed to until Sleg's agenda shifted to other more immediate sources of self-serving interests.

The report from the Great Hall was that in the wee hours of a particularly dark night, someone had moved aside several of the protective spearheads from the entrance to the village, allowing Ish to slither through. The squirrels in the colony were fortunately all inside of their burrows and protected behind closed doors.

Ish the snake knew where to find the opening in the ceiling of the Great Hall. Sliding down through the crack, he took the stone in his mouth and headed down the tunnel to the large double doors. Using the stone as a battering ram, he busted through and escaped with the precious prize.

Sure enough, the initial panic resulted in a rather large and disorganized search. Three young squirrels out searching never returned and were never found. The parents of these young squirrels made it quite clear that "this fate should have befallen the same young squirrels who had violated the rules of secrecy."

When this sentiment got back to the parents of the two young squirrels, there was great shame.

Now that the stone was missing there were no more storytelling nights, and the tight-knit community of Rimrock was not nearly as close and cordial. Fear was taking control of the colony. It eroded trust and the ability for squirrels in the village to care about one another. Rimrock had always been a vibrant, energetic, and caring community.

It was a place where "Hello, friend," "Greetings to you," and "How are you this fine day?" were happily called from one to another.

Soon, neighbors began to keep more to themselves. The colony had taken on an eerie silence reduced to paw-pointing and distrust.

The young squirrels in the village were becoming disconnected and disrespectful of their elder squirrels. For so long the village had been a place where colony members had made it their business to know the goings-on of their neighbors. Villagers that had once gone out of their way to offer their assistance, attention, or companionship now seemed to withdraw into their burrows.

Now everyone preferred to stay inside rather than socialize. Teek was particularly bothered by the changes he was noticing in the colony; he was all too aware of how important the Illumination Stone was and how the whole colony had seemed to change since its disappearance. He was no longer at ease, even when in the comfort of his own cozy burrow.

⋯⟨⟩⟨⟩⟨⟩⟨⟩⋯

Teek had inherited a beautiful and substantial burrow, Stonewood Place, a well-crafted and secure structure underneath and in between two great boulders.

Its beams were large and sturdy, yet its rooms were nicely appointed and neatly arranged. The entryway let in the bright light of day, which then reflected off a series of hanging wood-framed mirror fragments, sending light to rooms farther inside the dwelling.

It was a home that had been built by his late father, his late uncle, his friend Digger's father, and other burrow builder squirrels. Teek was considered by others in the village to be quite fortunate to have one of the finest burrows.

Although he would occasionally hear of back-channel conversations that questioned his right to be in line for such a fine dwelling, it had come at a most difficult price. Teek's family had suffered a series of tragic events.

Three cycles before, his father had been killed in a rattlesnake accident while out collecting food for a Story Gathering when he'd fallen into a deep snake pit.

Uncle Chip, his father's brother, lived another year and then failed to return from a long black slab of stone that the humans used for travel.

This meant Teek was in line for sole possession of the family home. Teek was the youngest in a small family, having two remaining older sisters who were both happily mated to prominent males in the colony. They both lived in their own comfortable burrows.

Teek's mother, Leese, had supposedly been lost when they were all quite young. She had left the colony to collect salmon flies near the river and had simply never returned.

Teek's father forbade him and his sisters to go searching for her. They obeyed their father's words. Teek's father, Seege, was a wise and well-respected squirrel in the colony, highly regarded by the elders for his wisdom and leadership qualities. He gathered the family together and told them that their mother had slipped and fallen into the river, had been swept away, and so had perished.

Teek had always wondered what had truly become of her and always regretted that he hadn't insisted that they conduct a more extensive search.

Because of the traumatic loss of his family members while he was so young, Teek had grown up rather quickly. From very early in his life, he would go out of his way to care for his sisters.

But they all knew how adventurous his spirit was. Born with a natural curiosity, an interest in his ancestors, a love for the canyon, and a deep love of the Rimrock colony, he knew how important the Illumination Stone truly was.

He knew that the storytelling had given them a way to all be together and share with one another. He knew that the colony had been a much stronger community because of it. Teek also knew that he could not comfortably live in Rimrock while these dark and unsecured times were upon them.

The return of the stone was more important to him than just about anything. There was only one thing for him to do, and it wasn't going to be staying within the walls of the colony. The parents of the two young squirrels who were responsible for the loss of the stone had agreed with the elders that their offspring should help in any and all search and retrieval attempts.

Teek happened to know these two young squirrels very well and had grown fond of them. Though they were young and naive, they were also very bright with positive inquisitive minds.

He was also quite close with their families. He tried to imagine what sort of future these two young squirrels and their families would face if they were always known for having caused the loss of the Illumination Stone.

8

THE DECISION IS MADE

Teek had made his way to his own bed, in his secluded sleeping chamber at the back of his burrow, much earlier than normal, and so awoke out of a longer-than-normal sleep.

He struggled to regain his faculties, feeling a little like awakening from hibernation. He was just able to hear the rapping on his front door. Teek made his way down the hall to the entryway and opened the door. It was Eechius and Seek, the story elders.

"Teek my boy, might we have a word?"

"Of course, Gent... uh, sirs... Your Honors... Please come in, come in," he stammered. "I will bring you seeds and something to sip."

The three entered the parlor at the front of Teek's home, a room off the front hallway, to one side of the front door.

"Make yourself comfortable, I will be right back."

Seek spoke up first. "No, no, we just have a short while. We wanted to make sure you knew that, well, we have been thinking about the way we just sentenced Cheeks and Peeps to an unsafe search for the *Illumination Stone*. Now we think that it is right that they be the ones to search for it, but maybe we need to give them a better chance for success."

"Yes, yes," Eechius continued, "Uh, and we understand that although you had nothing to do with the unfortunate occurrence, you were nonetheless of strong mind about this matter. In fact, of strong enough mind to have attempted to enlist the help of a human."

Eechius paused. "We do wish you had come to us first before showing him to our colony. Mind you, that gave us quite a start. We have concluded, however, that if properly handled, this just might be the only other time in our history that we *may* allow, or possibly require, a human's help."

"Well, sir, I...," Teek began.

"Now we know," interrupted Seek, "that counting on *any* human is not exactly easy. In fact, even getting through to them—"

"But, sir, he left. I do not know where he is."

Eechius and Seek were silent. This was new information that they did not expect.

Finally, Eechius asked in a low voice, "Did you manage to awaken him? What did you find, boy? Tell us, any sign?"

"Yes, I did. And I do know that at some point, probably when he was incredibly young, a ground squirrel had managed to awaken him. But it was a long time ago. He did have *the awareness*. However, it has been covered over with so much over so many years. It has been buried inside of him for so long. He had trouble recognizing it at first. But I found it in him, and I believe I reawakened him."

Both elders nodded and glanced at each other. "I see," said Eechius.

Teek began again, "I do have another thought, possibly a less favorable one, but it is still something to consider."

Without a word, the two elders looked up from their clenched paws and focused their gazes on Teek.

He continued, "Let *me* take Cheeks and Peeps and see what we can find."

Seek reacted. "Wait! What do you mean you want to accompany them in searching for the stone? Dear boy, there are few enough of your father's line left. We do not think that it would be a good idea for you to go!"

"I have given this a great deal of thought, and I believe that it is the right thing to do. I want to do this," maintained Teek. "And I cannot be comfortable here while the stone is missing. I think I can keep Cheeks and Peeps out of trouble. Otherwise, I fear that they may very well not stand a chance."

Eechius replied, "Well, that *is* most honorable. Hmm, I'm just not sure. We will have to discuss this."

"Eechius!" interrupted Seek. "I protest! This should not even be up for discussion!"

Eechius persisted, "Nonetheless, Seek, you and I should discuss this further and come back to Teek with our counsel. If you will excuse us, young Teek, we will go have a talk about this now. We will give you our final thoughts on the matter presently."

Teek watched from his front door as the two elders walked very closely together back down the path toward the Great Hall, verbally jousting back and forth and waving their arms as they dramatically punctuated their respective points with grand gestures.

Teek, now very awake, shuffled down the hall toward his larder to begin his day with a small bowl of crumbled pine nuts. Another sharp knocking on his door once again interrupted his morning.

Returning to his front door he found the two mothers of Cheeks and Peeps—Teese and Meep.

"Oh, Teek," Meep began in a high-pitched squeak, "We heard about your intention to accompany Cheeks and Peeps!"

"Well, we had not yet decided. Wait, how could you possibly...?" he began, quite dumbfounded.

"We just want you to know," Teese continued, "that we are most grateful."

"Well, we will just see how..." he began again.

"Now if there is anything that we can do to help you prepare, be sure to ask," added Teese.

"Yes!" Meep added.

"Well, I would if—"

"We heard Seek and Eechius arguing about it." Meep's words flew out of her mouth.

"You did?" Teek managed to say.

"And we will watch your home for you while you are gone."

"No, no, that is not necessary. I would ask Digger to stay here as he does work on it."

Teek was now peering from behind his door, attempting to close it.

"Cheeks and Peeps will be leaving in two cycles. Oh, Teek, thank you. We just do not know what we would have done," added Teese.

"Ahhh...all right then." Teek wanted to be very agreeable in the interest of concluding the conversation and closing the door.

After managing to finish his morning meal, Teek set off down the wooden pathway toward the Great Hall. The Village was unusually abuzz with activity.

It seemed that somehow the village had an energy that he hadn't seen in more than a great cycle. Many squirrels were out on their front porches cleaning, all the while chattering and cheeping. They all seemed to stop and look in Teek's direction.

Arriving at the double doors of the Great Hall, he found them unlocked and so realized that the two elders were expecting him. Entering, he followed the long passageway toward the large inner chamber. There stood Eechius and Seek, and a dim shaft of light shone down from the opening in the ceiling above, revealing their ongoing discussion.

Their whispers echoed, carrying their words softly to the recesses of the cavern. Seek stopped their conversation abruptly, and both the story elders turned to address Teek as he entered the hall.

"Teek my boy," Eechius called out, "we were just concluding our discussion about this expedition you are proposing."

"I see," replied Teek. "So, you have decided then?"

"We have indeed. We think that you are right. Without you, Cheeks and Peeps stand little hope of successfully accomplishing this task, and we think that your idea of going with them is a good one! Also, we want to thank you for your heroic effort. We believe that if you are successful, this would make you a very important member of the colony. Your choice will also make Meep and Teese very relieved."

"Yes, well, they visited me earlier and somehow already had the impression that I was going," said Teek.

"Jabbing Junipers! They must have been eavesdropping from one of the larders!" Seek exclaimed.

"They have access to the Great Hall because of the duties they perform," added Eechius.

"Listen, Teek, might we have a few moments more with you? Come and sit, please. Let us sit and talk for just a short while," said Seek.

He gestured toward the opening to a smaller room just off the great hall. As they moved away from the larger inner chamber, the shaft of light from the ceiling now fell on a noticeably empty space in the center of the floor.

Eechius spoke. "As you know, Teek, we are old squirrels and have seen many things in our lives. But the world out there is a whole lot bigger than even we can imagine. Many perils await you. We think that you may be about to see and experience things of which neither of us know. So, we are unable to warn you about them."

Eechius stood directly in front of Teek.

"Stay out of sight, lad, and tell Cheeks and Peeps that we want them to obey you! They are young and they can be rash. Know this, however, the entire colony goes with you. You will be in our thoughts. Our hopes and the future well-being of this colony are in your hands. You are an important part of our lives. Wherever you go, you represent this colony. You are an incredibly wise young squirrel, Teek. Both Seek and I believe that you will make a good story elder someday if you wish. We know you will return. Keep your eyes and ears sharp and bring back our stone, Teek! And this human that you have reawakened, you may very well have made a connection with him, and so you should not forget about him just yet."

As Teek left the Great Hall, he opened the large double doors and breathed in the fresh air.

Outside everything was clear, and the bright light of day was shining. He blinked as his eyes adjusted. Leaving the cool darkness of the inner chamber, he felt the warmth beaming down on his fur.

The village seemed almost dream-like as he made his way back toward Stonewood Place. In fact, so pleasant was the day that he decided to take a detour by way of the central grassy area. The Village was still somewhat busy with goings-on, mostly squirrels coming and going with foodstuff for the winter—seeds, grasses, nuts—and the last of the late-summer grasshoppers.

"Teek!"

He heard a familiar voice, the source of which may have been the very reason he had decided to take a detour through the central grassy area in the first place.

It was Cicci. Sweet Cicci. Her soft silky fur seemed to glow in the brightness of the morning light. Teek, reminded of how pretty she was, turned and did his best to portray surprise.

"Cicci! Good morning!"

She started right in. "I have been looking for you, Teek. I went by your burrow."

"Oh... Well, I had to spend some time with Eechius and Seek in the Great Hall."

Cicci's eyes looked knowingly into Teek's.

"You are putting yourself in great danger. Why you?" she asked.

"Why me what?" he asked back, wondering how much she knew about his decision to go with Peeps and Cheeks on their journey.

"You know what I'm talking about. The idea of you searching for the Illumination Stone with those two young squirrels!" she replied.

"How could you possibly know about this already?" he asked.

"The ears of Rimrock hear everything," she replied.

After a few moments of silence, Teek began, "Yes, well, Cicci, I guess that more than anything, I just want to help our colony. And also, I have some unanswered questions about who I am and what I am, um, made of. I think I can do this... I know I can!"

"Not without me!" she replied.

"Oh no, you are *not* coming with us!"

His reaction was more of an outburst. He should have known better than to blurt out his reaction before thinking first.

If there was one other intellect other than Eechius's and Seek's that Teek respected above his own, it was Cicci's.

Independent and feisty, she possessed qualities to be respected. She was quite a pretty squirrel, but for Teek, it was her honest passion for truth and her sensibility that he liked most. It shone like a fire in her eyes.

"You know, Teek, I also have unanswered questions about where *I* come from and what *I* am made of!" Teek wasn't sure that he should respond to that comment.

"Well," he began, but she cut him off.

"And you know I can stay out of trouble. In fact, I can help keep *you* out of trouble!"

Teek stood speechless before Cicci, thinking. These were certainly not the issues he was prepared to address. She could tell that he had no more argument to offer.

"Then it is settled," she added. "I am not crawling under a rock—"

"But you have a nice burrow...," he interjected.

"I am not crawling under a rock," she repeated, "all the while wondering where you are and if you are alive! When are we leaving?"

"We are supposed to leave two cycles from now," replied Teek.

"Let me see, I'll go home and get ready. Then I should come stay at your burrow and help get *you* ready. We can leave from there."

"But what about the colony? What will...?" he began.

"It does not matter what everyone thinks," she interrupted. "We are leaving, anyway, so that is of little concern! If we come back with the stone, no one will even remember or care! Do not worry. Teek, you know that I am better at tracking things down than you are. This will be a great adventure. Who knows, this might even be fun."

The debate was over before it had begun.

"I guess we will stop by your burrow so I can help you fill your satchel first then," was all Teek had left to say.

She hugged him so tightly that it felt as though his eyes would pop out.

"You do know that this is a concern for me," he added.

She hugged him again. "I know," she said affectionately, adding, "And *you* know that I am right on this one."

9

THE JOURNEY BEGINS

"You are a young squirrel, Peeps," said his mother Meep. "That is why I want you to listen very carefully to Teek, and do exactly what he tells you to do."

"Yes, Momma," Peeps replied.

She continued, "I have found, my dear one, that what ends up happening is usually somewhere between worst case and little or nothing at all. In other words, what is out there may not be either harmful or harmless. Most of the time, your imagination ends up being the worst part of it. So be brave, little one! Be confident in your own sensibilities but do follow Teek's lead! You are lucky that he has decided to accompany you."

"Yes, Momma. I will, I am, I will, I know," Peeps said with a twinkle in his eye.

"And none of your joking around. This is a serious matter. I will have your satchel ready first thing in the morning. Now go straight to sleep. You need your rest!"

Needing sleep was not the only reason Peeps' momma, Meep, sent him to bed early.

She was no longer able to hold back her tears and she didn't want Peeps to see her fear and concern. She was a single momma, having lost Peeps' father to a Koosagh Diaub (sky devil or hawk). She had always tried her best to keep Peeps out of harm's way. She knew that she could not bear to lose him.

Cheeks' mother, Teese, and his father, Pinion, prepared Cheeks' three satchels of food as Cheeks sat down to supper.

"I have a special surprise for you in one of your satchels, Cheeks," his mother sang out to him.

"I hope it is a big muffin crumb or a piece of a potato crisp!" he replied.

"You will just have to wait and see. Now are you bringing a satchel with anything other than food?"

This was a leading question that was intended to suggest to Cheeks not to bring so much food.

"Oh well, I don't want to carry four satchels!" Cheeks replied, beginning to understand what she was getting at.

He had started to realize that he might end up with one less satchel of precious food.

"Well then, maybe one of the three satchels should be for other things you might need other than food," his momma suggested.

"Momma, you cannot be serious!" Cheeks objected.

"Cheeks—think about it, son," said his father, looking up from his wood-chip plate of pine nut mash, just beginning to listen to the conversation.

With his mouth still full, he managed to mutter, "Where do you think we get all of *our* food? That's right, we have squirrels that go out and forage. They go to some of the same sort of places that you will be heading. Then they bring it to us! So, there should be plenty of food out there, son. Why, you might even find an entire bag of potato crisps! You never know."

The wheels turned in Cheeks' head as he pondered such an enormous bounty. It was difficult for anyone in Cheeks' privileged family to fully grasp the enormity or the true dangers involved in what Cheeks was about to undertake.

The morning for departure came too soon for everyone in the expedition party, but there were Cheeks and Peeps, as promised, banging on Teek's door at the break of dawn.

The last thing that either of their parents wanted was to keep Teek waiting for those whom he had so graciously offered to help.

Fortunately, both Teek and Cicci were already up and ready for departure. Cicci opened the door, and there stood the two young squirrels, mouths agape and speechless.

"Is she...?" began Peeps.

Teek quickly interrupted, "Uh, are all these your satchels, Cheeks?"

"Yes, well, you know my momma, she packs a lot of food."

"That is because she knows how much you pack in when you eat!" blurted out Peeps.

"Shut up, Peeps!" snapped Cheeks.

"Boys, come on, it is too early for this. Come in and we will sort this out," said Cicci.

They managed to redistribute the provisions so that each in the party only had to carry two satchels. After much rummaging about and a lengthy debate, they all assured Cheeks that *what was his would remain his*, and so they were finally prepared for departure.

As the group reached the outermost opening of the passage leading from the village, Teek stopped the group and spoke.

"There are many things out here that are unknown to me, so keep your eyes and ears open and stay alert. Tell me if something looks or sounds wrong, smells odd, or even feels strange, understand? Keep nothing to yourself."

The bright light of day had not yet crested the rim of the canyon. The dark blue and salmon colors revealed the first glow of light in the sky. Although it would prove to be a toasty late summer day, for now it was still cold, biting cold. During the night, the air mass had flowed down the icy slopes of the Cascade peaks to settle in the canyons of the high plateau.

"Let us see how much ground we can cover," Teek encouraged. "We can get warmed up if we simply keep moving. Then after we get far enough from home to get the leaving part over with, maybe the bright light of day will shine down on us and warm us up."

10

AN UNEXPECTED ALLY

"One thing I do know is that we are about to enter a world in which we are everyone's breakfast, lunch, and dinner, and right now, is their favorite hunting time. We have arranged for someone to meet us by the banks of the river and travel with us for a while."

"Who would that be?" Cicci asked.

"Fisk is meeting us. Seek took some of our guards to keep a lookout while he summoned Fisk from the river's edge. He asked Fisk to meet us and to divert predator attention away from us as we got started on our journey."

"Really? Fisk? He asked Fisk to divert attention away from us?" asked Cicci.

"Divert! That is a good word for Fisk," piped up Peeps.

Teek lowered his gaze at Peeps, who looked down sheepishly, struggling to keep from blurting out any further comments.

"You all need to realize that we are going to need all of the help we can get. We will be gathering information from some rather undesirable creatures just to even begin to figure out where we might be going. Does everyone understand this?"

"Well, we do now." Peeps covered his mouth with his paw. "Sorry," he said.

"Does everyone understand this?" Teek repeated.

"Yes," they all replied in unison.

"And when I say ditch, you ditch faster than you have ever ditched before, all right? Until we get to the river and meet up with Fisk, we are going to move from one protective cover to another. Now follow me."

Teek glanced at Cicci. She was staring at him with a new look that Teek managed to recognize as fondness. He could tell that Cicci wanted him to know just how she felt about him.

"Yes, all right then, uh, here we go," he stammered.

Darting from one cover to the next, they arrived at the bank of the river. They found a small muddy bank below a thick cover of willows. Many water-loving animals had used this hidden bank as a 'slide' to enter and leave the river. This included Fisk and his family. The river was dark and made gurgling sounds as it swirled by. Steam arose from the water, making the opposite shore hard to see from their low vantage point. Teek peered at length into the steamy mist in hopes of catching a glimpse of his delinquent friend.

The squirrels waited and waited.

"Where is he?" Cheeks asked impatiently. "Is this going to delay the morning meal?" he continued.

"Cheeks, you are not always going to be able to eat when you want," informed Teek.

"What? You are not planning the trip around Cheeks' meals?" interjected Peeps.

"Shut up, Peeps!" Cheeks shot back.

"Hey, no more 'shut up' from *you*, Cheeks. Shut up, Peeps," said Teek.

Teek knew that muskrat, nutria, and beaver used this muddy slide. He also knew that one very good sign that Fisk might be close by was that none of those animals would be around. They couldn't tolerate Fisk's frenetic personality for very long, and so they typically avoided him.

Teek's insight proved correct, and Fisk finally surfaced rolling over and over. Round and round he went, finishing up his crayfish breakfast.

"Crunch-crunch-crunch-crunch."

"Where have you been? We have been waiting," said Teek.

"Out 'n about, out 'n about. I watched a raccoon playing with a fish, you know, this 'n that. Been around."

"All right, Fisk, we have to depend upon you for a while. Can you stay close and look out for predators and, you know, pay attention?" asked Teek.

"Sure (rolling in the water), no problem (rolling again). I can do that (rolling even more). Got it (rolling once again)! No worries!" (rolling).

"Stop that!" cried Teek.

"Oh, sorry, uh, yup, I'll be here," answered Fisk, now floating at attention.

"Did you happen to find out anything?" Teek asked.

"Well, not really," answered Fisk, "but, but like I said, I watched a raccoon for a while, well, actually a few moments–well, less than a few moments, maybe just one moment, I–"

"All right, Fisk, what about him?" Teek interrupted again.

Fisk went on, "Well, he is just downriver. I could probably find him again. You could talk to him."

"Then it is settled, we start by heading downriver. We will start now," said Teek.

With that, Fisk rolled over again and disappeared under the surface with a flip of his tail. Cheeks stood staring at the water.

Peeps said nothing but, "Wow."

The group moved downriver, hugging as close to the bank as possible, darting from cover to cover. Fisk swam close to shore, off and on, struggling to keep an eye on his new responsibilities as he rolled around, darting after fish.

"Are you cold at all?" inquired Cicci.

"Oh no, the water is wonderful! Fun-fun-fun!"

"I guess his fur protects him from the cold," added Teek.

"How do you know that?" asked Cicci.

"I just kept asking him questions, and then one day, I actually examined his coat. Fisk had never given it much thought, so we sort of figured it out together. Oh, he'd dry off and preen himself, but I doubted that he really knew how it worked," Teek answered.

"So, he does dry out sometimes?" asked Cheeks.

"Yes," replied Teek. "It is his undercoat that needs to dry out mostly."

Peeps and Cheeks looked at each other and shrugged.

They hadn't gone far before they spotted the raccoon. He had been moving upstream, searching the rocks for crayfish, so they encountered him sooner than expected. Teek addressed the raccoon with as much politeness as he knew how.

"Pardon me? If you have a minute, uh, I do not mean to bother—"

"What?" the raccoon turned and hissed loudly.

"Uh, I said I do not mean to bother—"

"Yeah? Whadaya want? Make it fast!" he hissed again impatiently.

"Well, you see, my name is—"

"Look, do you have a point to make or some question to ask me before the morning is over and the crayfish are gone? Sorta busy here!"

Cheeks and Peeps looked at each other, taken aback by the abrupt abrasiveness of the large, grizzled creature.

"Hissss! Oh great, now where did it go? Ya see? Do ya see what you did? Trying to clean this thing and you show up! Now I've lost it! Which rock did that little bugger get under?"

"If you would, please...," Teek continued, attempting to remain composed.

"Are you still here? What do you want? Maybe a better question is, can you catch crayfish?" blurted the raccoon, now very agitated.

"I try to stay out of the water," explained Teek.

"Well, that must be convenient for you! Go away now, I gotta find this crayfish, then I have to wash it, then eat it... Oh, what am I talking to *you* for?" the raccoon concluded, resuming his search.

"Is it just me," began Peeps, "or do we think that this search may take an awfully long time?"

"We do not know, Peeps," replied Cicci. "It could take a *very* long time."

"So how did it go with the raccoon?" asked Fisk, reemerging from the depths.

"Oh! Fisk is still with us? It's a wonder!" commented Peeps.

"Of course, I am still here! I am still looking out for... Um, you want me to look for... Um, predators! Right? Yes, that is it. I am looking for predators. What fun!" *Sploosh*, down he went.

"All right, we need to keep moving now," said Teek.

"How about stopping for just a quick little something to eat?" added Cheeks.

"Pull some nuts from your satchel and eat them as we keep moving. We have hardly gotten far at all."

Teek clearly indicated that he wanted to move on without delay. Although he kept his feelings to himself, he *did* feel a little embarrassed about his encounter with the raccoon. He had let it get the better of him, and squirrels were supposed to be quick and clever creatures.

Cicci decided that it would be a good idea to leave him alone. And so, as they pressed on, she said nothing.

The group continued to travel farther downriver until they stood at the edge of a large ponderosa pine forest. It had grown right up to the bank of the river and then up the slope on the opposite side. Cicci felt that that it was now time to share her thoughts with Teek.

"You know," she said, "this journey will not be so much about how *far* we travel or how *long* it takes but what we learn about the whereabouts of the Illumination Stone along the way. That raccoon was probably just the beginning of the difficulties that lie ahead. I doubt that many of the creatures we encounter will be pleasant."

Teek stared into her eyes but didn't speak. Instead, he placed his forepaw on her shoulder and smiled–acknowledgement enough for Cicci.

"Where is Fisk?" Cheeks asked, sitting on a rock and peering into the river.

"I'm sure that the answer to *that* is obvious," answered Peeps.

Teek turned to the group and answered, "I told Fisk that once we reached the pine forest and the rapids just up ahead, he would be free to go. He won't be accompanying us from this point on."

"Who is watching our backs now?" Cheeks questioned in a worrisome tone.

"For now, *we* are," answered Teek, adding, "and the trees and the river."

They stood before a large, towering, and quite shadowy pine forest. They could just begin to hear the roar of rapids. It was a dark and formidable passage that awaited them.

11

KANTI'S FOREST

As they approached the first massive trunk, Teek stopped and asked them all to gather round. "Now that we are about to enter this forest, there are some things you should all know. First, it's made up of large old trees. There is not as much bright light here. There is also a thick layer of dead needles everywhere." He paused.

"This means that there will not be bunch grass and bushes for us to hide in. Owls will hear *you*, but you will not hear *them*. When they swoop down on you, they do not make a sound until it is too late. Move from one tree to another. Keep your backs to the tree trunks. Then at least, one side of you is covered. If there are rocky areas, we will hide in them. If you are out in the open and not paying attention, you will not hear an owl coming and they *will* get you."

"Well, that will not do," said Peeps.

"We need to get through this forest with great care, so at least *now* you know," Teek replied.

And so, they began to scamper from one tree to another. Halfway through the forest, they found themselves all huddled around the same large pine tree trunk. Cheeks and Peeps craned their necks, looking skyward, taking Teek's words very seriously.

"Ow!" All eyes turned to Cheeks.

"What?" asked Teek.

"Something just fell on my head. I think it was that pinecone," Cheeks said, pointing to a rather large pinecone now rolling down the bank below them.

"Hey!" This time the alarmed *"cheep"* came from Peeps. "I just got hit with that stick!"

Then came a shower of all sorts of forest litter from the trees above accompanied by high-pitched snickering, jeering, and shouting.

"Ha got one! I hit one too. Look at 'em run around! Hee-hee, hey you down there! What is the matter? Did that stick hit you in the head?"

Looking up, the group of ground squirrels could just make out small faces peering down from the branches above. "Why, those are young gray squirrels!" Teek reported.

"They sure are," said Cheeks. "What are they doing? Those nasty little tree rats!"

And so, it was. A band of young gray squirrels, completely alone and on their own, delinquent. The young squirrels climbed partway down the trees until they were close enough for Teek and the others to get a better look at them.

"They are so dirty, and they look like they are losing their fur. Do they have mange? They do scratch a lot, as if they are infested with fleas!" Teek observed.

Sometimes young ones get lost along the way. As you might imagine, decisions can be oh-so-difficult to make alone. Young squirrels, like young humans, believe that they know enough to always make the right decisions, and sometimes they must try whether they want to or not.

When there is no one there to lovingly tell them otherwise, they may have to make the best decision that they can. The future is hard to see, and so sometimes the right choice is hard to make.

Many times, young ones become misguided. What Teek's group did not know was that there was more to this story than they knew. There were no adult squirrels left to tell them how much they meant to the future of their clan, and so they had to strike out on their own.

Then it seemed from nowhere an enormous black bird swooped into view and began dive-bombing the squirrels in the trees.

"Croak! Kraw-hah-kkkkkk!" It was an adult raven.

The young band of delinquent squirrels scattered in all directions. With a thunderous whoop-whoop-whoop, the raven's massive wings brought the huge bird to a landing right in front of the group of travelers, who were now backed up against the large tree trunk, frozen with fear. The ultimate nightmare seemed to have befallen them.

"KKKKK, well, what do we have here?" the raven croaked. "Are you lost, little ones? What do you have in your satchels?"

"Uh, who... who are you?" Teek managed to ask, attempting to recover from the sudden arrival of the ominous winged creature.

"I am Kanti. I am the 'eyes' of this forest. Nothing goes on here that I do not see. And who then are *you*? Obviously not squirrels from around here. What could the reason be for you to be entering my forest? What are you doing here? What do you have in those satchels?"

Not certain of which question to answer first, Teek chose the last one. With bluffing bravery, he addressed the raven.

"Nothing that would concern you! We have ways of defending ourselves!"

"Oh, I doubt it," the raven chuckled. "You have clearly never seen the likes of *me* before. I am twice as large as a crow. There is no need to be scared, though. I will not harm you. I mostly eat meat that I find and try not to prey on other creatures. A personal choice, I suppose. I do love eggs, but you're not carrying anything like that, I'm sure. Some ravens hunt you squirrels, but I've never taken to it. I must confess, though, I was born with an insatiable curiosity. Everything interests me. In fact, I would say that it is more than an interest. It is more like an obsession. So, I must insist, you *will* need to let me see what you have in your satchels. I must persist until I know."

Teek spoke up. "We are merely passing through your forest, and as it happens, we are searching for something valuable that was stolen from us."

The ominous black bird hopped forward, cocked his head, and examined the outside of the first satchel.

"I see," he muttered. "Well, I *am* willing to help you travel through my forest, but only for a price, you must tell me what you are looking for and let me sort through your satchels."

Teek instinctively turned to Cicci for an answer. He knew that the raven might be a valuable ally, if only he could be trusted. This was very much an unusual situation.

Cicci nodded her approval and whispered to Teek, "Well, we *could* use eyes in the sky and a knowledgeable ally as we travel, and it is not really as though we have a choice, right?"

Once again, Teek considered Cicci's logic to be sound and most practical.

"All we have in the satchels is our food," began Teek.

"Then you should not have a problem with me looking through them, should you?"

Kanti was not going to take no for an answer, and Teek could see that this was indeed an obsessive necessity for the large black bird.

One by one, each of the party brought Kanti their satchel as he moved the contents of each around with his beak. Finally satisfied, he hopped back in front of the group and seemed to be more relaxed.

"Now tell me your names and why exactly you little ones are risking your lives here."

Teek explained the story of the stolen Illumination Stone and everything that was known about the events in the greatest of detail. So much detail that the raven had to occasionally interrupt him to find out what he really needed to know.

"Well, it sounds to me as though you may need my help. At least through this forest. I do like collecting shiny objects, and I notice everything. And I guess you could say that I am sort of on your side."

Kanti tilted his head. "Since the new humans have arrived, they have chased away a lot of the creatures in the canyon, especially predators. So now there is not as much to eat. And even when there is, I have to look out for the rats that the humans have brought with them."

"What about those young gray squirrels?" Teek asked. "Why have they been left alone? Where are the adult squirrels?"

"They have no adult squirrels looking after them," replied Kanti.

"What? Why?" Cicci was confused by this information.

"Well, you see, most of the squirrels in these parts died in the fire that tore through this forest."

"But I see no burned area," said Teek.

"The burned area is up there on the other side of that ridge." Kanti's head turned to point his beak up the hill. "It destroyed nearly their entire community."

"Poor young ones, what are they supposed to do?" asked Cicci.

"Nothing anyone can do," replied Kanti.

"How did it happen?" she went on.

Kanti turned back toward the group and said, "In a word, humans. They were riding on one of those monsters that blow smoke. It tore up my forest to make way for more shelters that the humans live in. Somehow the monster blew a spark on something."

"That is awful. Those poor young squirrels," she said.

"The only thing remaining of the village is the Pine Stone Inn," said Kanti. "It is still in operation. The locals depend on it for refuge and as a place to gather information. You will find the front door nestled down in the middle of a large island of boulders. Probably what saved it. But it *is* surrounded by the burned area and is difficult to get to if you do not know the way."

"Does the inn have food?" asked Cheeks.

"Yes, it is sort of a large tavern providing what it can during these difficult times. It is a refuge for defenseless creatures, no predators allowed, mind you. Maybe it will be a good place for *you* to pick up some information," replied Kanti.

"So how far is it as the crow flies?" asked Peeps, looking at Cheeks with a smirk on his face.

"Peeps!" squeaked Teek, sternly reprimanding him.

Kanti hopped up to Peeps, flapping his massive black wings with a whoop-whoop-whoop, backing Peeps up against the trunk of the tree.

"So, you are quite a funny little fellow, are you?"

"No, uh, I mean yes...um, sometimes?" Peeps stammered.

"Maybe I should fly off with you, and you could see for yourself," Kanti replied.

"I guess he must not like crows very much," Peeps whispered to Cheeks.

"Can you show us the way to the Pine Sone Inn?" Teek asked.

Kanti hopped back over to Teek. "Yes, follow me. I will be just above you, but I will stop and perch in the trees and keep an eye on you to make sure you do not lose your way." He flew off toward the crest of the ridge.

"You heard the bird—onward," Teek ordered.

They took the direct route, straight up the slope. With Kanti around, predator attacks were no longer weighing as heavily on their minds. Their thoughts were filled with unresolved questions regarding what lay ahead.

Kanti flew on, stopping here and there to peer down on them. The squirrels would catch a glimpse of him as he flew through trees until he was out of sight.

Pressing on, the squirrels could just begin to make out a dark form sitting in the mist on a low branch just long enough to watch him lift off and disappear again through the dark forest—a forest he called home. The four squirrels reached the top of the ridge. They all stopped at once in silence.

Before them stretched utter devastation. Through the mist and lingering smoke, as far as they could see, were the blackened remains of a once grand forest.

Death was everywhere. No bird chirped, just the windswept sound of desolation. An empty cold wind whipped the ground, stirring up the ash into dust, burning their eyes. The dust mixed with the cold fog, hanging like a thick blanket of death. Not a blade of grass nor bush was left alive, just blackness and gray soot. The large trees stood like large, charred skeletons.

None of them spoke a word. Kanti broke the silence as he dropped down behind them, startling the already frazzled Peeps.

"The going gets kind of tricky if you are not able to fly, so be careful."

"Good gravel!" Peeps screeched. "Where did you come from?"

Kanti continued, "If you fall off one of these downed trees, you could end up in a fiery furnace, and that might be the end of you. There is smoldering death waiting down there. This forest still burns underground. So, my advice to you is to be careful and stay on top of the downed trees."

"Yes, thank you, Kanti. We shall do just that," replied Teek.

Crack-pop-crackle-groan... "Ditch!" screeched Teek.

The squirrels scattered as an enormous old burned-out tree came down with an awful squeaking groan and then a deafening boom. The tree hit the ashen ground with such force that it created a massive explosion of hot sparks and ash. With a thunderous wump, billowing clouds of hot dust shot out in all directions.

Teek, Peeps, and Cheeks, hearing "Ditch!" had all scrambled down the length of one of the trees that had already come down. Cicci scrambled down the same tree but in the other direction. When the enormous old burned-out tree landed, it hit the downed tree they were scrambling down, splitting it in half, launching everyone high into the air. Teek, Peeps, and Cheeks propelled in one direction, and poor Cicci launched in the other.

Teek and Cheeks were thrown back over the ridge and back down the slope, through the trees, into the forest below. They were lucky enough to bounce off the soft duff of pine needles covering the forest floor. Down, and down they rolled, bouncing off tree trunks and boulders before a clump of grass stopped their chaotic descent.

"Teek! Cheeks!" Peeps called out. Having not been launched quite as far, he was farther up the hill than the other two and the first to recover.

"Teek! Cheeks!" Peeps called out again as he saw the two scrambling back up the hill toward him. "Wow, you two really flew!" said Peeps.

"Must have been quite a sight," replied Cheeks, huffing and puffing and staring wide-eyed at Peeps.

"Well, I guess I landed before you did," replied Peeps, adding, "I looked up and you two were still in the air!"

"Where is Cicci?" Teek asked.

Teek was now concerned about only one thing. His voice trembled with panic. "She must have been thrown in the opposite direction. This way!"

He bounded up the hill, leaving Cheeks and Peeps behind and still quite dazed from the tumultuous event.

With a *whoop-whoop-whoop*, Kanti landed.

"Are all you little ones here? Are you all right? The humans call that a widow maker. I overheard the humans who tried to put the fire out talking about them."

"Cicci is missing!" replied Teek, still trembling.

He stared past Kanti as he spoke, adding, "Kanti, can you please fly around and look for her? We will head over to the end of the fallen tree and call to her. Please hurry!"

Without a reply, Kanti launched from his perch with a loud *fwoop-fwoop-fwoop*. Teek and his two remaining companions scampered over the downed tree, running until the tree was too thin to continue, and then began to call to Cicci.

They called and screeched as loud as they could. Then they stopped and listened. But all that could be heard was the rush of the wind. The tinder dry ash hissed as it sanded their faces. Cicci was nowhere to be found. There was no answer.

A sinking shock hit Teek as hard as if the tree had fallen on *him*. He stared straight ahead, searching for a way to find any sign of her. Cicci was missing.

"I should not have allowed her to come," he concluded. "CEEE CEEE," he continued to call out as loud as he could, scrambling frantically from one downed tree to another.

Cheeks and Peeps did the same, heading in other directions. They heard Teek calling to them. "Stay with me, this way! We must stay in sight of each other! CEEE CEEE!"

The end of the day was approaching, the wind picked up, and the chilly evening air was heavy with smoke, fog, and thick dusty ash from the impact of the huge fallen tree. It burned their eyes, making it difficult for them to see any distance.

"Soon it will be dark," Teek said as his eyes searched through the dusky landscape.

The trees were becoming shadowy specters. The only sound between the echoing of their calls was the relentless whooshing and whistling of the wind. *Whoop-whoop-whoop*, Kanti landed on an exposed branch in front of them.

"Nothing," he reported, "and night is almost upon us. You know, Teek, she could have found a place to hide. You did tell everyone to stay hidden."

"CEEE CEEE!" Teek called again, ignoring Kanti's words, his eyes still searching out across the desolation.

He had a nauseous ache in the pit of his gut. "This is the worst thing that could have happened."

"That is just it," replied Kanti. "You do not know *what* has happened. Now listen, Cicci knows about the Pine Stone Inn. She heard me tell you all about it. Maybe she is headed there right now."

Teek thought for a moment, considering Kanti's words. "You may be right," he concluded. "She *would* think to go there. What can I do? What if she is hurt?"

Still panicky, Teek needed answers from Kanti.

"The best thing for us to do right now is to find the inn before it gets too dark for you to see where you are going," advised Kanti. "If she is not there, from what you have told me, maybe she had enough sense to find a place to hide for the night. I can just barely see that rocky pile of boulders out there. I want to get the rest of you to the inn while we still can," he urged.

"He is right, let's head to the inn," said Cheeks.

"Quiet!" Teek screeched. "You just want to eat!"

Cheeks lowered his head.

"I am sorry, Cheeks," Teek added, placing his paw on Cheek's head. "I... I...," he began.

"I know, it is all right. I am worried about her too," Cheeks whispered.

"No, I was wrong," Teek continued. "I am not angry with you. I am angry with myself."

Teek was particularly sensitive about losing those he felt closest to. He felt helpless about there not being anything that he could do about it. With great reluctance, Teek agreed to head in the direction of the Pine Stone Inn, nestled in the middle of a hazy silhouetted island of boulders, now barely visible in the distance. Kanti landed periodically in front of the small group to make sure that they were still on course.

"I should let you know," he warned, "it is going to get pretty tricky for you through here. By flying, it is easier to see from up above, but it *is* beginning to get dark."

Teek didn't like what he heard. His mind was consumed with the whereabouts and well-being of Cicci.

THE PINE STONE INN

They crossed the expanse of charred ground, scampering over downed trees and hopping over many large boulders. Arriving at the edge of the rocky island outcrop, they found one last narrow and perilous branch that barely reached the edge of the first boulder. Helping and encouraging each other across, they huddled together at the edge of the large island, looking back at where they had just come from. Kanti was quite pleased to see that they had all made it safely.

"Well done, little ones! Just scamper up over these next two boulders and we're there."

Scaling up one side of the large island of boulders, they soon reached the top and were able to look down into a large open bowl area. With what little light remained, they could just make out a flat stone porch with a heavy wooden door tucked under two enormous boulders—the front door of the Pine Stone Inn.

Cheeks began to scramble down toward the door, cheeping, "There it is! There it is! I wonder if they are still serv..." He stopped himself before finishing his words.

"Wait, Cheeks," ordered Teek, "we should approach this together."

Upon closer examination, they noticed that there were markings on a flat rock face to the right side of the large wooden door. They revealed carefully rendered and quite accurate representations of the footprints of many creatures.

"It appears to be a kind of message," said Teek.

"Yes, in fact, it is," replied Kanti. "If your footprint is represented here, then you may enter. If not, then you are not allowed inside mostly because you happen to be, well, a predator."

Here is what was drawn on the stoneface (except the identifying titles underneath):

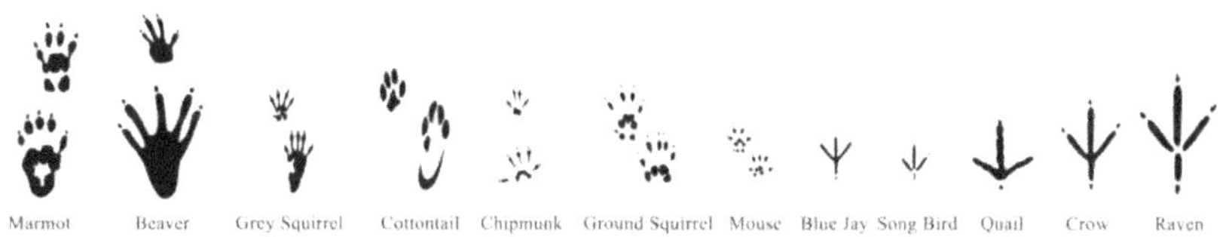

"Well, we are ground squirrels, and I can see our footprints on the wall." reported Cheeks.

"Are your footprints up there, Kanti?" asked Teek.

"Yes, they are over there at the end, but not all crows and ravens are welcome. I happen to know the innkeeper very well. Remember, this was all part of *my* forest. And besides, I am not as much a predator as I am a scavenger. At least..."

"At least what?" returned Teek.

"Oh, nothing," replied Kanti. "I know the innkeeper very well. He'll let me in."

"Do we knock first?" asked Peeps.

"Well, the door *is* locked," said Cheeks, trying the handle. Locked. They knocked.

No one answered at first. Then after a time, a small peephole door opened in the upper middle part of the large door, and a nose appeared. It twitched as it sniffed the outdoor air, and then the nose moved to one side, and a large eye appeared. It rolled around as it scanned the group of travelers. Then the little peephole door slammed shut.

"What was that? A big gopher?" Peeps asked.

"No, that was not a gopher. That was a marmot," replied Kanti. "His name is Wuchak, the keeper of the Pine Stone Inn. And this inn, I am here to tell you, is the only comfort you little ones are likely to see for quite some time."

From within, they heard what sounded like a thick wooden beam being lifted and slid aside. The heavy wooden door opened with a creak.

"Well, Kanti!" said the giant innkeeper. "It has been quite some time. Come in, come in. And who are these ground squirrels? They are most certainly not from around here."

"No," answered Kanti. "This lot is from an upriver colony called Rimrock. I will tell you all about it once we're inside and get settled in."

"Well, come in then. You are most welcome. Not all that cheery in here lately but it *is* a lot safer than out there," said Wuchak.

Kanti continued, "I have been keeping close to what is left of my forest."

"That *is* wise. Everyone is stayin' low and hidden these days," replied Wuchak as he bolted the door behind them. "Uh, I'll be right back."

He shuffled off toward another group of wayward patrons who had just arrived and were now huddled around a stone table.

The squirrels followed Kanti into the main room of the inn. It was quite spacious. Although the ceiling was not as high as their own Great Hall, it was still quite a large room.

As they entered, they began to make out their surroundings. The only sources of light were from small flames flickering from piles of rocks on each flat stone table and from an opening to an underground cavern at one end of the room.

The cavernous furnace held glowing embers and was tended to every so often by Wuchak. The forest fire had smoldered through a large tree root and had hollowed out a subterranean fiery pit. The resourceful marmot had moved stones, creating an opening to the pit. Then he piled up some stones in front of it, creating a fireplace. There were pieces of wood stacked by the opening that Wuchak used to keep the embers glowing and hot.

Although the smoke found its way up through a crack in the rock to the open air above, there was still a smoky smell to the place. As soon as the squirrels were better able to make out more of their surroundings, they could see the thick wooden beams that supported portions of the ceiling of the spacious main room. Most of the wooden beams were used for the construction of an expansive bar structure. It appeared that gnawing had shaped much of the wood.

"How was this done?" asked Teek.

Kanti answered, "When this inn was being built, Wuchak was given a lot of help by his friends. These friends happened to be beavers. His beaver buddies have not been around much since the fire. They stay close to the river now."

Warm light from the hearth flickered against the stone walls and the wooden beams. Straw had been laid over the floor. All in all, it was quite a cozy and protected sanctuary. Teek and his group found a large flat stone table and gathered around it. They looked up to see the marmot standing over them with a small towel draped over his shoulder.

Wuchak the innkeeper shuffled up to take their order.

"Hello," said Teek. "If you would be so kind, we—"

"Are you still serving?" Cheeks interrupted, blurting out what he felt was most important to him.

"By all means possible," the innkeeper replied. We're not what we used to be, as you might imagine, in keeping with the circumstances, but I think I can manage to put somethin' on the table fer ye."

Looking about the room, they could see other patrons begin to appear. All eyes were on the newcomers. Another small group of ground-squirrels was huddled together at the far end in a small nook. They had all turned to stare.

Now their gazes turned back to each other and their private affairs. They had lost everything—loved ones, homes, way of life, everything. There were also a couple of chipmunks at the opposite end of the room. They, too, returned to their muffled chattering.

There was a stellar's jay finishing off a plate of grubs, next to two robins all "billed up" to the bar.

"We have a very nice fermented pinenut brew, and I can bring you some seeds and nuts in a bowl," continued Wuchak.

"That sounds good. We will have that," said Cheeks before anyone else could speak.

Teek looked up. "Actually, if I may, we need to ask you... have any young female ground squirrels, that is to say, have you seen..."

"Oh, jumpin' juniper berries! You all are the Teek party! Great corn kernels, yes! There is someone waiting for you. I should have thought of that!"

Teek's heart felt as though it would leap from his chest. "Cicci?"

Sure enough, there she was at the opening of a passageway at the far end of the room.

"Cicci! Oh, Cicci!"

Teek scampered over to her, nearly knocking her over when he reached her. He hugged her as if he would never let go. She realized at that moment just how important she was to him.

"Kanti said you might be here! One of your legs is bandaged, and some of the fur on your back is burned!" Teek gasped as he looked her over.

"I am fine now," she replied. "I remembered Kanti mentioning this spot, so when you were nowhere to be found, I thought it would be best to come here."

"We looked and looked, but we could not find you! We called and called and searched and searched! You scared me terribly! You just do not know!"

"Well, Teek, I think I am beginning to," she said.

They joined the others at the table, greeted by hugs and pats.

Shortly the marmot returned from the back room carrying a large flat piece of wood. On it was an enormous nutshell filled with fermented pine nut brew, five nutshell cups, and a big bowl of seeds and nuts.

"What can we give to you in return for all of this?" inquired Teek.

"Well, times are pretty hard around here as you might imagine, but if you can spare something to replace the food, it would be good for those that come after you," said the marmot.

"We can indeed," said Teek, adding, "and thank you."

"Uh, Mr..." continued Teek.

"Wuchak is just fine, Master Teek."

"Uh, Wuchak, do you think that we could trouble you and your patrons with a couple of questions? Our colony was plundered, and we are searching for answers."

"That would be just fine," Wuchak replied. "Go ahead. I only ask that ye not pester them if they do not want to talk. This is their last refuge for quite some distance. Ye see, at first, everyone showed up to find out, well, who was alive... and who was dead. Now they just want to know about, oh, ye know, goin's on. But there is not much goin' on, doncha know."

Teek glanced around the room. He had been so consumed with worry about Cicci that he had not stopped to think about those poor creatures at the other tables that had lost their homes and their loved ones. They had no place else to go.

"Sort of gives me a better understanding of *our* situation," commented Peeps.

"It most certainly does. It really does," Teek acknowledged.

As Teek gathered his thoughts about these lives, now torn apart from all the devastation, he realized that he had never felt such relief before in his life.

As his gaze returned to Cicci, he added, "I am never letting you out of my sight again."

"No more worrying now. I am fine. We made it this far, and we are all still here, so stop all this fuss. We can do this," replied Cicci.

"Well, we have much to celebrate," said Cheeks as he raised his nutshell cup for a toast, breaking the moment of silence.

"Hey, where has Kanti gone?" asked Peeps.

Sure enough, he was gone. As they looked around the room, they found him sitting next to the jay at the bar. It appeared that Kanti and the jay already knew each other.

The group turned back to their table. It was their first taste of the pine nut brew. It was most pleasant and refreshing, and it had a curious warm feeling going down. They all agreed that it provided a sort of satisfying happiness.

Cheeks dove into the seeds and nuts as though he hadn't eaten in days.

"Cheeks, please stop stuffing those nuts into your mouth for later," Teek corrected. "Leave some for the rest of us."

Kanti returned to the table; he lifted his nut cup with his beak, dipped it in the bowl of pine nut brew, and set it in front of him. All eyes were on Kanti as he stood with his head down at the table. He dipped his bill into his cup and drank for quite some time. Finally, he raised his head and pondered before beginning his foreboding message in a low subdued tone.

"Well, KKKKK! Not good."

"What did you find out?" asked Teek.

"I *am* hearing things, dark and strange things. I feel that I need to tell you..." Kanti paused, looking directly at Teek. "I advise you to turn back."

"What? No, we are not turning back! We are not returning home! We are not going to give in to fear!" Teek proclaimed. "We made it this far, and Cicci is safe!"

"Yes, you are all safe for now. I will grant you that."

"What is it, Kanti?" asked Cicci.

Kanti began again, "There are hidden dangers out there, very hidden but very serious. These dangers are far beyond the predators that we all know about. I have been keeping to my forest with no attention paid to the dark forested mountain country to the west and to the north, but the jay *has* been farther out in that direction."

"What is it, Kanti?" asked Teek.

"We do not know exactly," he continued. "You see, we birds stay at the top of the trees at night and keep silent. It is difficult to see under the canopy, and we do not want to see."

"See what?" Teek urged.

"I am just not sure. They come in the night when it is dark. No one sees them. They are so hard to find that some believe that they do not exist. There are those that have gone missing, though. But one thing is certain, something is out there, and if it finds you, you are in great danger."

The group sat waiting for Kanti to continue, but instead he said simply, "You should get some sleep now. We will talk about this again in the morning."

Peeps looked at Cheeks, saying, "Well, that is most reassuring. Nothing like a horrifically frightening story just before sleep." Kanti continued, "There are sleeping chambers up that passageway. Cicci, you can show everyone where *yours* is."

"Are you staying with us?" Peeps asked Kanti.

"No, I sleep better high in the trees, and I am a light sleeper."

"I will keep one eye open and trained on the forest floor. When you are done here, follow Cicci up the passageway to the sleeping chamber. I will return in the morning."

The innkeeper opened the front door for Kanti and bid him good night. Kanti spread his wings and took flight. A chilling wind blew in as the innkeeper slammed the heavy door shut with a deep boom and slid the wooden beam into place. Teek was noticeably shaken by Kanti's cryptic words of warning.

Wuchak walked up and wiped their table, adding, "As Kanti said, when you're ready, head straight up the passageway. Your sleeping chamber is at the end, on the right. It is easy to find."

Teek and his reunited friends finished their repast and then headed up to the chamber.

At the top of the passage, there was an open door to a cozy room with a thick carpet of straw and feathers. Filled and contented for the moment, they all curled up together and slept with the soundness that only comes at the end of a long hard day.

13

INTO THE DARKNESS

"Kraauuk! KKKK-quiulup!" The raven arrived early and called up the passageway to awaken the small group of travelers.

Teek appeared at the top. "We are just now stirring and will be down shortly, Kanti."

Teek was down first, anxious to hear what Kanti had to say from the day before and what he might have seen or heard during the night. He found Kanti near the fire warming his feathers, staring into the embers.

"Tell me, Kanti. Tell me, what is happening?"

"I wish I could, but I am still not sure," he replied.

"You told us to turn back, but we must not," continued Teek.

"Then you said that we should know that the way ahead is not safe. We knew that this expedition would not be safe when we started," he added. "So, I have known this would be dangerous... Cicci has too. I'm not completely sure about the other two, but I believe that I have warned them about most of it... or *you* have, right? Right?"

"No, no," retorted Kanti. "There is something else. Not one of the usual dangers. This is not something that you know about or could ever prepare for."

Teek sat waiting in silence, hoping that Kanti would continue. He did.

"Last night I heard many things but could only see shadows. I was not able to make them out."

"What did the jay say?" asked Teek.

"He said that there have been howls and screams, some far off, some closer. They are quite loud and sound like they come from a very large creature. If you insist on continuing, keep together and stay hidden. You may soon find out more than you want to know about why you hide in burrows after dark."

Teek reached out and turned Kanti toward him, asking, "Will you travel with us and keep a lookout from up in the trees?"

"For a time," Kanti replied. "I can look down on you for a time, but I have other serious matters to attend, and I do not know how I can protect you from this."

The other members of Teek's party now filtered into the room, satchels in hand, ready to resume the journey. Teek motioned them over to the hearth where he and Kanti were huddled. Kanti addressed the group.

"It is very still right now. The fog has not lifted, and it is quite cold. As it is still just now dawn, your path will be hard to find. Be careful, little ones."

Wuchak, the marmot innkeeper, brought the group a round of hot pine nut brew to send them off. He had been listening in on their conversation, and to others passing through, and knew all too well that what lay before them was very dangerous.

With a knowing smile, he said, "All the best to ye, Master Teek. Ye take extra care. Make sure ye stay safe and find your way back this way again."

Thankful and full, they gathered themselves together, standing in front of the large Pine Stone Inn door, ready to resume their search.

Teek spoke. "We are so incredibly lucky that we are all still here, but I must remind you that this is only the beginning. In fact, it is likely that our toughest times lie ahead of us. Stay close and do not think for one minute that you are safe. Remember, stay sharp. We still have no idea what has befallen our sacred Illumination Stone, and we are not turning back without it."

Reaching the top of the boulder island, they scanned the great expanse of land ahead. It was deathly quiet. The cold air lay close to the ground in a thick fog. The blackened burned-out trees loomed above them like ghostly specters.

"Is everyone ready?" asked Teek. He turned to Kanti, who spoke.

"Once you get to the forest, you will need to head to the river and follow it north downriver. I will be overhead for a time but know this—it is a different forest now. You will soon reach the edge of my range. There are things here that even *I* do not know about."

The squirrels looked at each other and then out across their unknown future. With a little nod to Teek, Kanti lifted his wings and was airborne. His departure whipped up the dusty ash and soot that had collected on the ground where they stood. They covered their faces. When they were finally able to look up, he was gone.

As the squirrels reached the base of the boulders, they all managed to successfully hop onto the outstretched branch from the night before.

All, that is, except Cheeks, who lost his grip for a moment, slipping underneath the branch. But Peeps was ready, grabbing him by the scruff of the neck.

"Teek, help!" he screeched. Together they managed to pull him up.

Following the downed tree, the squirrels climbed carefully over the burn. The foggy smoke was still thick in the air.

They traversed the dangerous devastation below, passing over the hot, dusty soot that covered the ground. Teek made sure Cicci was in front of him all through the burned area.

She made a mild fuss about him watching her so closely, but deep down in her heart she liked the fact that he cared so much.

Hoping to keep the group below him on course, Kanti occasionally called out to them as he flew.

Following his calls, they reached the end of the last downed tree. Now at the edge of the burn, they dropped back down into the shadowy forest and into the unknown journey ahead.

As Kanti had warned, this was indeed an entirely different forest from what they were accustomed to back up the river. The cover, the way was confusing in this unfamiliar territory.

They moved silently, weaving under, over, and around the roots and low-hanging gnarled branches. The silence was as penetrating as the icy mist that enfolded them. The air was now free of smoke and ash, but a new kind of heaviness had taken over. It was thick and dense. It seemed to smother them.

Breathing seemed labored. No birds sang, nor was there the sound of the rustling wind; all was strangely silent. The woods were deep and dark.

"If I didn't know that the light of day was rising, I'd say it was, well, night," whispered Peeps to Cheeks.

"Where has Kanti gotten off to?" Cheeks asked.

Teek stopped the group to listen—nothing, not the slightest sound. They waited. They listened. With little warning, the silence was broken by a *whoop-whoop-whoop*.

"Funny you should ask," said Peeps.

The squirrels huddled under some bitterbrush at the edge of a thicket, peering into the clearing before them.

Whoop-whoop- whoop.

This time the sounds were lower and closer.

Whoop-whoop.

It was close enough for them to feel the rush of wind from dark shadowy wings. Pine needles and pinecone pieces kicked up.

"Caw-caw!"

The clearing was filled with dark shapes. Three crows landed in the middle of the clearing. They bobbed up and down, stretching their necks out with each caw. With a whoosh, Kanti landed behind them; he was twice as big as any of the three crows, with a wingspan twice as wide. "KKKKKK, qiulup! Settle down and listen up!" he croaked.

He cocked his head and peered into the thicket. "Are you in there, little ones? I brought you some news. These crows are under my instructions to tell you all of what they know."

Teek turned to his group, directing them to stay put. He hesitated and then entered the clearing in short jerky steps, ready to ditch at the slightest sign of trouble. One crow is something that a ground squirrel may be able to face, but three was quite unnerving.

"Teek, it is all right," said Kanti. "I'll make sure you are safe. Go ahead now, speak! Tell Teek what you told me!" Kanti clearly had an attitude about crows, considering them to be inferior to ravens.

"Why do you care about this squirrel?" one crow cawed.

Kanti croaked loudly, lifting himself off the ground and landing on the crow's back.

"All right, all right, no need to get your feathers ruffled!" The crow pleaded.

"Tell him!" repeated Kanti.

One crow hopped closer to Teek. "We know where a rat encampment is."

"What about the snake?" pressed Kanti.

"We have overheard the rats mention a snake. They were saying that the snake would eat more ground squirrels so that one day all of the ground squirrels would either be eaten or driven out, and then they would take over the colony upriver."

"Rimrock!" added Teek.

"What else did you hear?" Kanti prodded, looking serious.

"That was all that we heard!" cawed one of the crows.

"Where is the rat encampment?" Kanti prodded again.

"It is located at the north end of the burn, just at the edge of the ridge, where all the human things were left."

Teek managed to ask, "Human things? You know, long tubes, stacks of stuff?"

Kanti hopped around the three crows. "Is that all of it then?" he added.

"Yes, yes, that is all," they said.

The crows stood nervously, keeping their eyes on Kanti's every move.

"All right then, take off!" Kanti ordered.

The crows looked at one another and wasted no time in taking off, without a single squawk, up through the trees.

Kanti launched himself after them before Teek could ask him where he was headed and when he might be able to return.

"Can you see anything, Cicci?" asked Peeps.

Just then, Teek reappeared, reporting, "Those crows said that they knew where the rat encampment was and that they heard them talking about our colony."

"Where is Kanti?" asked Cicci.

Teek replied, "I think he needed to chase the crows away, but then he kept going. He might have had other things to take care of."

"I wonder if he has a mate somewhere and maybe a nest and some offspring of his own," she added.

"I've heard of a crow's nest. Is there such a thing as a raven's nest?" asked Peeps.

"I believe that ravens build large stick nests near the treetops," Teek answered. Teek thought out loud as he spoke. "I get a strange feeling about this forest. I do sense what Kanti was referring to. It seems there is a different kind of danger here."

"Not just predators?" asked Peeps.

"No, something different. Have you noticed how strangely quiet it is? Even Kanti flew off without a word. No, it is decidedly something else. I wonder if it might be better to find somewhere to hole up for a while," Teek answered.

Cheeks had been poking around on one end of the thicket chasing a beetle, and he waddled up to report that he had found a couple of rocks to crawl under.

So, they followed him back to the spot and wedged their way into what turned out to be a very tight space.

"Well?" began Peeps, looking at Teek. "Are we just going to sit here?"

"I do not know yet, Peeps. Something is strange. It is not yet something that I am able to determine. I think we need to stay here until the light of day gets brighter and things have settled down."

They huddled together for what seemed like a long while until shafts of light filtered down to the forest floor.

"Listen!" Cicci said suddenly.

They stopped and sat quietly. They could hear the crunching steps approaching them. Two humans marched down the hill and stopped next to the hiding place of the squirrels. They had hard white shells on their heads. One of them was pointing and speaking, while the other stood with his arms folded. As they came closer, the squirrels overheard their conversation.

"I suppose the fire sorta saved us the trouble of clearing out all the trees for the lots. Now we can just push out the boulders and topsoil and put in some ornamentals," one said.

The other replied, "You may have to change the name of the development from Forest Glen to something else. How about Burnout Bluff?"

"Good one." The other man chuckled and then continued, "Hey, once we clear out all these charred dead trees and brush and put some houses in, nobody will know the difference. Don't worry, we'll still make plenty of money."

It wasn't just the fire itself that created problems for the creatures of the canyon. The land had caught fire numerous times over hundreds, even thousands, of years.

In fact, many times fire had been a way for the land to renew itself.

No, the real culprit was the loss of habitat by the enormous increase of human subdivisions. Humans have had an increasing need for enormous dwellings with groomed yards, golf courses, farms, and ranches.

Above all, they have an insatiable thirst for water. Humans seemed to have been unaware of their effect on other creatures. For the most part, they had little or no awareness of the needs of other living things nor even spent much time considering it. They busied themselves building habitat for their own kind, carving out more and more areas of land suitable for humans only.

"So, the trail will start here where the cul-de-sac ends, and over here where it drops down, we'll pour in some cement stairs. Then the trail continues down closer to the river where the picnic area will be. I've already talked to the commissioners, so we have the go-ahead to start clearing land for that. Then we'll plant some grass and put in some picnic tables and benches."

It was quite some time before Teek, Cicci, Peeps, and Cheeks found the right moment to attempt to scurry away from where the two humans had been sitting.

The first attempt was thwarted by the loud clack of a soda can that was thrown by one of them, hitting the rock just above the squirrel's heads. It was so alarming the squirrels shot back under the rock and hid, frozen in fear.

Then one of the men flicked a burning cigarette that bounced into the opening right in front of where they were hiding. It lay there smoldering while the smoke drifted into the area under the rock, filling it with the toxic fumes of burning tobacco and chemicals, making the squirrels nauseous.

Finally, the two men got back on their feet and headed back to the machine that had brought them and rode away with a roar, kicking up dust and rocks.

Teek and the other squirrels resumed their journey downriver. Because they had spent most of their precious time hiding from the two developers, they were now quite anxious to get as far away as possible from flying cans and burning cigarette butts.

"That might have been why Kanti flew off so fast," said Peeps. Then he added, "Teek, you know how you can look into a human's eyes and make them understand us? Well, I have a feeling that it would not have worked on those two."

Teek stopped to address Peeps' observation.

"That is quite a perceptive conclusion. There *are* humans who can be reached in that way, but there are most certainly humans who can *never* be reached... in *any* way. If I had to describe what it feels like, well, I would say that every living thing has a different vibration, and I can tell when a human is vibrating in a way that allows them to connect with our world, the natural world. I can also tell when a human does not vibrate in a way that allows them to connect. I believe that this force comes from another place, a place that we all come from and will probably go back to someday. That is about the best way for me to describe it, Peeps. Anyway, I am most impressed that you think of these important things."

A pebble struck Peeps on his hind end. "Ow! Cheeks, what did you do that for?"

"Dunno, I just... felt like it."

"Well, stop it!"

"Hey, hold it down. We have a long way to go. No fooling around!" directed Teek.

14

IT COMES IN THE NIGHT

Deeper into the northern end of the pine forest they went. They continued without rest, water, or food for the remainder of the day. They were entering an area where the forest became darker as the ponderosa pine trees became even larger and taller.

They traveled by the bank of the river—across the river the towering cliffs were higher than they had ever seen. This was a shadowy world of deep dark canyons, deep dark swirling water, and a deep dark forest. They were intruders in a foreign land.

As the bright light of day faded into dusk, dusk faded and was replaced with the cool light of night, they felt anything but welcome. This was a far more mysterious land, a land of strange noises and strange shadowy movement. A cold wind funneled through the canyon walls swaying the top of the tallest pine trees.

Soon the large round cool light of night shone down over the forest, reflecting a silvery luminescence, and casting dark shadows.

"We need to stop and hide for the night," Teek concluded.

They had just stopped underneath a manzanita bush while they looked around when *crack pop*! There was something moving through the underbrush just ahead of them. Teek and Cicci stood very still, scanning the darkness for the source of the sudden noise.

The forest grew very silent, no crickets, no frogs, just silence. This heavy silence continued for quite a long while. And then... it began. It started quietly, as Cheeks was just beginning to suggest having a nibble of food.

Teek's sudden "Shoosh!" interrupted him.

They all listened as a deep rumble rose in pitch and intensity to a bloodcurdling howl. It was so loud it rebounded off the walls of the canyon.

"What in the pine needles was that?" Peeps whispered.

"I do not know... I really don't," replied Teek.

Peering through the thick undergrowth, Teek continued carefully looking for any movement.

Nothing.

Then, ever so faintly, he heard something. Something large and heavy was trying to step closer without being noticed. It was moving oh so carefully, staying hidden so that it couldn't be seen. But the squirrel's sharp ears picked up a crunching sound in the soft pine needle duff. The sound became more pronounced the closer it came. And then it stopped.

Teek stared into the darkness under the trees. Was something out there hiding in the dark? Nothing. And then something began to move again.

Two glowing white eyes appeared. They floated high above the forest floor. They moved behind a tree and then reappeared. Teek froze to listen for more sounds. It was deathly quiet. He wondered if maybe this creature was up in the tree.

He waited. Then he heard something moving on the ground, as though it were creeping up on them.

A growing sense of dread welled up in Teek. Cicci clutched his side. He could feel her squeeze tightly.

What sort of creature is this? he thought. He could feel his heart pounding in his chest and could hear a deep rumbling sound. Something very large was huffing and puffing heavily. The shadows were dark, and the light of night filtered through the branches in beams.

Through these beams of light, Teek could just make out a steamy snorting breath gliding through the spaces between the branches. Teek knew he would have to ditch if it came any closer. He noticed that another beam of cool light was shining down on a large mound of boulders just a few bounds away.

Teek chirped a quick "Ditch!"

Grabbing Cicci, he scampered toward the closest opening, hoping it would be large enough for all of them to fit.

Finding a small door, they quickly opened it and scurried inside. And then in that instant, they were charged.

Crashing and cracking through the branches, a giant dark figure leaped into the clearing. It shook the ground, smashing through the undergrowth just over their heads.

As Teek and Cicci slipped through the door, a loud slapping sound hit the rock they had just dove past. They had come close to disaster, closer than they had ever been. There was a deafening roar, loud snorting and breathing, as if air were being drawn into a large drum. The enormous creature scraped and clawed at the ground.

"That was too close," whispered Teek. "I hope Peeps and Cheeks found a place to hide."

"No need to tell *us* twice." The voice of Peeps standing right behind Teek caught him by surprise.

Teek spun around, searching for them in the darkness. "How did you...? I did not see..."

"Thanks for the 'Ditch!'" Peeps replied.

The very same doorway that Teek had chosen was in fact, the entrance to a passage.

Teek peered into the darkness, adding, "Well done, you two! If you had not scrambled after us then, well, who knows what would have happened to you. I think that you two just might survive this trip!"

Their moment of relief was interrupted by another deafening roar.

"What in the stinging nettles is that?" asked Cheeks.

"Unknown. Maybe it was what Kanti was referring to. We had all better be absolutely quiet until it is gone," added Cicci.

"If you think that is scary, you should see this!"

No one recognized this voice coming from the dark recesses of the passage.

"Who said that?" asked Teek in a harsh whisper.

He had gone through quite enough surprises for one day and had no room for more.

"Not me."

"Nor me."

"Nor me," added Cicci.

"Now hear this," Teek insisted. "If it was none of you, then—"

"Hello, I am Tibbs."

They all spun around. In the darkness, they could just barely make out a silhouetted shape—the source of the unrecognized voice.

"What are you? Show yourself!" Teek squeaked.

Teek realized that in this part of the forest, it could have been just about anything.

"Well, you could say I'm a kwitshie." A large rabbit with warm brown eyes and moved out so they could see him.

Teek was quite surprised. "Really? A kwitshie? This is your burrow? You must be terrified living here!" he said, now recognizing what was before him.

"Like I said, follow me. There is something that you need to see. You will want to make sure to avoid this."

"A kwitshie, huh? Hey, Peeps, what is a kwitshie?" Cheeks asked, struggling to keep up with the situation.

Peeps whispered back, "Big ears, big feet, and friendly."

The group followed behind Tibbs the kwitshie through a narrow passageway to the other side of the boulder mound. A small crack of light began to appear ahead of them. As they approached, they could see that a break in the trees was allowing the light of night to illuminate the clearing on the other side of the mound of boulders.

"Look," said Tibbs.

Teek and Cicci were the first to peer through the opening. The clearing was lit by the cool light of night. They could just make out a large mound of something. The mound appeared to be moving. Not from one place to another, instead the surface of it seemed to be crawling and pulsating with many things.

"What *is* that?" Teek whispered his question.

"Just wait and look very carefully," replied Tibbs.

Teek kept looking. Forms began to appear. He saw things wriggling, ripping, and fighting. Then they heard screeches ringing out, echoing off the surrounding trees. The movement soon revealed itself.

"Rats?" asked Teek.

"Yes, feeding rats," answered Tibbs.

"Feeding?" Teek continued.

"Yes, on a deer carcass," Tibbs answered.

"Pine nuts!" Cheeks exclaimed, a note of horror in his voice.

"That is disgusting!" added Peeps.

"Get back!" ordered Tibbs, but none of the squirrels moved.

Teek, noticing the lack of response, chirped, "Ditch!"

Tibbs was surprised to see how quickly the use of this word caused the squirrels to disappear back into the darkness of the passageway.

Teek nodded his head once and gave Tibbs a little smile.

Three of the rats looked up from their grizzly feast. Their faces were soaked in blood. They thought that they had heard something, but they were feeding so ravenously that they were only distracted for a moment.

"Best to remain hidden. Maybe you should stay here tonight," suggested Tibbs.

Peeps and Cheeks were now peeking through the opening in the rocks, horrified by the scene before them.

"No, I do not believe there will be any scurrying around for you out there until the light of day comes again. I will show you a chamber at the back end of the burrow where you can stay hidden," said Tibbs.

"You are most kind. Yes, we should stay hidden. It is too dangerous for us to travel right now," said Cicci.

Tibbs piled up dirt at the opening with his large hind feet, just in time for what was to happen next.

Crack-boom, boom, boom! The ground shook with a heavy impact.

An enormous boulder had been tossed on top of the feeding rats, crushing several of them, snapping some bones in the carcass, and then rolling onto the ground. Rats scattered in every direction. All was quiet, and then they heard the sound from before.

Only this time there was more than just the crunching of the soft pine needle duff. Something heavy was walking, and heavy footfalls shook the ground. The creature was so close that it sent tremors through the burrow.

The earth shook, and pebbles fell from the ceiling. Tibbs showed Teek a small opening in the rock wall, just large enough for him to peer through.

"You will also want to see this," Tibbs said.

Teek peered through the opening. He could just make out a massive shadow moving by, blocking out the beams of light as it went.

With popping, snapping, and scraping noises, the dead deer was dragged away. Heavy breathing and a low guttural growl could be heard as the carcass was dragged over the gravelly ground.

"You should go to your sleeping chamber now. You have probably had enough of this for one evening. By thump, I know I have. Head down this way and go into the second chamber on your right," directed Tibbs.

"What way? I am unable to see much of anything," said Teek. He felt a large foot on his back, shoving him forward.

"That way, follow your leader, friends!"

The others followed Teek to a cozy sleeping chamber.

All through the night, they huddled together, listening to the sounds of the deep dark forest. They could hear terrifying sounds, some far off, some so close as to sound as though they were just outside, howling, growling, snarling, thumping, and clacking.

All sorts of unimaginable creatures patrolled this forest. At times, they shivered together in fear.

Cheeks turned to Peeps and whispered, "I do not want to go out there tomorrow!"

"Well, you have no choice in the matter, so try not to think about it. We *will* make it. You wait and see. Tomorrow everything will seem easier. With Teek's help, we *will* make it." Peeps' words of encouragement were a comfort to Cheeks.

They awoke to the chirping of birds. Light was peeking through a crack in between the rocks on one side of their chamber.

Teek and Cicci were the first to rouse, and so they made their way down the passage to a larger chamber toward the end of the burrow that had looked out on that frightening clearing the night before.

The chamber was now bathed in the golden early light of the new day, and the family of rabbits was up and gathered on the straw-strewn floor, munching on their first meal, almost as though nothing had happened.

There was a simple wooden table and a slab of wood that served as a doorway that might have gone to a larder of some kind. They lived in very sparse surroundings compared to what Teek and the other squirrels were used to.

Tibbs, his mate, and three little ones were munching on somewhat wilted green shoots. Tibbs' young kits were startled as they looked up suddenly from their morning feeding.

"Oh yes, there you are," greeted Tibbs. "The others, are they still sleeping?"

"They are," replied Teek.

"I would offer you some—"

"Oh no, we have our own provisions in our satchels," Teek interjected.

"Well, please do join us," returned Tibbs. "This is my mate, Nibble."

"Hello," said Nibble timidly.

"And our six little kits, Dibble, Bomba, Bopple, Tibbs Junior, Teedy, and Kittle," Tibbs continued. Dibble and Bomba and Tibbs Junior were busy rolling around on the floor in a wrestling match. Teedy was watching as she nibbled on a leaf, and Kittle, who was younger, hid behind Nibble.

"Can you say hello, Kittle?" asked her papa.

Kittle managed to peer out at the visitors from behind her momma.

"We do not let her out of our sight," added Nibble. "We have to be so careful now."

Noticing the difference in the ages of their young ones and being somewhat familiar with rabbits, Teek wondered if maybe some kits in their litter had not survived. But he said nothing about it.

"This is a pleasant home you have here, Tibbs," said Teek.

"Thank you," Tibbs replied. "It *has* been a lot safer in the past. Now it is pretty scary. But if we go out, we do have thick underbrush nearby to hide in. The clearing out there occasionally gives us some new fresh shoots, roots, and blooms, particularly when the great cycle is new. That is, when there is no dead deer and a large band of feeding rats! That big fire up the hill ruined many burrows, you know, and many sources of food went with it. No, this area is not what it used to be, but it will sprout again when the great cycle is new."

Teek began to realize that Tibbs was a stalwart sort, who tried to maintain and present a positive outlook on what he and his family had been going through.

Clearly times were tough for this family. They had little to eat and were no doubt living in constant fear. But Tibbs was a "chin up, ears forward" sort of fellow.

Teek admired his stout heart and positive, gentle nature. He thought of how he might be able to help this brave family.

"You know, Tibbs, we have a friend here in the forest that might be able to help you," Teek began. "What do you think of... ravens?"

"Ravens! Well, they are dangerous, no doubt!" Tibbs reacted with alarm. "I have seen them feeding on dead creatures, even my kind. Those poor creatures that have been hit by the large moving things the humans ride in on the long strip of black rock!"

"Yes, yes, I know," Teek reassured. "But this one is our friend, and there is no need to fear him. You see, Tibbs, these days you may have to accept some rather unusual creatures as allies. Some of them you might even consider to be... dangerous. I know you want to get Nibble and the kits to a safer place. Let me tell our friend Kanti about you. He *is* a raven, but he is a grand fellow, and I think he will help you. I will ask him to check in on you. He is sort of the 'eyes' of his forest. Back where we come from, it is dangerous as well, but I know that with help from other creatures, you can make it through. Maybe there will be something that you can do for *him* too. It is important for well-intending creatures to help each other these days. Working together might even be the only way to survive."

Tibbs stood and listened thoughtfully, and then he turned and looked back at his family. In a low, resolute voice, he replied, "Tell him that when he lands here, he can call to me. Go ahead and tell him my name. I will listen for him."

"Good, he will help you. Now, my new friend, we must return to our journey," Teek said as he turned to leave.

Then he turned back to Tibbs, adding, "I will not forget you and the help you gave us. I have a strong feeling that we will be seeing each other again."

Cicci had gone to rouse Peeps and Cheeks. Now they had returned, satchels in hand, ready for travel.

"We are ready to go, Teek," said Cicci.

"One last thing, Tibbs," Teek inquired. "What was that giant shadowy thing that dragged the deer way last night?"

Tibbs glanced nervously in the direction of the clearing from the night before.

"We do not have a name for it. It is always too dark to see them when they come. We know that they are large and very dangerous. I am noticing that *most* creatures are on edge and seem more dangerous now. I am not sure whether it is hunger or fear. Many creatures appear to be on the move and less predictable. They show up in unexpected places. It might be because of that fire. Or maybe it is because of the increase of new humans that is causing the behavior of the creatures of the canyon to change. We never used to spend this much time hiding. We stay mostly in our burrow now. I have not left it in days, except when I absolutely *had* to quickly gather more food for the little ones. It is much harder to prepare for winter. We have to be so careful more than most other creatures."

"Yes, I understand," said Teek. "That is the reason you will need more help, and from all sorts of different creatures; otters, geese, marmots, and yes, as scary as he is, a raven named Kanti."

"Wherever *he* is," added Peeps.

"He will return, Peeps!" corrected Teek. He then turned back to Tibbs. "You live beyond the border of Kanti's end of the forest, but I know he will find you. I dare say he has saved *us* more than once."

"I do hope you find what you are looking for," said Tibbs. "Do be careful."

Teek and his group took one last look at Tibbs and his family and then cautiously moved through the passage and out into the brush, heading down the slope toward the river.

15

THE LANDING POOL

When Teek and the group arrived at the river's edge, it was still very early. The morning light was just peeking over the rimrock. The air was colder than the deep dark swirling water of the large, pond-sized pool before them. Steam rose from the gurgling surface as the river rolled by. It smelled of wet mud and sweet water plants.

Ground squirrels never ventured into the river itself, but they were known to frequent the banks to drink and to collect various delicacies, like salmon flies and other aquatic bugs. Every so often large trout interrupted the gurgling sound of the river as they sipped flies from the steamy surface of the water. Wriggling and rushing through the shallows after minnows, the trout's glistening backs slipped through the reeds. Then with mighty flips of their tails, they wriggled away, returning to the shadowy depths and out of sight, leaving bubbling ripples slopping up on the muddy bank.

"Honk-honk-honk!"

They all spun around toward the loud trumpeting sound behind them.

"Good gravel!" exclaimed Peeps.

"There it is, up there!" Cicci turned Cheeks around and pointed to the top of the rimrock.

A quite large and commanding Canada goose was standing atop the rimrock cliff above the large pool.

"Follow me," directed Teek.

Cheeks looked at Peeps with alarm. "Where is *he* going?" he asked.

"Well," Peeps began, "up where the goose is, I guess!"

They all followed Teek, scrambling up the rocky cliff to the top of the rimrock.

Approaching the goose, Teek addressed him. "Hello and greetings!"

"Honk-honk, one moment, please. I have to land this flock!" said the goose.

"Flock?" Cheeks asked.

The goose's beak was pointed back upriver and toward the sky. The squirrels all turned their heads, following the direction of the goose's beak until they could just make out a flock of Canada geese in their final approach to the large pool that lay below them.

"Oh, this should really be something," Teek said, looking at Cicci.

The arrival of a flock of geese on the river was clearly a far more complicated process than one might imagine. It should now be made known that even in the lives of animals, numbers and measures are a kind of 'universal language' and are also of vital importance.

In fact, although many things that animals do are attributed to instinct, there are some things that simply could not be achieved without careful calculation—a fox's accurate pounce on a mouse in three feet of snow, for example, or landing a flock of geese in a pool on a river, for another.

As the flock came within earshot, the squirrels began to hear the approaching geese honking out to the pool's control goose standing at the top of the cliff rim; most of the honking came from the lead goose, the flock commander. The other geese in the flock had been honking largely in a show of support, but now they were silent, allowing the flock commander and the pool's control goose to communicate and safely land the flock.

The flock commander honked, "This is flock three-three-five, heading two-zero-zero northbound, descending into final approach."

The pool's control goose replied, "Flock three-three-five turn to heading one-eight-zero, drop to fifty-foot level and begin reducing air speed."

"Roger that," came the reply from the commander. Moments later, he was heard again. "Maintaining fifty-foot level, landing pool in sight."

"Affirmative," answered the pool's control goose. "Flock three-three-five cleared for final approach, reduce airspeed to fifteen knots, and drop to twenty-five-foot level."

"Three-three-five," came the reply. The commander honked back at his flock, "Maintain formation. Tighten it up, flock! Three- three-five requests confirmation for flock heading."

The pool's control goose came back with, "Flock three-three- five, maintain heading one-eight-zero, descend, and hold at twenty-five-foot level."

The flock commander then responded, "Confirm, heading one-eight-zero, descend and hold twenty-five, flock three-three- five." A long pause and then, "Final approach, flock three-three- five dropping flaps, landing gear down."

Their large, webbed, black feet stretched out below them in anticipation of the touchdown onto the dark smooth surface of the large pool.

The control goose began again. "Flock three-three-five, you are cleared for landing—on landing pool number seven."

"Roger that, three-three-five," was the reply.

"So, three-three-five," Peeps began.

The pool's control goose lifted his wing quickly, maintaining his concentration on the task of landing the flock.

"Not now, Peeps," corrected Teek.

The pool's control goose continued, "Flock three-three-five, you're coming in a little hot, drop airspeed to five knots..."

The flock command goose responded, "Dropping to five knots, three-three-five."

Then with a swoosh and a splash, the flock command goose reported, "Splashdown landing pool number seven, three-three-five."

The pool's control goose, still holding up one wing to the squirrels, completed his instructions. "Flock three-three-five continue to the cattails on the east side and base end of landing pool number seven.

"Roger, three-three-five," the flock signed off.

"All right, may I help you?" The pool's control goose now turned his attention to the small band of squirrels.

They were impressed with the goose and had been watching his every move and listening to his every word in amazement.

"So, Peeps, go ahead, ask your question," said Teek.

"Uh, oh yes, um, wow. I had no idea there was so much—"

"Peeps, your question, please?" Teek urged.

"Yes, so...so why are they called flock three-three-five?"

"Well," said the pool's control goose, "in this flock, the front or lead row has three experienced adult geese on one wing of the commander and three experienced adult geese off the other wing. This lead goose or commander is not included in the number on either the left wing or the right wing. Also, there are typically two geese that take turns being the flock commander, depending on the situation. Some are better at landing, others better in bad weather, and so on. Then in this flock, at least, the second row had five geese. These second rows are typically made up of less experienced, younger geese or geese new to the flock. We use only one number to represent them—in this case, five. Understand?"

There was a long pause.

"Oh," Peeps replied.

He looked at Cheeks a bit bewildered to see if he had understood.

"May we trouble you for some information?" asked Teek. "We have some questions we would like to ask you."

"All right," said the goose. "And then I need to head down to pool number seven to welcome the flock and check them in."

Teek began, "We are squirrels from Rimrock, from up the river and—"

The goose trumpeted, saying, "Oh yes, Rimrock, I have heard of you! You are a long way from your colony, are you not? Congratulations for making it this far. Kanti mentioned that—"

"You know Kanti?" asked Peeps.

"Oh yes. Kanti mentioned that you might be traveling through. Here is what I know, and then I must go. At the north end of the burned area just up the hill, that way," he gestured with his wing, "there are piles of human-made things, long black tubes, and other stacks of stuff. Humans were getting the area ready for more of their dwellings by digging out—well, ruining, really—the homes of all kinds of creatures. Then the fire destroyed everything else, and then the humans left. Now there are rats living in those long tubes and in the other piles of human things. And there has also been a large snake around. We geese hate snakes, you know. We chase them when we see them. Anyway, this one goose that landed in pool number eight a while back, chased this snake, and that goose told me that the snake had something in its mouth. It looked to him to be a large clear golden egg or rock. That is all I know. Now I really must get down to the river."

Teek began to thank him. "Well, may I just say for all of us..."

The large goose had already launched himself off the cliff and was gliding down to the water's edge before Teek could finish his appreciation.

"Clearly the goose was referring to Ish!" commented Cicci. She continued, "I would imagine that the horrible rat Eek is part of that, that clan in that encampment!"

"This is really good news," said Teek.

"It is?" blurted Peeps. "A gang of large, nasty rats has possession of our Illumination Stone, or a large snake still has it. What was the *good* news?"

"Obviously, we are going to need more information first," replied Cicci.

Teek thanked Cicci for her answer. "Cicci, it is good to know that we can rely on you for clarity," he said. "Now listen, the point is, we *are* getting closer. But the closer we get, the more dangerous it will be. It is more important than ever that we be especially careful as we close in. You might all feel anxious to find the stone but stay close and do not get ahead of yourself. That could get you and the rest of us in serious trouble."

"No need to worry about that! I *am* anxious, but it is not so much about finding the stone," Peeps replied.

Teek continued, "Listen very closely to what I tell you to do, and as always, when I say *ditch*, you find the nearest hole, crack, or crevasse and ditch. Any questions?"

"I ga' one," said Cheeks with his mouth full.

"What is it, Cheeks?" Teek asked.

Shifting the food, a bit, Cheeks did his best to reply. "Hwdoyo poposto ake thstonbaa?"

Cicci looked at Teek and then closed her eyes. "Cheeks!"

Teek shook his head, "Please finish whatever it is that you have in your mouth! I am unable to understand what you are saying!"

Peeps piped up, answering for Cheeks, "He wanted to know how we are going to take the stone back. I think he is asking if there is a plan."

"If Cheeks wants to ask me a question, he should finish what he is eating first! We must go now, and please stay close!" With that, Teek turned and departed.

The squirrels headed north along the rimrock in the direction in which the goose had spoken. They scampered from cover to cover.

As they neared the burned area, they could see that the only plants that hadn't been unearthed were clinging to life near the edge of the cliff. So, this was the direction they traveled. It was a very narrow route. On one side of them was a sheer cliff. On the other side of them all the trees and brush had been uprooted and pushed aside.

The light of day was setting over the mountains to the west. They had been scrambling for quite a long while, and so they stopped to rest high on top of a cliff face.

They peered over a ledge that jutted out and afforded a view of the canyon and river below. They were all silent as they looked for great distances in both directions. It was a view none of them had ever beheld.

They sat in silence, watching the river wind its way on its journey northward, disappearing into the evening haze of the canyon. The towering basalt wall across the river provided a cool shadow for a flock of swallows.

They flitted just off the edge of the rim, chirping, and chasing undulating clouds of flies. The sound of a distant chute of rapids thundered quietly.

Teek whispered to the others, "Look over on the other side of the river, above the cliffs. There are open areas of green grass. And look further up the hill. Are those the large dwellings of humans? I have never seen such a sight."

"Nor have any of us, I imagine," Cicci added. "It looks like it goes on forever."

"The world is a very big place," said Teek, "and yet as we continue our journey, our world seems to be getting smaller. I would like to have seen this during better times. Smells funny, though. Does anyone else smell that?"

The group sniffed the air.

"Yes, it does smell rather rotten," commented Cheeks.

"Hmm, well, we need to keep moving," Teek directed, picking up his satchel. "All right then, onward."

Turning around, they were terrified to find themselves facing the source of the odd smell, a large band of rats. These weren't just any rats. These rats were the remnants of the very same band that had been feeding on the deer carcass from the night before near Tibbs' burrow back in the old dark forest. These rats were returning to the encampment where the humans had left their building materials in piles.

The squirrels could see that some of their heads were still red with blood.

The rats sniffed the air as they inched closer. Having happened upon Teek's small group by accident, they weren't exactly sure what their next move would be.

"Well, well," said one exceptionally large and bloody rat. "We find ground squirrels snooping around. We think they look lost. Maybe we bring them with us back to camp!"

Humans call a colony of rats a "mischief," but that term is, of course, not used by the rats.

"What are you doing here so near to our camp? What are you up to? Speak up! Tell us!"

Teek and the others were in shock. They were speechless. They feared for their very lives. They had no answer to offer.

"Well? Nothing to say?" the large rat pressed. "No? Bring them!" he hissed.

The rats circled around the squirrels, closing in on them. Not wanting to be touched by the bloody creatures, Teek's group quickly moved ahead, herded in the direction of the rat encampment. They soon arrived at the end of a large cleared-out area just above the cliff.

The rats had arrived at this spot by stowing away in freight shipped in from large cities by truck or by train. After gathering at nearby shipping centers, they then wandered to temporarily occupy the dumps, vacant lots, and the piles of unused debris left at construction sites at the end of the abandoned subdivisions. Here was desolation.

Everything was either dead or dying in large piles. As the band of returning rats arrived at the opening of the pipes with their captive squirrels, other rats poured from the opening to see what the commotion was about.

With them came an overpowering stench of decay. It was a putrid odor that slapped Teek's group squarely in their faces.

The mass of rats pouring from the opening of the pipe squealed loudly while shoving and rolling each other over and biting each other's necks.

"We found these squirrels poking about, so we brought them. Tell Sleg that we have arrived!" Eek screeched.

Three rats rushed back into the pipe, while the rest of the rats poked about the new captives. Deep inside the cavernous black tube, they could hear scratching and screeching that echoed out of the opening.

In the blackness of the tube, they could just make out a large dark figure emerging from deep within– "attendant rats" were leading it. A set of glowing eyes appeared. Steam began to swirl out of the top of the tube as the scratching noise became louder.

And then it emerged from the tube, an enormous dark gray rat with streaks of darker grease in its fur, as if it had been rolling in some black oil. The group of attendant rats swarmed him, crawling on him, pawing at him, and whispering into his ears. He was a terrifying sight. Years of primitive, violent gluttony had warped and twisted his visage into a mangy, gnarl-toothed old rodent.

"Tell me, what have you brought us? Who are these creatures?" His squeaky raspy voice was surprisingly high-pitched for a rodent of his size.

Eek (one of the rats that had eavesdropped on Cheeks and Peeps and had survived bringing the news to Ish the snake) was the rat that answered him. "We know who they are! We took their golden rock from them, and we mean to take their colony over as soon as the snake gets 'em all! They are from upstream, a colony called Rimrock. Oh, it is a fine place! We will take it!" He went on.

"Well, hee hee, we have them now," declared Sleg, the enormous alpha rat.

He let out a hissing, wheezing laugh as he peered down his long, pointed nose at the travelers. Extending a long, thin-fingered claw, he poked Cicci. "We will have to fatten you up a bit," he said.

"You do not touch her!" cried Teek.

"Well, listen to this one." He turned his attention to Teek. "Oh, we are going to do a lot more than that," replied Sleg. "Take those packs of theirs and bring them!"

"If you do, you will never have what you need to take over our colony!" declared Teek.

"He is lying to us!" accused Eek.

"Maybe, but you will never know unless you hear this!" Teek parlayed.

"Speak then," screeched Sleg, "before we tear you apart!"

Teek continued, "You took a valuable part of our colony, a large stone. We came to get it back."

"Oh...well, *did* you now!" Sleg replied.

"Yes! That is why we are here," answered Teek.

"How could a stone be so important? How does it help us?" Sleg's voice became whinier as he interrogated Teek.

"Uh, well," Teek began again, "if you find the clear golden stone, you... you can use it again, you see, to... to draw more ground squirrels away from the colony!"

"Teek!" shouted Peeps.

What Peeps did not know was that Teek was stalling to gain some precious time. Teek had glanced up toward the sky and noticed some rather large birds circling. One was black. He hoped beyond hope that it was a bird that they knew very well.

Sleg screeched at Eek, "Eek, tell me, where is this stone?"

"Ish the snake had it," came his squeamish reply. "He... he was grabbed by a large bird. He must have dropped it."

"Well then, find it!" screamed Sleg. "Then we can move out of these tubes and into this Rimrock! Meantime, bring them into the tube."

Three rats began to close in on the group of squirrels to grab at them. Cicci had noticed a stick at her feet with a pointed end. She picked it up and thrust it at an advancing rat, poking him in the eye. The rat screamed in pain and reeled back.

As he did, he was jerked into the air with a mighty swoosh and a scream. He felt the terrible needle-sharp claws of a raptor sink into his back.

Swoosh!

Another rat was taken and then another! The rats scattered.

Sleg lifted his head toward the sky, blinking and squinting to find the attackers. He spun around, screeching, and waddled quickly back into the darkness of the tube.

"Ditch!" Teek squeaked.

Without hesitation, the squirrels scampered for cover. A familiar *whoop-whoop-whoop* made Teek peek back over the rock from which they had just ditched. It *was* Kanti!

"Teek, stay hidden until the Muhas are gone. They might just as easily snatch you!" Kanti croaked.

Teek ducked back down until all the commotion had stopped. Kanti hopped down over the edge to join the squirrels.

"You saved us! Are those Koosagh Diaubs?"

Kanti turned back to him, puzzled, "What?"

Teek thought again about the term "sky devil" and changed his question. "Uh, what were those birds?"

"Oh, those were Muha. It is a big bird with a red tail."

"How did you get them to help us?" asked Teek.

"Food! Alive and wriggling!" Kanti answered. "I just told them that I would guide them to it if they made sure to only grab gray rodents and leave the orange-yellow ones with the stripes alone." Kanti chuckled.

"Oh, can they see color?" Teek asked.

There were a few moments of silence from Kanti, except for an initial KKKKKK, as he stared back at Teek and silently reviewed his plan of attack. Finally, he drew his conclusion. "Well, it worked! I did mention your stripes to them as well."

"Yes, you did," Teek confirmed. "We really thought we were finished."

"I have been watching you from above. We ravens notice everything. Most animals, either on the wing or crawling, look to us for finding things and for finding things out," Kanti replied.

"How fortunate for *us* that we can count on you," added Teek.

"All right now, I mean it, little ones. You must head down to the river and stay hidden. I will try to join you there."

Teek gathered up his group and headed down the steep slope, hopping from rock to rock, through sage, nettles, fescue, and finally into the rushes at water's edge. He caught up with Cicci. Leaning toward her ear, he said, "I had no idea you were so dangerous with a stick."

"You'd better stay in line," she replied with a quick smile.

"I shall," he replied.

They reached the base of a towering rock at the water's edge, where they caught their breath and collected themselves.

16

KEEPING WATCH

Fwoop-fwoop-fwoop! Kanti landed.

"Were we ever glad to see you!" said Peeps.

"Seems like you arrived just in time. We thought you were gone for good," added Cheeks.

"Nonsense. I was looking for more information and preparing for the air attack."

"A goose told us that Ish was chased by another goose," Teek reported. "They thought that a rat had picked up the stone, but it turns out that the rats did not know where the stone was either. We heard the rats say that Ish had been grabbed by a koos, um, a muha."

"Yes," said Kanti. "That is what I have been told. The muhas say that the snake was carrying the stone in his mouth at the time. But he dropped it so that he could bite the muha in the leg, which caused the muha to drop the snake. So, we think that the snake may still be alive somewhere. Sorry to tell you this, but we think the stone was dropped... in the river."

Silence fell over the group. If this *were* true, there would be no way of ever locating the stone, let alone recovering it.

"We need to find a place to stop and think," Teek concluded. "We came so close," he added.

"You are brave squirrels. You did everything you could, including risking your lives." Kanti's words were low and quiet.

"You have helped us more than I can say," said Teek. "Yet with all of that, I do have one more favor to ask of you, my friend. Hopefully, it is not too troublesome. It is right on your way... on the edge of your forest."

Kanti cocked his head to listen closely.

Teek continued, "There is a family of rabbits living in your forest...at the north end. They live in a boulder pile."

"Yes, I've seen them there, but they are very fearful," Kanti replied.

"Well, I told them about you," Teek went on. "They are afraid to leave their burrow, with all of the dangers around them, but they need fresh food and a better place to live."

Kanti interjected, "Teek, I am not sure I can—"

"Could you just stop by and check in on them from time to time, see if they need anything? They are expecting to see you. So... so Tibbs, he's the male rabbit. I told him all about you. He said he would talk to you."

Kanti could tell that this was particularly important to Teek.

"Well, I suppose I could fly by and check in on them," he said.

"You are a true friend and a great bird, Kanti," said Cicci.

"Yes, well, you know me, I am not happy unless I know what is going on in my forest. That *is* what I do. I will watch for you on your way home, little ones."

With that, he leapt into the air, lifting himself skyward with two mighty beats of his strong black wings, and was gone. He headed south, back upriver.

"He is something, that one," sighed Cicci.

Teek looked at her and rolled his eyes. Cicci slapped him playfully.

"Good thing you don't have a stick," he said.

The small group of squirrels stood looking at each other without a word. Finally, Cheeks spoke.

"Well, there is no way to think clearly on an empty stomach. On the way down from the rim, I gathered some seeds, some grasshoppers, some beetles, and some pine nuts."

"You know, Cheeks," Teek began. Cheeks expected the worst from Teek. "That is a good idea!"

Cheeks was relieved, he looked down and humbly shuffled his hind feet in the sand.

Teek noticed a towering boulder just a short distance away, by the river's edge. It was a pillar-like roost with some boulders on top of it. It looked like it might serve as a good hiding place. It also had a large bush of sage growing right out of the top.

"We can scramble up there under that bush, eat some supper, and see what the morning brings. Maybe there is some room under a rock up there where we can hide out for the night. We can huddle together for warmth. I would not be at all surprised if, when it gets dark, the rats come looking for us, so we should take turns standing guard," said Teek.

Once they found their way to the top of the towering rock, they were better able to view the surrounding area. It was a perfectly defensible position. Atop the enormous stone tower, under three boulders, was a place for them to crawl into, huddle together, and find warmth. They ate well on what Cheeks had gathered. Cicci made a point of thanking Cheeks profusely. Cheeks nodded in acknowledgment. His mouth was full.

After they had eaten up the evening's meal, they huddled together and began to assess their seemingly unsolvable problem. Teek began, "All right, let us talk now about what we do next."

Peeps jumped in, "I would just like to say that it sounds to me as though the Illumination Stone is most likely in the most inaccessible place possible, never to be recovered, and we have come all this way to find out that there is no hope of finding it."

"Well, thank you, Peeps, for that inspiring summary!" said Teek.

Cicci then pointed out that the situation they were in had always been part of the risk from the very beginning. Teek listened to their comments and quickly deduced that it was probably not a good time to talk about what they should do next.

"We will discuss this again in the morning. It has been a very traumatic day for us all, to say the least. We are not out of danger in this location. So, who wants to stay up and keep lookout first?" asked Teek.

"I can keep watch first," declared Cicci.

"All right, Cicci, then Peeps, then me, and finally Cheeks. Is that agreeable to everyone?" Teek asked.

Nodding heads proved it was.

Teek continued, "Cicci, we will all really need your clear guidance in the morning. Peeps and Cheeks, you need to be particularly alert tomorrow. You need to stay focused and keep a good lookout. When your turn comes, if you see anything approaching our position, sound the alarm."

Cicci and Teek walked to the edge of the towering rock. Teek wanted a quick look before he rested.

"You get some sleep, Teek. You look tired," she observed.

Cicci took her position, staring unblinkingly at the slope that stretched up to the top of the cliffs, looking for any slight sign of movement. Just over the rimrock was the rat encampment.

Watching Teek return to the group, she wondered how difficult it would be for Teek when the time came to awaken Cheeks for his turn to stand watch.

She could hear Cheeks' heavy breathing; he had already conked out. She wondered if Cheeks would be able to stay awake while at his post. She returned to her place on the rock and stood watch.

Cicci's ears swiveled like antennae as she listened to the sounds of the canyon at night. Her full attention turned in the direction of each sound. A biting cold wind had picked up.

Cicci drew herself up into as tight a ball as she could. The wind blew at her fur. Ground squirrels don't tolerate cold wind as much as other creatures, and Cicci was no different. She wished to take refuge underground but stood fast at her watch.

The night was filled with all sorts of alarming sounds. Many of them were unfamiliar to Cicci. The one thing she *was* sure of was that there was a lot of activity taking place all around her, even strange bird sounds. She had expected creatures like birds to be quiet at night.

So then, who could have been creating all that commotion? What was causing all that noise in the dark? She could hear strange snapping of twigs, muffled growls, squeaks, and screeches.

Yeeap! Yeew! Aaeee! The scream of a fox was an alarming noise that

Cicci was unprepared for. It startled her so that it made her jump. It was sudden, loud, and a call that wasn't what one might think would come from a fox.

Oow, oo, oo-oow!

She could hear the call of a barred owl. Remembering what Teek had said about owls, she moved back from the edge and put her back against the nearest rock. Whatever was going on below was, for now thankfully, going on below.

The cool light of night was full. This brightness compelled a northern mockingbird to provide an extensive and varied repertoire of calls that it had learned and had found abundantly entertaining to mock.

Cicci thought as she listened, *how could all of those different calls be coming from one location?*

She was grateful they were making plenty of noise so she would know where they are.

Finally, Cicci made her way back to begin the process of waking up Peeps. Returning to where they were all tucked in between the rocks, Cicci found Peeps wedged between Teek and Cheeks—he had one eye open.

As Cicci reached out to let him know that it was his turn, Peeps sat up. He was ready to go. He looked back down at Cheeks. Cheeks was mumbling in his sleep.

Peeps whispered to Cicci, "I wonder what sort of nightmare he is having. Maybe he is unable to locate something to eat."

Then he turned to Cheeks and whispered, "Cheeeeeks, there are corn crumbles over near the edge of the cliiiiiff. Mmmmm, they are soooo gooood."

"Peeps!" Teek roused from a very light and restless sleep and mumbled his orders. "Just take your post, all right?"

Cicci was ready for sleep and snuggled in next to Teek.

Peeps scrambled out bravely to his post. As his eyes adjusted, the slope stretching out before him began to be revealed. All was quiet now...quiet, cold, and very early. He huddled tight and thought, as if he was remembering a dream.

If it hadn't been for his careless words with Cheeks, outside of the walls of the village on that fateful day, none of this would have happened. He thought of his mother and her well-being, of their home, of the colony of Rimrock.

Peeps felt something change in him, something much bigger than himself. He thought of the colony members. He felt... responsible. This feeling gave him a renewed spirit and a renewed strength of purpose. He began to realize that he had an important part to play in making sure that the stone was found and returned. He didn't know how or if they could find it, but he suspected that this just might very well be the most important thing that he would ever do.

Teek and Cicci had drifted back to sleep for what seemed like a very short time before Teek felt Peeps poking him.

"What is it now?" mumbled Teek, still half-asleep.

"It is your turn to watch, sir, unless you want me to continue—"

"What? Really? Oh no, dear boy, my turn. You take my place here where it is nice and warm."

Teek looked down at his group and gave voice to his thoughts. "Maybe Cheeks and I should both stand watch for the rest of the night. It is almost morning anyway."

Peeps heard Teek's words, and so he was eager to rouse Cheeks. He poked and prodded him, squeaking in his ear. "Hey, hey, Cheeks... get up. Hey, Cheeks! Teek wants you to join him."

"Peeps, I shall rouse him," muttered Teek as he rolled Cheeks over. This awakened Cheeks with a jolt.

"Who, what, hey!" he exclaimed as he struggled to gain his senses. "Hey, Cheeks!" squeaked Teek. "I want you to join me now for the watch!"

"Yes, I am awake, I am ready," said Cheeks.

"Yes, but for how long?" asked Peeps.

"Just give me a minute!" grumbled Cheeks.

"Peeps, how *is* it out there?" Teek asked.

"Noisy," Peeps answered.

"Hmm, curious. Well, that should help Cheeks stay awake," Teek said, patting Peeps on the back. "You get some sleep, young fella. Cheeks and I will take it from here."

Peeps curled up next to Cicci as Teek led the still drowsy Cheeks out to their post. Cheeks shuffled along with his eyes half open.

He whispered dreamily, "Cruuumbles... no... pass the chips... you gonna finish that?"

"Cheeks! Wake up!" Teek nudged Cheeks again.

"Huh? Oh, sorry, where do you want me?" Cheeks murmured.

"Cheeks, are you going to be able to do this?" Teek asked.

"Yes, yes, just give me a minute," Cheeks replied.

Teek sat with Cheeks so that he could assess what was going on out there for himself. "Tell you what, Cheeks," said Teek, "you post yourself over there for a little while, and I will look out this way. I will keep an eye on you to make sure you stay awake."

"I can do this," said Cheeks.

Teek added, "I know you can, and *you* know that you can do this."

Teek sat and focused his eyes on the dimly lit slope below the cliff.

Was he seeing things? The undergrowth appeared to be moving, or was it just the shadowy play of the light of night on the leaves? He could not be sure. The occasional squawks, chirps, cackles, and growls continued.

He returned to check Cheeks. Cheeks' head had dropped down and he was just beginning to fall over.

"Cheeks!" chirped Teek.

"Huh, wha—" Cheeks rolled over and then stumbled to his feet.

"Cheeks, you head back and get some sleep. You can relieve me in a while," said Teek.

"All right... sorry," Cheeks replied.

"I will come and get you soon, so try not to sleep too soundly," Teek added.

"Oh, I will be ready..." His dreamy, half-conscious voice trailed off as he headed back to where the others were curled up.

Teek's attention was now directed out to the cliff and slope below it. There *was* movement most definitely now just under the cover of the brush. The rats *were* actively searching for them. He kept perfectly still, not making even the slightest noise.

His face whipped around to the left upon hearing a sudden burst of sound. A rustling and snapping of twigs interrupted the smaller sounds, and then he heard growling and screeching. He could see branches shaking, and they were moving erratically in all directions.

The screeching stopped, and from the thicket, a large form appeared trotting up the slope. The moonlight revealed the silvery coat of a coyote! It had caught one of the rats and was making off with his prize.

Even better, he had scattered the other rats. They were scrambling back up the slope and back over the rimrock toward their encampment.

After some time, Teek returned to the slumbering group to try to rouse Cheeks.

"I am awake, Teek. I can watch again for a while," Cicci whispered.

"No, you sleep now. I'll need you in the morning. I am here for Cheeks," he said.

"Hey Cheeks, get up."

"Yes, yes, I am up," said Cheeks, shuffling back out toward his assignment.

He truly wanted to fulfill his obligation. Teek nestled in next to Cicci. As he dozed off, he noticed how comfortable he felt snuggled up next to her soft warm fur.

"Sir! Sir! Teek!"

Teek opened one eye and saw Cheeks peering down at him. "There is something in the water!" Cheeks announced.

Teek sighed. "Yes, Cheeks, I am sure there are lots of things in the water. Maybe you should just jump in and find out what it is!"

"No!" insisted Cheeks. "I mean something is really splashing about, making a lot of noise!"

Teek arose with a groan, asking, "How long have you been on watch?"

"Oh, I have been up listening and watching for quite a spell," he replied. "Hurry, this way!"

They headed over to the other side of the rock that faced the river. Sure enough, there was something of some size moving through the water, splashing about, gurgling, and making croaking noises.

Cheeks exclaimed, "Good groundhogs! What could that be?"

"Whatever it is," replied Teek, "if you keep hidden and try not to make any more noise, you might not give away our position. The light of day is just beginning to show up in the sky. Can you hold on for a little while longer?" asked Teek.

"Yes, I am most certainly awake now," Cheeks replied.

"Yes, well, unfortunately so am I," Teek added. "I will check back with you soon. You should not worry so much about the river. Keep your eyes on the cliff and the slope."

"Yes, Master Teek," Cheeks answered.

17

THE LEAST EXPECTED

Soon, all too soon, it was getting light. The group arose and stretched in the warmth of the bright light of day, just hitting the top of the large, towering rock earlier than the ground below.

"I will go check on Cheeks," said Peeps.

When Peeps found Cheeks, he was propped up on one of the rocks, a position that reflected his best efforts to not fall back to sleep; however, despite these efforts, he *had* slumped over and dozed off.

"Cheeks!" Peeps screeched.

"Pine nuts!" squeaked Cheeks as he jolted awake. "Yes! Yes! All right!"

"Cheeks, you are just lucky that we were not all captured or killed during your watch!" Peeps barked.

Cheeks offered a pitifully weak excuse. "I drifted off for only a moment, just before you walked out here!"

Peeps simply stared at him through squinting eyes and then said, "Get up, we are discussing our current situation and whether there is anything that can be done about it or not."

As they approached Teek and Cicci, they began to hear the discussion. Teek was in the middle of weighing their options.

"On the one paw, we probably should not leave until we have at least searched around the bank a bit... but on the other paw, we should not be sticking around here with all those rats so nearby. They *will* start looking for us again now that it is light."

Another commotion back on the slope caught their attention. They scurried over to look. There was a shape moving along the top of the cliff. Looking up, they saw the coyote from earlier trotting and traversing the rim. The hunting being good, he had come back for more.

"Well, *there* is our answer," commented Cicci.

"How is that?" asked Teek.

"Well, the coyote is not going to just hop down off the cliff and come after us. He is not aware of us. And I am quite sure that right now, he is hunting for rats. We can slip down the river side of this rock without being noticed. So, the coyote just provided us with a diversion! You see?" asked Cicci.

"All right, yes, that makes sense. It was good that you got *some* sort of sleep last night," Teek concluded.

"Well, it would have been had I been able to sleep with all the noise from you males fussing about," she replied.

"Grab your satchels, everyone. This way."

Teek led them down the riverside of the large rock tower to the muddy shore. The river had its usual early morning steam rising off it.

Directing the group, he said, "Now look, stay close. We will search the banks for a while, but we should not be too long. So be ready to move out soon. Now go!"

They moved through the rushes and underneath the willows. There were all kinds of prints in the mud. Teek recognized tracks from a raccoon, a beaver, and a mink. This muddy bank was no doubt frequented by many different creatures, but the freshest track was that of an otter. They combed the bank in both directions, but there was no sign of the precious Illumination Stone.

Splash! Gurgle sploosh!

"What is that?" Peeps chirped.

"Hey, Teek!" *Sploosh.* "Teek!"

"Fisk? Fisk, is that you? What are you doing here?" Teek asked.

"Fishing, of course! I am up and down the river all the time! Up and down, up and down, up—" he croaked.

Sploosh! He was underwater again.

"Oh, terrific, Fisk!" commented Peeps, shaking his head.

"Fisk!" Teek screeched. "Can you be still?"

"Sure, crunch, crunch, crunch," he replied, finishing off the end of a trout tail. "The larger trout are up early but not too early for Fisk, no, sir! You know what they say, an early otter gets the fish!"

"Do they?" replied Peeps.

"Say—uh, Fisk!" Teek began.

But Fisk had already submerged.

Peeps looked at Teek with a little smile and said, "Follow the bubbles."

Fisk resurfaced.

"Fisk!" Teek called out again.

"Speak up, speak up. No hearing you when I am underwater!"he replied.

"Clearly," said Teek. "Where is your family, by the way?"

"Oh, they are just a couple of pools upriver. They stay in shallower water, yeh see. A real"—*splash*—"surprise see'n"—*sploosh*— "you here!" Fisk said, as he rolled on the surface. "So, what are *you* doing here?" he asked. "That is the question, yup, it is."

"If you stop for a moment, I will tell you!" barked Teek.

"Oops, sorry, sorry, go ahead." Fisk bobbed to attention in the water.

Teek began again, "Do you remember when we started our journey farther upriver?"

"Oh, sure, sure I do. I—"

Teek held up his front paw to stop Fisk from going on and on and continued, "Do you know *why* we are here, Fisk?"

Fisk spun around a few times as he thought.

"Do not tell me, I know this, I do, I do. You are looking for something... yes, you are looking for something very important, yes?"

Peeps looked at Teek, amused by his frustration. Teek did not return the glance. Cicci stared at the ground. Cheeks was nearby, stalking something crawling through the grass.

"Yes, Fisk, we still *are* searching for something, something very important. A bright, clear, yellow-orange stone. It is very important to us, and we have not been able to find it. We fear it may be lost forever."

"Oh yes, that. I think I saw it," Fisk reported unceremoniously.

"Right, and so—wait, what?" Teek began.

But Fisk was gone again. He did a surface dive with another gurgling sploosh and disappeared into the dark depths to the river bottom.

"Well, I guess that just about wraps it up for Fisk," Peeps concluded.

And then after only a short while, Fisk resurfaced. In his mouth was the Illumination Stone!

"Yoo mea iss?" he said with his mouth full of the large gem. He dropped it on the muddy bank in front of them.

"I wondered what that was down there," he added.

Teek and the group of squirrels stood on the edge of the river, staring, speechless, mouths agape in amazement.

Finally, Teek managed to gather himself enough to speak.

"Fisk! I... how... where did you... how did you...?"

"Well, what do you know about that?" said Peeps. "Fisk found it. How about that?"

Fisk explained, "Yes, well, you see, this beam of light was shining on this bright thing at the bottom, and so I swam down to get a closer look."

There was a long pause as they all waited for Fisk to finish his story.

Finally, Teek asked, "Yes, then you remembered that we were looking for it?"

"No, then I saw a fish and I chased it. Anyway, there you go."

There was silence, and then Cicci spoke up. "Well, he *did* find it, so... so thank you, Fisk!"

"Uh, yes, thank you for bringing it, um, to us, Fisk," said Teek, still attempting to recover enough to offer some formal expression of appreciation.

"Yup," he croaked, "gotta go now!"

Bloop! Fisk was gone onto his next chase.

"You know, I am not sure that he even understands what he just did," said Peeps.

"Oh, probably not," replied Teek, still staring down at the long-lost treasure at his feet.

The group stood around the precious Illumination Stone in disbelief.

"It is hard to believe that it is actually sitting in front of us," Teek continued.

"I had nearly forgotten how wondrous and beautiful it is," added Cicci.

After all the trouble, the distance, and the danger, the rediscovery of the Illumination Stone seemed to Teek like such an underwhelming moment for such an important object. Teek wondered how Fisk's discovery could have been so haphazard and incidental.

Could it possibly be that this was, in fact, just a stone and no more? Could it be that nobody, but the ground squirrels held any reverence for this precious source of information? Did others not realize that it contained the historical stories of their colony? Did no one realize how valuable it was?

Teek stood looking out over the river. Cicci, suspecting that she knew what was troubling him, felt that it was time for a comment.

"Well, that *is* how these things happen, is it not?"

"Yes, I guess it is," replied Teek. "It is just that I feel as though I do not understand something here."

Cicci continued, "Well, the task we have before us is to bring it back to the colony, and we are a long way from that. We still have the second half of the journey ahead of us."

Teek redirected his attention to the entire group. "Listen, all of you, it is now more important than ever that we do not underestimate the dangers that lie ahead. We are only halfway through this journey, and the going will now be slower with the weight of the stone."

"Well, I, for one, am very thankful," commented Peeps. "I mean, what were the odds of finding it, anyway? This is more than a small victory!" he continued.

"He *is* right, you know," added Cicci.

Teek responded, "Yes, of course, I just do not want us to underestimate the task ahead."

Just then, Cheeks returned from chasing down a cricket, explaining his absence with an excuse that sounded useful.

"Hey, I managed to find an opening in the—oh, you found it! What happened?"

Cicci answered, "Fisk pulled it from the river bottom."

"Really? Fisk? Down here, this far? He must have been the one splashing around in the water earlier this morning! Oh, I found an opening in the boulder down here."

"Good," said Teek, "we should get out of sight while we determine our next moves."

Cheeks led them to a place between two boulders and under a thick cover of willow. Peeps helped Teek drag the golden stone to the hiding place Cheeks had found.

"Great juniper berries, we could be heroes!" declared Cheeks.

"Well, you are no hero yet, Cheeks, and it is more likely that you will simply regain some credibility in the eyes of the colony," corrected Teek. "It *is* always good to be able to repair your mistakes, but again what we need to focus on right now is being very careful to make sure we all get home safely...with the stone. Cheeks, go gather some reeds that I can use to tie our stone to my back for travel."

"You're going to carry it?" asked Cheeks. "How else were you thinking that we were going to get it back to the colony? You? Peeps?

Cicci? Do you think I would ask Cicci to take on this burden?" He wished those words had never left his mouth.

"What do you mean by that? I can do it!" She jumped all over his comment.

"Yes!" Teek stammered. "I mean, you can... of course."

Teek took her arm and ushered her to one side, whispering, "What I mean is, if *you* do it, then the two youngsters over there are less likely to step up, and since they are the cause of it all, well, they should not be let off so easily. I will just take this on for now while I figure out how to handle it. If you have any ideas about it, let me know."

"I have one!" she returned.

Teek shut his eyes and listened.

"Tell them plainly what you just told me!"

Teek opened his eyes and turned his face toward Cicci. "Funny how I always seem to need reminding of the simple way to do things," he concluded.

"Yes, funny," she replied.

Teek, Peeps, and Cicci managed to drag the stone over and lift up one end, leaning it against the side of a rock. Cheeks returned with the reeds to tie it to Teek's back. It would prove to be quite a heavy burden for Teek. Although Cheeks was "well rounded," Teek was the eldest and strongest of the group. But even for a young and strong ground squirrel, it was going to be difficult.

"What do you think? Is it secured? Do you think this will stay on?" asked Teek.

Peeps attempted to hide his amusement. "What is it, Peeps?" Teek insisted.

Peeps hid his face in his paws.

"What?" Teek repeated.

"Well," began Peeps, "I *am* sorry, but I cannot help thinking that..."

"That what?"

"Well, I cannot help thinking that you look like a very fancy turtle!"

Cicci had to turn and walk away, not wanting to laugh in Teek's face.

"Come on!" Teek retorted. "I want all of you to keep an eye on this. If something comes loose or slides to one side, try and help me out, will you? Cicci, are you going to join us now?" Cicci scrambled back to catch up with the departing group.

It was not long before Teek realized that it was going to be a very long painful journey with the Illumination Stone tied to his back. Along with the sheer weight of the stone, the reeds that they had used to tie it in place were so binding and restrictive that Teek found it quite difficult and painful to move.

The others were all too aware of Teek's difficulties. They felt rather helpless in their inability to offer any assistance. Cicci, Peeps, and Cheeks would scamper along and then stop by a log, rock, or bush and wait for Teek to gradually catch up.

They found that they had to stop frequently, as every step Teek took he was straining against the weight of the stone on his back.

Ratchety-Ratchety-Ratchet!

A kingfisher streaked right over Teek's head. Teek was so startled he lost his balance and rolled over.

Overturned, his legs were in the air, very much like the fancy turtle that Peeps had described earlier. He was unable to right himself. The group rushed over and helped him. They moved Teek over to a large clump of reeds next to a fallen tree to rest and make an assessment.

"This is not working very well, is it, Cicci?" Teek said in a quiet, labored voice.

It was during this stop that Cicci began to think very hard about any other possible solutions to their situation. They had used up most of the day struggling to get only a short distance. It simply was not enough. At this pace, it would take too long for them to make it back to Rimrock. They would have to move more quickly to be successful. Teek appeared to be nearing his last steps of the day.

"What about Kanti carrying it?" she began.

"I thought about that," Teek replied. "I do not know Kanti's whereabouts, and I am just not sure about letting him fly off with our Illumination Stone. He *has* been a wonderful guide, he has saved our lives, and I am beginning to trust him, but he *does* prize bright shiny objects, and I also think that this task is ours, and ours alone. But I also think that this is probably not the way to be carrying it back. There has to be something that we have not considered yet."

Peeps was standing close, ready to assist.

"Peeps, help me get this off." Teek's voice was quiet and a bit shaky.

The day was waning. They clearly needed a new way to transport the Illumination Stone. Cicci searched her thoughts.

"Teek, do you remember back, oh, two great cycles ago, a story that Eechius was telling about the original humans of the great plateau, humans whom our ancestors knew about?"

Teek stared into Cicci's eyes as he tried to remember the event. Having a ground squirrel's ability to remember details, he began to recall the story.

"I believe so, what are you thinking of?" he asked.

"Well, the Illumination Stone had given Eechius a story about something that humans had used, and so our early colony members had ended up building this tool to move dirt and rocks while creating Rimrock. I remember them saying that it really helped in hauling away dirt and rocks so we could build our burrows. Let me show you."

A long time ago, the native people would transport their belongings on a structure that consisted of crossing two small tree poles. Then they would tie branches across that structure on which to place their belongings.

One end of the structure crossed over the back of a horse, a dog, or a human. The other, wider end was dragged along the ground. The native people referred to this contraption as a *travois*. Neither Cicci nor any ground squirrel, for that matter, knew the name of this contraption, but their ancestors had observed its construction and its use very carefully. And so, during storytelling time, the stone had illuminated this information to Eechius, the story elder.

Cicci, being a particularly acute listener, understood the basic structure and the function of it. She began to draw a diagram in the sandy soil at their feet.

"Yes, Cicci, good thinking!" Teek exclaimed. "You may have found the answer." He embraced Cicci with appreciation and much relief.

"We need to go gather the right sticks," Cicci directed. "Peeps? Cheeks? Can you collect the sticks?", holding her hands out to show the proper dimensions needed.

"We can do that!" declared Cheeks.

The two had been listening and watching Cicci's diagram in the sand. They started off immediately.

"Don't go too far," Teek called to them.

As Teek and Cicci began to gather more strips of reeds and rushes for tying the structure together, Teek happened to notice some movement on the opposite bank of the river.

A quite unexpected ambush had rustled the brush near the bank. They both stood frozen from under a thick clump of bunch grass. Soon the rustling from the bushes was revealed.

It was a fisher, which looked rather like a large weasel, impressive, and as well suited for predation as any cat. He had just caught a vole, a little rodent that was a staple of the fisher diet, along with, unfortunately, ground squirrels.

A fisher is one predator that is quick enough to regularly catch ground squirrels. He stood for a moment with the vole in its mouth and then headed back up the opposite hill with its prize. The poor little rodent had been adequately dispatched and was now a meal. They both stood shocked and horrified.

Presently, Cicci whispered, "You know, something has just occurred to me. This idea of staying close to the bank of the river—well, what if we stuck close to the base of the cliffs instead? That way we could ditch into the rocks if trouble found us. It just seems to me that there might be a lot more predators down nearer the water."

Teek glanced back across the river as he pondered her idea. They had been driven down to the river by the rats. Initially he had thought that maybe the bank of the river was better because there were more grasses and willows to hide in.

But then again, Cicci was probably right. Although there was more vegetation to hide in where they were, there were also more predators, and up nearer the cliffs there were more boulders to crawl under or between.

"It might be tougher going... and what about snakes?" he asked.

"Well, it will be dangerous any way we go," she replied. "Where are Peeps and Cheeks?"

No sooner had he asked than they both showed up, dragging some straight sticks.

"Did you see it?" exclaimed Cheeks. "It was across the river, but there is just as likely to be one on this side!"

"Yes, not to mention Bobcats and Coyotes!" added Peeps. "We were watching it, hoping that you two stayed hidden.

"Fortunately, it caught a small mouse, poor thing," replied Cicci.

"Listen, Cicci has mentioned that we should change our course," Teek said, sharing Cicci's idea of traveling closer to the rocky base of the cliffs for the rest of the journey.

Peeps revisited the concern that there might be more snakes, but soon they all decided that by traveling near the cliffs, they would be able to ditch into a small space in the rocks, be less accessible to most predators, and not be quite so visible. Having all agreed, they set about assembling the travois.

Cicci supervised, provided instruction, and helped to tie the reeds to the frame and secure the stone. Working quickly, as squirrels do, they managed to build a structure that pleased them, and they were satisfied it would carry the stone securely, with far less effort than before. Once the stone was secured, they fastened the two main sticks across Teek's back.

"How is that? Better?" Cicci asked.

18

REST AND REFLECTION

"At this point, we have to find a place we can all fit into for the night. I am so very sorry I have been holding us up. It seems to have taken all day to get this far."

"Teek, for pine nuts' sake, we have the Illumination Stone! We are doing fine!" said Cicci.

"Yes, in fact, we owe you everything, maybe even our very lives," added Peeps.

"Well, we are not home yet," replied Teek.

Cheeks then asked if it might be good to get started finding a place to stay for the night.

"Yes, you are right," answered Teek, "so we should find a place to crawl into and see what, if anything, is left in our satchels." They had been searching the base of the cliff when Peeps finally looked up.

"Look," he said. "There's an opening in the rock up there." They followed his gaze upward.

"You mean that ledge halfway up the cliff, Peeps?" said Cheeks. "For all we know, it could be a hawk's nest, or worse, a snake den. And how would we drag the stone up there?"

"We would not," answered Cicci.

"Exactly," continued Cheeks. "So that settles—"

"No, actually we would hide the stone down here for the night," she continued.

"Leave the stone down here?" Teek asked.

"Yes! Nobody will know," she replied.

But Teek was worried. "You cannot be sure. The rats could be watching us right now!"

Cicci responded, "Well, I guess I am thinking that the attacks by Kanti and the hawks and then the coyote were enough to keep them occupied for a while. Besides, we are pretty good at hiding things."

Teek was quite reluctant to leave the stone out of his immediate care.

"Where would you hide it, Cicci?" he asked.

"Well, if we slide it behind this rock,"—she identified a large rock that was leaning up against the base of the cliff, "then we could pile some sticks, pine needles, and other things over it. If we do a convincing job, nobody will know."

With no further objections, Teek began to coordinate.

"Peeps, can you climb up and see if this opening is occupied? Be sure to peek around into it very cautiously first. Hurry, before it gets dark."

"Cheeks," Cicci called out, "help me get the stone out of sight for Teek. You really should rest, Teek," she added.

"Hello down there! It appears that there is a nest up here with eggs, but they are all broken and there is nobody home. It appears that they have all left for good," reported Peeps.

"That was fast, Peeps. Is the space big enough for all of us to stay out of sight?" asked Teek.

"I think so, and there is an easy way up that I found."

"Then that settles it," said Teek.

"What do you think?" asked Cicci, redirecting Teek to the hiding place of the stone.

"I think that you two did such a good job that we had better make sure we remember where you put it, or *we* will never find it!" he replied.

As the bright light faded away, Teek posted himself just inside the opening, next to the ledge, and looked out from his new vantage point halfway up the cliff. He wanted to keep an eye on the area around the stone's hiding place.

He could see the last glimmerings of the light sinking behind the mountains, silhouetting the dark peaks. It cast a yellow-orange and deep pink glow, which faded into the deep dark blue of the evening sky, revealing a pale silvery crescent moon. A chilly breeze picked up and carried the pure sweet fragrance of the canyon to gently brush his face.

He watched and listened to the birds as they hurried to make the most out of what remained of the dusky light, rushing from branch to branch, as though they had a sense of urgency and last-minute things to attend to. Their songs and calls echoed through the canyon.

As the sky grew darker, little bats fluttered in zigzag patterns over the river, occasionally zipping close to the cliff where Teek was positioned. Trout slurped and swirled at the surface of the deep dark gurgling river below. Teek's evening was quiet, pleasant, and serene. For now, all was well. They had recovered the Illumination Stone, and Teek was at ease, knowing his traveling companions were safe.

"Teek," Cicci softly called to him, joining him at the ledge. "Do you want something to eat?"

"No thank you. I think I will just sit quietly and enjoy this beautiful evening."

"Mind if I sit with you?" she asked.

"That would be nice," he replied.

They huddled together, both knowing somehow, with no words spoken, that they would never leave each other's side for the rest of their lives.

19

SUMMONED BELOW

It was early when Teek, Cicci, and Peeps began to prepare for the trail below the cliff.

"Uh, Peeps?" alerted Teek. "I hate to break this to you, but you will have to climb back up there and rouse Cheeks. Cicci and I will uncover the stone and get it ready for travel."

Peeps nodded once, and up he scampered.

After a bit of prodding, they had gathered Cheeks and were all assembled. Cicci had decided to haul the travois for a time, and so Teek helped affix the sticks to her back.

"It should be Peeps or Cheeks taking this for a while!" commented Teek.

"Well, I tell you what, when I get tired, I will hand it off to one of them. I'm sure that they will be more than thrilled to take it from me," reasoned Cicci.

They followed a small deer path that hugged the base of the cliff face. The forest that they had traveled through on their journey downriver was now below them.

The trail at the base of the cliffs was anything but smooth. And with Cicci having to drag the travois laden with the Illumination

Stone, it was still slow going and quite cumbersome. Any rocks in the trail had to be traversed.

It seemed that they were always either climbing or descending, and occasionally they would lose control of the stone-laden travois. Teek hung back with Cicci and her burden. He said that he wanted to be close to her so that they could talk.

The unspoken truth was that it was difficult for him to watch her struggle so and wanted to be close to her in case she needed help. Although the cliffs still sheltered them from the bright light of the early day, it would prove to become unseasonably warm.

Peeps, who had taken the point, stopped.

Before them was a massive Talus slope, which showed where a landslide of boulders had occurred. The cliff had given way, and tons of rock had slid down toward the river. It was not, however, a recent event. This landslide was a little over a thousand years old. Cicci dropped the heavy travois and looked out over the vast field of boulders.

"What now?" she asked Teek.

"There *is* a bit of a trail," Peeps observed. "It is not much of one, see there?"

There was a small slightly trampled deer trail through the middle of the boulder field, but it was quite treacherous for small squirrels. It was made up of branches, pine needles, and some other rubble with fissures that any of them could easily fall into.

It dropped off in some places enough so that trying to carry the travois across it would be nearly impossible for them. As Teek sized up the ominous obstacle, his attention became redirected and drawn to a particularly noticeable boulder with one flat side. It sat just where the cliff face stopped, and the boulder field began. He noticed that it had red markings on it.

"What do you suppose that is?" he asked.

The others turned toward him to locate what had caught his eye.

"Where?" Cheeks asked.

"Over here? It looks like some sort of a stick human."

Teek had found a pictograph, a painted marker rendered by original people from an ancient time when a tribe had called this canyon their home, far before the arrival of Europeans and Americans.

Teek lifted the heavy travois off Cicci's shoulders and leaned it up against the base of the cliff. They both moved closer to the pictograph. As Teek stared at the image, he placed his front paw on the stone. As he made contact, he thought he felt something. It was almost undetectable at first, so faint, so distant. But it was decidedly something Teek was feeling and hearing. It moved through his entire body. He could just make out a very faint and very regular beating, a faraway rhythm. It sounded as though it were emanating from deep underneath the boulder field.

"Teek... Teek!"

It was Cicci's voice behind him. He turned back to her as if returning from a faraway place.

"Teek, what is it?"

"I do not know," he replied. "There is something here. I feel that something is here."

"What are you sensing?" she asked.

"I hear them... I feel them."

"Who?" asked Cheeks.

Teek turned to them as he sorted through his impression. "Humans. Humans... that were here... a long time ago," said Teek.

Peeps watched Teek and then turned to Cicci, asking, "Can we *all* do that?"

"Ah, no. Teek's abilities are... unusual," she replied. "Teek happens to have a very special ability," Cicci continued.

Peeps and Cheeks did not understand this, of course—at least, not at that moment.

"Look over here!" chirped Cicci. "An opening of some kind, like a burrow!" She poked her head into the entrance. "There is cool air coming out of it, and it smells like, well, it smells like the underground smells."

Teek had noticed that Peeps was now staring over the edge of the trail into some bunch grass below.

"What is it, Peeps?" he asked.

"Something is moving. I cannot seem to... *ditch*!" he screeched.

A bobcat charged up the hill with lighting speed, hitting the edge of the trail in an explosion of dust and flying pebbles.

When the dust cleared, the ground squirrels were already gone.

The bobcat spun around, scrambling to search the ground all around her for the squirrels, but she found nothing.

From the opening of the small passage in the rockslide, Teek and his group watched as the cat sniffed the Illumination Stone. Looking up, it continued to search for its owner.

"Thank you, Peeps. Your alertness probably saved our lives. My attention was clearly focused on *a rock*! I apologize. We all owe Peeps our deepest appreciation."

Teek leaned against the rock wall of the burrow and took a few long, deep breaths.

"And thank you, Cicci. If that stone had been fastened to one of us, then that one would not have made it."

The bobcat approached the entrance to the burrow, and the squirrels backed away farther down the narrow passageway. The cat sniffed at the burrow opening, which was too small for her to squeeze into. There was no longer any benefit to continuing her search for the squirrels.

She did sit for a moment or two and began grooming herself as if to show that she was completely unfazed. Like most smart ambush predators, she knew that she had lost the element of surprise, and so she headed back down the hill to search for her next opportunity to pounce on an unsuspecting meal.

As Teek and the others caught their breath, Teek spoke up.

"We should probably stay put for a while." Peering back out through the opening of the burrow, he continued, "I have just remembered that I have to go back out there and retrieve the stone!"

"I will go with you and watch for the cat," said Peeps, now energized by his newfound success.

"Agreed," replied Teek.

Teek and Peeps stood at the opening of the rocky burrow for quite some time, discussing the challenge before them.

They waited until they were satisfied that all was clear, and then Peeps stepped out, rearing up on his hind legs, to peer over the edge of the trail. Teek sped for the stone-laden travois. Teek and Peeps returned to the burrow passageway in what seemed to Cicci and Cheeks to be so fast that if they had blinked, they would have missed the maneuver altogether.

In fact, it took much longer for Teek and Peeps to plan the maneuver than it took for the actual retrieval itself.

The group was silent. The four travelers crouched in the opening of the passageway. Then from deep within the darkness of the tunnel, Teek once again began to hear the soft distant sound of drumbeats. Nobody but Teek heard it at first.

"Am I the only one who hears that?" he asked.

They all kept still and listened. None of the others heard a thing, so they all kept listening.

And then oh so quietly, from deep back in the recesses through the darkness of the tunnel, it came. They all began to hear the rhythm of the soft distant drumbeat.

They peered down the blackness of the passageway. It was a cold, dank, descending pathway. The chilled air carried a musty smell.

Cheeks spoke first. "Well, this is all quite interesting. So, we should probably be getting on with our journey now."

"No, Cheeks," Teek corrected. "There *is* a reason we hear the beating. I felt something, I still do. The way forward is down this tunnel."

"What? The way forward is back to the colony!" chirped Cheeks.

"Cheeks, remember, we are supposed to obey Teek's direction and follow his lead," said Peeps.

"Yes, but that was to retrieve the stone, not chase unknown sounds down abysmal tunnels!" Cheeks replied.

"Would you prefer to wait here, Cheeks?" asked Cicci.

"What? You too?" replied Cheeks, huffing, puffing, and wheezing with each breath.

"Do not fret, Cheeks," said Peeps. "Settle down. Calm yourself! You always pass out when you do that!"

"Fine, fine! Down 'the tunnel of unknown peril' we go!" Cheeks replied reluctantly.

"Very well then, everyone, single file and follow me," said Teek.

They headed down the passageway and into the unknown. They searched for each other in the dark.

"Stay close. Put your paw on the back of the one in front of you!" he instructed.

The passage was small but not too small for the squirrels. As they descended, they all wondered what sort of creature had dug out the dirt in between this rubble of boulders and for what purpose. They knew that it had been dug out by some small animal.

"Anything could be down here!" continued Cheeks. "You do not know what awaits us! It could be a weasel or worse!"

"Quiet, Cheeks!" chirped Teek. "If there *is* something dangerous down here, we do not want it to hear us chattering!"

They carefully crawled deeper and deeper. It jogged in all directions along the way. It was particularly rough going for Teek; he had once again insisted on dragging the heavy Illumination Stone.

They would reach what they thought was a dead-end but would then feel their way around a large rock until finding a way through.

This happened several times until Cheeks began to conclude that it was about time that they turn back. They had just struggled around another protruding rock when the burrow opened up abruptly into a large cavern, an opening big enough for humans to walk through.

The air that hit their faces had become even chillier than the small burrow passage. They stopped and listened carefully. The now massive cavern continued on around a corner to the right. The drumbeat also seemed to be coming from that direction. The walls were dimly lit from some undetermined source. The light wasn't flickering like a flame; it was more of a constant dim glow. They kept silent and listened.

The sound of the distant drumbeat now seemed a little louder. All of them could hear it—a single rhythmic beat that echoed through the walls of the passages.

Cheeks shook his head and sighed. "What are we doing?" he muttered to himself.

The floor of the cave, although covered in a thick dusty dirt, was now fairly level. They entered the cavern. As they did so, Teek peered up at the walls of the passageway. He noticed that they had the same sort of markings on them as the rock at the entrance, the same human figure depicted in the same reddish color.

As they turned the corner, more and more drawings came into view. Teek noticed that the cave drawings appeared to reveal some sort of story or a series of events. Here are the drawings as Teek and the others saw them on the wall of the cavern:

"Hey, some of those markings look a little like us!" said Peeps.

"Yes, they do," answered Teek. "Those are not just markings. I think that they show events. Do you think you can all help me remember every detail of these markings? We will need to redraw them so we can try to figure them out after we get back."

"Yes, I will remember them completely," said Cicci.

"Then I will hold you to it," replied Teek with a smile. "Well, let us see where this goes then," he encouraged.

They continued around the corner and down the now cavernous passageway. Eventually, they approached what appeared to be an enormous, vaulted chamber. If they had known what a cathedral was, it would have reminded them of one.

Standing in the entrance, the glowing light was now much brighter. This chamber was, in fact, the source of the glowing light! As they stepped in, Teek began to hear other sounds that were new and strange, more than just the distant drumbeat, and it wasn't the sound of Teek dragging the travois with the Illumination Stone on it. Was it the sound of the wind, or was it the sound of whispers?

The whispers might have been words, but if they were, they were of a language that neither he nor any of them could understand.

"It is so cold in here I can see my breath!" said Cheeks.

THE ANCIENT ONE

As they reached the inner chamber, they stopped in their tracks. The distant drumbeats and the windy whispers had ceased. They stood in the silence, filled with wonder and amazement.

Before them lay all sorts of amazing things—ancient things. To them the room was gigantic. This great chamber reminded them very much of their own Great Hall back at Rimrock, only much, much bigger. The ceiling had several cracked openings from which poured streams of the bright light of day.

They couldn't help but notice the same familiar golden glow that used to fill the Great Hall at story time; yet with *more* shafts of light streaming down through the massive ceiling casting light onto many more golden jewels, it was far brighter and bedazzling. The precious clear golden stones glowed with brilliance, refracting golden light in all directions.

It was quite clear to the squirrels that this was a very important place and a significant discovery. It was, without doubt, the most impressive sight they had ever beheld.

Teek was quite positive that he had been purposely drawn toward this chamber, that he had been called upon to find it.

As Teek looked around, he made more and more important connections, mainly that this amazing chamber was most likely the source of their own prized Illumination Stone!

The squirrels spoke ever so softly to one another, yet their voices still somehow echoed off the chamber walls. They were frozen in time, gripped by a quiet, mysterious power that resonated through the entire room.

"This is a wondrous sight," whispered Peeps. "Teek, what sort of place is this?"

As they looked around, they tried to understand their surroundings. It was difficult for them to identify what most of the artifacts were, having little or no frame of reference. But somehow, something crept into their memories from the stories they had been told by their story elders—of their forefathers and an ancient clan of humans. Was it possible that this chamber held some sort of great story regarding the origin of their colony?

Throughout most of his life, Teek had frequently wondered about their origins. He had pondered what might possibly be behind the power of the Illumination Stone and the elder's ability to tell every detail of those great stories.

They were old tales, so fantastic, so detailed, and so ancient as to test the memories of even the wisest old squirrels. This chamber was all too overwhelming and difficult to understand, and yet to Teek there was something strangely familiar about this place.

Now from the perspective of the original native humans of the canyon, it would have been regarded as a burial chamber for someone very important. Ancient artifacts filled the room. These were personal belongings that held much more importance and value than mere treasure; these artifacts told a long-forgotten story from a time long past. It was a time when humans and other creatures had lived alongside one another.

These ancient humans had shared the same spirit with the other plants and animals that depended upon the river. The ways of humans had changed much since then.

This quiet time capsule now lay hidden from the modern world, echoing a faint whisper of what once had been. It existed now only as a silent oasis in a world that had become so noisy as to all but drown out the sounds of the wind or the calls of birds and the other creatures of the canyon.

The sweet spicy smell of pine and sage—and all growing things that called the canyon home—the very breath of life, was being replaced with the exhaust of a new human population that was vastly increasing in number. Now this fragile ecosystem was being bought and sold for profit—a false profit.

As for this small band of ground squirrels, the chamber was as difficult to understand as any alien world. A human would have recognized bows and arrows with obsidian and jasper spearheads and arrowheads; war clubs with eagle and hawk feathers tied with leather straps; beautifully woven baskets, many filled to overflowing with gold, some in nuggets, and some in the form of flattened coins.

There were large scraping and pounding tools, all made of different colored agates and obsidians. Necklaces hung on the far wall, glorious necklaces with beads, claws, teeth, and feathers.

At another area of the chamber sat pottery that had been filled with grains, seeds, and flour—no doubt long since eaten or simply decayed and unrecognizable. Woven blankets hung on the wall. Beaded cords and beautifully woven leather ropes hung on bone hooks from the ceiling.

Teek's attention was now drawn to the center of the chamber. There lay a circular rug with an elaborate spiral design, the same design that he had seen on the wall of the passageway. The spiral was made up of the large clear golden Illumination Stones.

Forgetting their fear, they approached the center of the chamber. They felt drawn toward the stones and could not resist their attraction.

As Teek gazed down in wonder at this arrangement of glowing stones, his suspicions were confirmed. He began to piece together the mystery behind the existence of their colony. It was bigger than he had ever imagined.

This place was the source of the power that had given their elders the stories and the ability to remember. He began to suspect that in this place, he might find the answers that he had sought for so long.

Cicci, Peeps, and Cheeks stood with Teek around the chamber centerpiece. They were seeing things they could not understand—and yet somehow knew that their lives, and their colony, were closely connected to it.

Teek looked up and searched the surrounding chamber. The others redirected their attention to where he was now focused. He noticed something significant over in a dark recessed area.

They followed him as he moved closer, starting and stopping in the usual cautious manner of squirrels, ready to ditch at the slightest sign of sound or movement. But none came, and so they inched closer.

In the shadows, seated up against the far wall, they saw him. He was one of the ancients and clearly one who had been an important member of a tribe of original people. He had passed to the other side long ago.

All that remained were bones and his beautiful vestments and adornments. Peeps, startled at the sight, let out a squeak.

"Easy, Peeps," said Teek.

The ancient human had been placed among the artifacts that represented the celebration of his life. He still had remnants of his long gray hair. It was tied into braids that hung down both temples. He had worn large flat, round silver earrings that were now lying on his collarbones. He was clothed all in elk skin, including moccasins, adorned with fringe and beads.

Next to him lay a long ceremonial staff showing the same symbols as those seen on the wall of the cave. He wore an elaborate headdress of eagle, red-tailed hawk, and woodpecker feathers. The headband was lined with gems. A hair-pipe breastplate made from buffalo bone, complete with leather fringe, agate, and beaded tassels hung from his neck and draped over his ribbed chest.

The squirrels stood together, and Teek began to whisper.

"Do you remember that story we were told about the one who brought us the Illumination Stone? This is how he was described in the story, dressed like this. Could this be? He was an important man who could talk with the creatures in the canyon. He and his colony of humans had respect for ground squirrels and other animals. A group of these humans lived here, along the river."

"Are you sure that this is him?" Cicci asked.

Teek paused before replying. "Well, looking at the other Illumination Stones in the center of the chamber, I would say that it *is* very likely."

The canyon and the world had been a much different place in the distant past. In this chamber were the last remnants of a time when humans and the creatures of nature were all part of the same world, a time when they depended upon each other. Not like today.

Modern humans have only seen the earth as something to own. Humans, both native and immigrants, have tried to control the earth. But the new humans had acted in ways that had been the most contrary to the well-being of the natural earth.

They burned and cut down forests, encroached on habitat to build their homes, or, for recreation, dammed the rivers for more power. They killed living things simply for sport and entertainment.

Their numbers increased, numbers beyond the ability to count. They only saw the earth and nature's creatures as something to be controlled.

They had lost senses that, in times past, had been of a subtler nature, senses that had been used back in the time when humans still lived among the other creatures of the earth. They must not have known what they were doing.

How could they not understand that they were destroying themselves? They would come to realize, only too late, that this wisdom was as fragile and as hard to understand as the knowledge of the creation of the earth itself.

All these things were not of Teek's understanding, but somehow, he did have the feeling that there was more to know. He approached the ancient human and placed his front paw on one of the moccasins. He hoped he would be able to make some sort of connection, like the one he felt at the entrance to the passageway.

"Teek? What are you doing?" asked Cicci.

"I don't know, I just thought that I should touch him. I felt something from the stone outside, so there must be more to this," he replied.

"Do you feel anything?" she asked.

"No, but I do believe that there is more, I just know it. We should not leave here without finding it."

"Teek, we have our stone, and we now know where it came from. Now you are saying that there is more?" asked Peeps.

"There must be," Teek said as he circled around the feet of the ancient human.

Looking back at his group of confused friends, his front paw came to rest on the long ceremonial staff. As he did this, the drumbeats returned and were closer than ever.

"Do you hear that?" he chirped.

"Hear what?" asked Cicci.

"What?" repeated Cheeks.

Teek looked down at the staff and saw inscribed the same cave drawings that he had seen earlier. Physical contact with the ceremonial staff was the connection that Teek had been looking for, and yet he was not at all prepared for what happened next.

It began as a vibration but quickly grew into disorientation. A powerful energy surged through him, much like an electrical current, had he been familiar with such a thing. The world around him seemed to move, becoming a dizzying spin.

Teek saw other places, or was it another moment in history? Everything around him appeared brighter, and the world now had a luminescent quality. The beams of light from the cracks in the ceiling moved across the floor of the chamber, as if the light of day were passing quickly, either advancing or receding.

He would soon discover that it was, in fact, rapidly receding. There began a low rumbling sound all around him. Although physically he had been deep underground in the cavern, he now somehow became very aware of the world outside and of the entire canyon.

How very strange. I am completely aware of everything around me. I am here and I am there at once! he thought.

Before him was a vast and wondrous vista, a view of the entire canyon. Beyond, he could see the mountains of the Cascades.

"It seems that everything is all just one thing."

Now Teek was both inside and outside of the cave.

How could this be? he wondered.

He looked down on the river far below. He was up high where the muhas flew. "I am not afraid," he said softly. "Should I be?"

He was thinking that he should be terrified, and yet he felt peace. He could hear the drumbeats again, now calling to him from a ledge at the top of the rimrock. The same whispering of the windy words met his ears. It was in a language that he still could not understand, yet it was soothing and welcoming.

He turned to look. There, standing at the edge of the cliff with his arms outstretched, stood the ancient one, fully alive and vital. He appeared to be welcoming Teek to join him. He was dressed in the same beautiful vestments and adornments that Teek had seen in the burial chamber. His hair was no longer gray but black. It was tied into the same braids that hung down from his temples. He wore the same large flat, rounded silver earrings; the same elk skin and moccasins adorned with fringe and beads; the hair pipe breastplate; and the same beautiful headdress.

He held the ceremonial staff out in front of him, as though he commanded the very wind. In his other hand, he held a stone. It was a large, many-faceted, golden Illumination Stone.

Teek, unaware of whether he was flying or floating, knew only that he was soon close enough to be able to peer into the many-faceted crystal. He could see his own face looking back at him, repeated many times in every facet. He noticed how liquid black and penetrating his own eyes were.

As Teek peered at his many reflections, he realized that the eyes looking back were not just from his own reflection; they were, in fact, looking back at him, peering into his thoughts, and they were whispering to him. They were telling him stories!

Teek felt himself surge with an energy that seemed more powerful and more real than the physical world itself. It was an energy drawn from a force that existed everywhere around him. He felt connected to all things.

A thought filled his mind, as the force filled every cell in his body.

As one thing was created, all things were affected by it. When something was destroyed, everything was also affected by it.

The words encircled him and connected him to everything.

The ancient one had summoned Teek and given him the stories of the Rimrock colony, of the canyon, and of all the creatures that called it home. He directed a power with his ceremonial staff, a power so great that it flowed through all things. Teek had been chosen to receive this power, a power that was now channeled through him, an energy from ages past.

At that moment, he realized, as clear as the stone itself, that he knew the stories. He held the power of the stories. And there were many stories, as many as the faces in the facets of the Illumination Stone staring back at him, and more; the stories were already all around him. The stone was also reflecting the stories that Teek was creating with his own life.

"Teek! Where did you go? You were there, and then when I looked again, you were gone!" exclaimed Cicci.

Teek, now realizing that he had returned to the chamber, was aware of the others once again.

He asked Cicci, "How long was I gone?"

"For a moment or two," she replied.

"You mean you were gone?" asked Peeps.

Teek's only reply was, "I saw him."

"Who?" asked Cheeks.

"This ancient human! He was alive."

"Alive? How? What happened? What did he say?" Cheeks pressed.

"I am unable to explain it yet. It does seem as though I have been gone for quite a while," Teek said, staring back at the seated figure.

Their echoing whispers were suddenly interrupted by sounds of shouting and barking. Humans were up above on the cliff, running by.

Dusty dirt and small pebbles spilled down from the ceiling onto the circular ceremonial centerpiece. It startled the squirrels, causing them to ditch toward some collapsed rocks at one side of the chamber.

They soon realized that the sounds were coming from outside and above. Like the seated ancient human, they were hidden; but it was another worrisome reminder that humans were once again intruding, and that they could easily change life as they knew it forever.

"This way!" Peeps squeaked as he darted through a small opening.

They had all come to appreciate Peeps' ability to think quickly, so they all reacted without question to his alarms. Without a second thought, they all followed. This time his quick decision appeared to result in a blocked passage.

But Cicci then called out, "There *is* something here!"

She noticed a small opening over to the right of where Peeps was looking. This seemed to have been burrowed out similarly to the passage that had been dug leading *into* the chamber from the other side.

But this passageway was closer to the surface than the passageway that had led them into the chamber, and fortunately this opening was located on the other side of the boulder field, in the upriver direction.

As they reached the outside opening of the passage, Peeps ventured a bit farther, cautiously poking his nose out into the bright light of day.

He soon returned, reporting an energized, "All clear."

The actual opening to the outside was small and hidden well behind a very large boulder. No one, including the squirrels, could have noticed it from the outside.

"Wait!" chirped Teek. "In all the excitement, I forgot the Illumination Stone!"

He spun around. To his surprise and amazement, he found that the stone, still fastened to the travois, was lying just behind him, just inside the tunnel. He spun *back* around to Cicci with a look of confusion. Cicci was staring down at the travois, her face also showing confusion.

They looked back at each other with the unanswered question still on their faces. The message was clear to them—they were still supposed to complete the mission of returning the stone no matter what they had learned back in the burial chamber.

Cicci turned to leave but stopped and spun back around to face Teek. She positioned herself nose to nose with him, saying, "You do realize that you will be telling me what happened to you back there, right?"

After a brief stare down, Teek finally replied, "Yes."

She lifted her head, peering down her nose as if to scrutinize his word. They then proceeded through the opening and into what was now afternoon. The light breeze was a refreshing change to the cold, ancient, musty air of the burial chamber.

The sounds of the canyon returned with the familiar chirping birds and the distant roar of the rapids below them. It was good to be outside again and on their way.

In front of them, the small deer trail continued and disappeared around a corner at the base of the cliff. The downhill side of the trail was thick with bitterbrush and bordered the edge of the pine forest.

As they continued their journey, Teek took one last glance back at the massive talus of boulders. He would never be the same. As for the rest of the canyon, he decided for now not to try to imagine.

CHEEK'S LESSON

As the squirrels rounded the trail at the base of the cliffs, they were met squarely with their next challenge. There stood five white-tailed deer—a buck, two does, and two yearlings. Normally, deer would flee in a moment if approached by a predator or a human but noticing four golden mantled ground squirrels was no alarming matter for a deer.

So, for the squirrels, the question became—how do you get by them without getting stomped? The deer hardly acknowledged the new arrivals. Most of their attention was focused on the lush grass at the edge of the trail, on which they eagerly grazed with ripping and munching sounds.

They were frequently distracted by flies, but the flipping and flopping of their enormous ears and large fluffy white tails seemed to take care of most of them. A deer's ears take on a lot of responsibility, especially while the deer is focused on eating. If their ears aren't batting at flies, they are acutely turned and tuned to any sound that has01 been "earmarked" as a potential threat.

They also speak with their tails. Each flip is a very efficient way of signaling to the others. Deer tails deliver relatively simple messages: "I found something good to eat over here," or "You are very attractive to me," or "Hey, I think I hear something," or, most importantly, "Run!"

You might say that they developed the ability to raise the original "warning flag."

"Well, they do not appear to be going anywhere, do they?" declared Peeps, reporting back from his point position.

"Is there no other way around them?" asked Cheeks.

"No, not unless we head to the top of the cliff or into the heavy brush down off the trail," said Teek.

Cheeks sighed. "To be honest, I have not wanted to go near the brush below the trail since that Bobcat ambushed us."

Teek sighed. "The cliff it is! I had almost forgotten about that bobcat," Teek whispered to Cicci. "It will be difficult to carry the stone up this cliff. Do you see a way up?"

Just then, Peeps appeared from a ledge halfway up the rock wall.

"This might be the way," he squeaked down to them.

"How will we get the stone up there?" asked Teek.

"There is a steep slope between these two cliffs just inside this crack in the rock. I think the stone will fit," Peeps replied. "Get it started and I will come down and grab it."

"Peeps is not big enough to pull it up by himself, Cicci. Cicci?"

She had already climbed up the shoot through the crack and was now looking down on Teek, saying, "Just see if you can lift it up this far, Teek. We will take it from here."

"Cicci!"

"Just hand it to us, Teek!"

Teek managed to slide the travois into the opening, get under it, and shove with his back legs enough for Cicci and Peeps to reach it. Teek and Cheeks reached the top ahead of them and helped get the stone to the top. They all stopped to rest, feeling quite good about their accomplishment.

"Cheeks, I think that you might actually be looking a little thinner! Your mother is not going to recognize you," Teek pronounced.

"Well, I *hope* I look thinner! With all this climbing and scrambling about, and we have not had a decent meal in three cycles, hiking to the far end of the canyon and back!" Cheeks replied.

"Poor fellow," said Peeps.

Teek stopped next to Cicci and scanned the skies. "I wouldn't mind knowing where Kanti is right about now," he muttered.

Cicci spoke softly into Teek's ear. "I think that he *has* been looking down on us. He *does* have the whole pine forest to look after. Besides, you will do fine."

Teek thought for a moment and then replied, "Well, this is the part of the journey when we should start to be more cautious than ever. Just when you think that you are almost home. You know what we prey animals say, 'It is always the most dangerous when you are closest to home.'"

"You are a survivor. You'll know what to do," she replied.

"Where is Cheeks?" asked Cicci.

Looking around, they found him at the edge of the cliff teasing the deer, chattering away, and kicking small stones off the ledge at them.

"Are you enjoying yourself?" asked Teek.

"Oh, uh, just seeing if they are still down there," Cheeks said.

"It is a little late to try to move them out of the way, is it not? Tell me, Cheeks, did you learn nothing from getting hit in the head by a pinecone?"

"Well, I..."

"If you want some supper, Cheeks, you can get busy finding it since I doubt that we have anything left in our satchels."

A look of sinking realization fell over Cheeks' face as he heard that he would once again not be eating unless he got busy. And so off he went with two empty satchels to fill.

"And keep your ears up! And do not go too far!" Teek called after him.

It was now early evening and time to think about another place to shelter for the night.

Clinging to the top of the cliff was a very old and very large juniper tree. She had sent roots down through the cracks in the basalt cliff in search of reliable water and nutrients.

The old matriarch had made her living doing this over many long years to the point that she was able to support some very old and very full branches.

Heavy with greenery and berries, the old juniper revealed the story of her growth in gnarled and twisting shapes. Her roots provided the perfect spot to crawl up under and hide for the night. Teek called to Cicci.

"Cicci, can you and Peeps hollow out a place for us while I go check on Cheeks?"

As Teek set off after Cheeks, he became aware of a dog barking not far off. This was not a "Who's out there?" sort of bark, but this was more aggressive. It sounded like the bark of a dog that had something cornered.

Accompanying the dog were the same humans whom they had heard passing overhead above the burial chamber. They were returning from their hike, and their dog—a stocky, heavily muscled and aggressive beast—had unfortunately noticed Cheeks before Cheeks had noticed him. Poor Cheeks was cornered in the crook of a large boulder.

As Teek scurried up, he got a better look at the situation. The dog had a large black leather strap of some kind around his neck. There were shiny metal points stuck to it.

"Blitz! Get over here!"

Blitz wasn't listening.

"Blitz!" the humans repeated, marching over. "Whaddya find, boy?"

Teek bravely positioned himself behind the ruckus and started to screech at the top of his lungs. The dog, delirious with excitement, spun around to chase Teek.

This gave Cheeks the break he needed. He shot back over the slope toward the cliff. Teek ditched into the nearest crack under a boulder just as the dog pounced and started digging frantically.

"Come on, Blitz, you've had enough."

Blitz was jerked back by the collar and pulled away as he strained to stay on his attack. He struggled to get free of his owner's grip in much the same way a schoolyard bully is restrained from a brawl. Teek listened carefully as the humans moved on.

"Did you see that?" one of them said. "It's almost as if one of those rodents was trying to save the other one!"

"What? Yeah right," said the other human.

"Yeah, well, maybe not."

Their loud voices finally drifted off, Blitz was hooked back up to his leash, where he should have been all along, and Teek was finally able to poke his head out from under the boulder.

Sneezing the dust from his quivering nose, he cheeped one last time to help release some of the remaining tension and aggravation with Cheeks' carelessness.

"What was the last thing I said to him? Keep your ears up! Does he not know what that means?" he grumbled to himself.

Teek left his hiding place, starting and stopping in the usual cautious manner of squirrels when not sure of the danger. He noticed that Cheeks had left the two satchels in the spot in which he had been cornered. To his surprise, they were half full.

Returning to the base of the great old juniper, Teek found Cheeks being attended to by Cicci and Peeps. He was rolled up in a ball and had stuffed himself as far under the roots as he could squeeze.

"Good gravely groundhogs! That was too close!" Teek exclaimed. "Is Cheeks all right?"

Cicci held up her front paw to quietly let Teek know that it was probably not the time for loud exclamations.

"Is he hurt?" Cicci asked in a whisper.

"I think he will be fine. He is just scared and needs to recover," Teek replied, "and I as well."

"What happened?" asked Cicci.

"Oh, those humans and their dog! Remember hearing them above the chamber of the ancient one? They were returning from whatever it was they were doing. When I found Cheeks, the dog had cornered him. So, I screeched as loud as I could, and the dog turned on me instead. Then I ditched, and the humans pulled him away."

"You saved his life," she said, nuzzling his face.

Teek looked at the ground in shyness.

"Ahem," Peeps intruded, "the stone is over there out of sight. I dragged it in."

"Ah, good, that was my next question. Uh, thank you, Peeps," stammered Teek. "It looks like Cheeks may have managed to find some food before the attack, but I have yet to look in the satchels."

"Well, if there is one thing Cheeks knows how to do, it is to find food!" Peeps blurted.

"I heard that!" came a whimpering chirp from under a root.

"Ah, he is back!" said Peeps, very pleased to hear signs of recovery.

The morning found Cheeks up early and situated at the opening of the tree roots, gazing straight ahead toward the edge of the rimrock.

"Cheeks?" Peeps noticed him and crawled out to see how he was doing.

"I doubt that I can do much more of this, Peeps. I am not cut out for this. I just want to be back in the colony and never venture out again."

Peeps listened carefully but was not sure how to reply to his friend or how to comfort him.

"Well," he said, "it sure is not for everybody, this adventure thing. But just think how sweet it will be when we're rounding the corner of the passage to our village again after all of this. We will be there before you know it. And then you will look back and you will be so proud of yourself, and your family will be too! Think of the next story time in the Great Hall! Maybe they will want you to tell of this journey. Just think of how much better Rimrock will be now that you have left and come back. I think that we will have a better time there than if we had never done this. In fact, I think everyone should go away and then come back home. I know *I* grew up a little bit—"

"Peeps?"

"Yes?"

"I feel better now. Please stop talking."

"Sorry. It looks like Teek is getting ready to head out now," added Peeps. "Maybe you should stick closer to him as we go."

"Yes, you may be right, maybe I should," admitted Cheeks.

THE RETURN OF KINDRED SPIRITS

"Wait, Grandpa, I should go ahead of you in case you stumble." Sofia squeezed past Grandpa Prudy to position herself on the downhill side of him.

"I'm not going to fall," he replied.

"Well, you did last time. You know we're not even supposed to be here," Sofia scolded.

"Oh, nonsense, Sofia. Nobody can expect me to stay away from this place. This is where I spent my childhood."

"Yeah, well, in case you don't remember, you're an old man now."

"Yes, well, you know what that means?" he replied. He continued without her answer, chuckling, "That means there are things that you're too young to know and that I'm too old to remember!"

"Oh yeah? What things?" she asked.

"Oh, many things... never mind."

Walter soon learned not to make idle comments around a teenage girl, especially this one.

"I would like to show you a very special spot," he announced.

"Really? Where is it?" she asked.

"Down next to the river."

"All the way down there? That'll take forever. We don't have time for that, do we?"

"Sure, we'll be there in no time."

"Well, be careful. If you fall again, we'll be in big trouble."

"Sofia, I've been in trouble off and on for most of my life, hon. Just tell your mother I forced you to come along. Blame me. I can't be in any more trouble than I have been in for the last forty years."

"The way I hear it, that's your fault, isn't it?"

"I suppose so, Sofia. Partly my fault, anyway. Let's sit here for a minute. Grandpa has to take a rest for a little while."

Walter Prudy had returned to visit his favorite spot in the world— the Deschutes River Canyon. It had only been a day since his last visit, but he had to show his granddaughter this special place below the rimrock. Sofia walked down the hill ahead of him.

With each switchback, she turned around and waited to watch her grandfather navigate the steep rocky trail.

Walter used a walking stick and moved slowly, choosing his steps carefully. He knew that if he didn't, he might very well put Sofia in a difficult situation.

Sofia was a plainspoken yet thoughtful thirteen-year-old girl. She had spent most of her young childhood separated from her grandfather. Her mother, Helen, had been the only product of Walter's failed marriage. While Walter had spent time in Portland devoted to his law practice, Sofia had lived with her mother and grandmother Abbot in her grandmother's home in Central Oregon. Most of what Sofia knew about him was through comments made by her mother and grandmother.

Now Grandpa Prudy had finally retired from a life away from his granddaughter, Sofia, and for the first time was giving her his undivided attention.

Sofia was surprised to find out how adventurous and fun to talk to her grandfather was turning out to be. But it would be a long day before she would *tell* him that.

Halfway down the trail, Walter and Sofia sat down to rest under a juniper. As they began to get reacquainted, Sofia was taken with how different he seemed from what she had imagined. He was not at all how she had been thinking of him over the years. He had rarely come to visit, but Sofia began to wonder if possibly it might have been because her mother and grandmother hadn't wanted him around.

After some silence, Sofia asked her Grandpa Prudy very directly, "Why didn't you visit more often, Grandpa?"

Walter turned his face away from the river and looked at his granddaughter directly.

"You know, Sofia dear, one can't change the things that are already done. We can only decide what to do from this moment on. I did want to visit you more often. What is important is that we have the chance to spend time together now, so we should make the most of it. You're only thirteen, we have the rest of our lives," he said.

"Not the rest of *my* life!" she replied.

"Don't you worry, I'm not going anywhere for a long while."

Sofia thought for a moment as she listened to his way of thinking.

"Did Mom and Grandma keep you from visiting?" she asked. Walter took great care to answer her question truthfully and yet not place blame.

"I suppose I should have tried to find out how we could have worked things out. Family is always a challenge, isn't it? The important thing now is what we do with the time we have before us. I know that I haven't been there to repair your owies or tell you what a smart girl you were," he said.

"Well, my *dad* wasn't around much either," Sofia added.

Walter continued, "Sometimes the choices we make are further reaching than we realize at the time we make those choices. I'm here now. And I want you to know that I love you and I want to spend lots of time with you."

"Well, it's okay. I have friends at school." Sofia needed her grandpa to realize how much she had lost because of her family's difficulties. Deep down, she wanted very much to be a big part of her grandpa's life.

"I'm sorry that I haven't had as much time to spend with you as I do now," Walter replied. "One of these days you may look back and realize how lucky you were that I was here with you now. There's something else you may come to realize," he said with a smile. "You're a lot like your grandpa."

Sofia got up suddenly. "Are you rested yet? Let's go!"

Without a word, Walter hoisted himself up. Sofia was already walking down the trail ahead of him. He knew that he had a lot of catching up to do if he was going to reacquaint himself with his granddaughter.

He had decided that he wouldn't explain to her how her mother and grandmother had purposely kept him away from their lives for so long. If the two of them were to become fast friends, there would be no blame. He would not place her in the center of the conflict.

Besides, Helen was beginning to realize how important it was for Sofia to be able to spend time with her grandfather, specifically this weekend.

Grandpa Prudy had made a special trip down from Portland just to spend a weekend with his granddaughter. Helen had sat down with Sofia to gauge her interest in spending the entire weekend with him.

She could tell how important it was to her daughter that the two of them be able to have a closer relationship. And so, she agreed to let them spend both weekend days together.

And Sofia was just beginning to realize how precious each minute of time was when spent in the company of her grandpa. She realized that she was fortunate to be gifted with something very rare and very valuable. She was also beginning to realize that it was quite possible that they were, in fact, as he said, very much alike.

23

THE BIRDCALL SPELL

"It starts to level out down here," Sofia reported back. "Can you make it?"

"Sure, I can make it."

"Well, just remember, we have to climb back up," she went on.

"We'll worry about that when the time comes. Just remember to pace yourself so you don't poop out on me!"

"No way!" she answered.

But she was remembering what her mother would say about him. *There's no fool like an old fool, especially when it comes to your grandfather!*

She wondered whether her mother was right. She was just beginning to suspect that it was possible that her mother had been mistaken.

Down they went at a slow and careful pace until they reached the riverbank safely.

"What do ya say we sit and have some of that ice-cold pop we stuffed in your backpack? Let's sit under those trees over next to the bank," Walter urged.

It was a glorious morning, somewhere between late summer and early fall—dry and warm with a cool breeze. They heard the sound of the river swirling and gurgling by. They stopped to listen to the bird calls overhead.

One made a *"Pssst-a-dee-dee-dee-dee"* call; another went *"Wip wee weer"*; still another went *"Psst psst ree ree ree ree"*; and so on.

"How about we play a little game?" suggested Grandpa Prudy. "I used to play this when I was a boy. Every time we hear a new birdcall, we take turns trying to spell it. Then the other one has to try to pronounce what was spelled."

"That's silly!" Sofia declared.

"Come on, give it a try. I'll spell the first one."

Grandpa Prudy took out a pencil and paper and waited. Soon a call came. He wrote: "Pssst-a-dee-dee-dee-dee."

"Okay, you read this," he said.

Sofia grabbed the paper from him and began to read aloud, but she didn't get far before she burst into laughter. Then it was Sofia's turn to write what she heard, and it was Grandpa Prudy's turn to pronounce it. They laughed together.

Soon Sofia realized that she was enjoying the company of her grandpa immensely.

"Now it's my turn again!" said Walter.

After a time, when all the laughter had stopped, they sat in silence and listened to the gurgling river. Sofia gazed quietly at the dark swirls passing by. Grandpa Prudy waited patiently, watching her sort through her thoughts.

"Grandpa," she began, "was the canyon always like this, like, when you were a kid?"

"Oh, in some ways but not in others."

"In what ways was it different?" she asked.

"Well, there were fewer people, and there was more water," he replied.

Sofia commented, "I bet the critters in the canyon were happier then.

"Yup, I suppose they were."

Grandpa Prudy was quite tickled when he heard Sofia use a word he had used, like *critter*, when she referred to animals. He chuckled when he heard it.

He asked her about what was going on in her life, with friends, school, and other interests. He listened carefully to her enthusiastic answers and made sure not to judge.

He accepted her perceptions unconditionally. Occasionally, being an old lawyer, he would interrupt and attempt to correct the way she phrased her answer.

Sofia would reply to his correction with, "Oh, Grandpa, that's just the way old people say it."

Sofia went on, now more comfortable with his company, "If you ask me, there are too many boys at my school. Boys my age can be really mean and dumb!"

"It's a tough age, for sure," he replied with understanding.

"I wish you could come visit more often, Grandpa!"

"Well, I plan to. I'm retiring from my practice now, so I think that such a thing just might be arranged. In fact, I'm looking forward to moving out here near you."

This news was the best thing that Sofia could possibly hear, but she didn't dare let on. Inside, deep down inside, she felt a stronger feeling of belonging. She felt more loved. Walter had given her two of the greatest gifts he could give—unconditional love and a feeling of being connected to a family.

Everyone needs to be part of a pack or clan. Sofia was no exception, and young Sofia would ultimately give Grandpa Prudy a precious gift as well—unconditional love in return and the exuberant enthusiasm and optimism that only a young person can show an old man.

"Why is a law firm referred to as a practice, Grandpa?"

"Oh, I suppose because, well, I guess each day you have to keep practicing so that you get better. Our work requires practice so we can perform properly."

She paused and thought for a long time. Then she simply replied with, "Then you must have been very good."

"So, the boys are giving you grief, huh?" he continued.

"Oh, some of them are okay, I suppose."

"Uh-huh."

"Actually, I sorta like this one boy."

"Oh?"

"He's kinda quiet and sorta gentle."

"Sounds like a nice boy."

"Yeah. Well, we'll see."

Grandpa Prudy pulled a long thin stick from his coat. It was smooth and a beautiful amber color. He had tooled it with great care. It had interesting curves and gnarled shapes with agates, arrowheads, and many carved markings on it.

Sofia's eyes grew bigger. "What's that?" she asked. She knew that the answer would most likely be wondrous.

"This, dear Sofia, is one of my prized possessions. This is a tapping stick."

"A tapping stick? What is it for?"

"Well, when I was young, I used to tap a rock to let the little critters know that I was near. I made these a long time ago. Last week while packing, I found them again in my attic in an old chest."

"Are there more of them?" she asked.

"Oh yes, but this one? This one is my favorite," he said, holding it up. "I'm going to let them know we're here right now."

"Let who know?" she asked.

"Oh, you'll see. In all those rocks behind me, there are a lot of critters that humans walk right by, but *I* let them know that I'm here. Many of them are golden mantled ground squirrels. After I tap this time to let them know we're near, I'll give this tapping stick to you—that is, if you promise to take good care of it and appreciate what it's used for."

"Oh yes, I promise," she quickly replied.

With that, Grandpa Prudy tapped a rock at their feet three times and then three more times. He then handed the tapping stick to Sofia.

"It's beautiful, Grandpa. Thank you!" she said.

"Let's see if that's enough to get one of them to visit us," he continued.

24

SOFIA'S AWAKENING

Very soon Grandpa Prudy's efforts were rewarded.

"Look, Grandpa, *there's* a squirrel!"

"That's a golden mantled ground squirrel," he added.

"It's coming closer. Look how bold it is," Sofia observed.

The squirrel moved in cautious starts and stops as it approached the two humans. It seemed to stare unblinkingly at Walter Prudy.

"He's looking at you, Grandpa."

"Yes, he appears to be."

Walter and the squirrel stared at each other. The squirrel stood unblinking only a few feet away. It began chirping, peeping, and cheeping.

As the squirrel continued to chatter, Walter began to realize that his previous experience had been authentic, for soon he began once more to hear names and words.

"Hello, are you Walter Prudy? Hello? Walter Prudy?"

"Yes, that's me," he answered.

"What's you?" asked Sofia.

Grandpa Prudy turned his attention back to Sofia, realizing that she was unable to understand what the squirrel had just said.

"Uh, why, I meant to say that it sorta looks like me, doesn't it?"

"No," she replied.

"Walter Prudy?" the squirrel repeated.

Walter turned back toward the squirrel with a "Shhh!"

"Did you just shush me or the squirrel, Grandpa?"

"Uh, no, I, uh, I was just, uh… Oh, for heaven's sake, didn't you hear it?"

"Well, yes, I heard it squeaking…"

"No, it's not squeaking, it's speaking! It asked me if I was Walter Prudy."

"Grandpa, stop teasing me. I'm not a gullible little girl anymore."

"Listen, Sofia, do you remember when I told you about when I came down here, lost my balance and fell? Remember when I told you not to tell anyone that I had seen a small village and met a squirrel named Teek?"

"Well, yeah, but I thought that you were either kidding me or that maybe you had, well, had some… well, you know, dementia. Or maybe it was just because you got hit on the head?"

"Okay, I did *bump* my head, but what I experienced was real! I know that your mother wouldn't want me to talk about it, and I wouldn't want her to think that I was crazy. So, I guess I just don't want to share any of this with her."

Sofia sat and stared at her grandpa.

He continued, "I'm not teasing you, Sofia. It's all true. But you mustn't tell anyone!"

"Oh, Grandpa! I've heard of this sort of thing, but I didn't know it would happen to you so soon!"

"Sweetie, I promise you that I'm not getting dementia! Apparently, there's a whole world out there that not many people get to experience. I suspect it's mostly because over thousands of years, humans have told themselves that certain things just weren't possible and that someone would have to be crazy to believe it."

"Believe what?" she asked.

"Oh, something I used to think about a lot when I was young. I guess I sort of forgot about it myself. It has been so many years… I had almost forgotten."

"Forgotten what?" Sofia now needed to know more.

"Well, something I think humans have refused to acknowledge or understand. I think that there is an ancient universal language, a quiet, natural language. Somewhere along the way, humans just forgot about it. Maybe if we had just kept an open mind, we never would have lost it. It seems that people sort of tuned it out. Then the world simply became too noisy."

"I don't understand! It all sounds like a bedtime story."

"Okay, well, I don't think that everyone is born with this sort of thing. Most people think that it *is* nothing more than a bedtime story. The truth is that some people have the ability, but they just need to be awakened. I think this happened to me when I was a young boy. But somehow, over time, I had forgotten. I may have covered it up. A long time ago, one of those critters saw it in me. If they notice it in *you*, then you may be lucky enough for them to awaken it in you."

"Hey! Hello! Did you say that you *are* Walter Prudy or not?"

"I am," replied Walter.

"Ah, good. Well, I am Seek. I am one of the elders of the Rimrock colony."

"Hello, Seek. I'm afraid that if you want me to continue talking with you, you'll have to try to get my granddaughter to hear your words, or she's going to think I'm crazy."

"Grandpa, please tell me that you're not still talking to that squirrel?"

"Did you hear that, Seek? Like I said, if you want to talk to me, you need to make her understand too!"

"What is her name?" asked Seek.

"Sofia," Walter replied.

"What is her other name? You humans have two names, right?" he added.

"Just call her Sofia. That'll be enough."

"Grandpa, stop it. You're scaring me!"

Walter looked at the squirrel and raised his eyebrows. "Well?" he urged.

"All right!" Exclaimed the squirrel. "I need to look into her eyes first."

"Sweetheart," started Grandpa Prudy, "If you want to understand what he's saying, you need to let him look into your eyes now."

"I... What? It's going to stare at me?" she said in disbelief.

"It was pretty hard for me to believe, too, dear. Now remember, this must be something that you don't tell anyone about, no matter who they are. This is one thing that I must ask you to keep just between the two of us...well, us and the squirrels. Other people just won't understand. Can you do as I ask of you?"

"I, uh, well, yes! Sure, I can, Grandpa." As she said these words, her eyes met Seek's, becoming intently transfixed.

Seek's thoughts entered Sofia's thoughts. Seek investigated Sofia and found her spirit to be in a good place. So, he allowed her to understand.

"All right then, I have to listen to the squirrel now."

Sofia stared at her grandpa with a whole new perception of him.

"You can blink now, dear," said Walter. Walter now turned to the squirrel. "So, your name is Seek?"

"Yes, I am one of the elders of the Rimrock colony, a story elder. I do not usually show up outside of our walls, but lately I have been walking near the passage opening to our village with the hope that, well, we've lost some of our own recently. Anyway, I heard your tapping and I remember learning about tapping sticks from stories about an ancient human."

"The Illumination Stone?" inserted Walter.

"We mustn't speak of it out here. You have returned. I was surprised to see you again so soon."

"Where is Teek?" asked Walter.

"Well, he is on a journey, along with three others. They have been gone for several daylights. We sent them to try to retrieve, uh, to retrieve... that which I dare not mention."

"That's all right. I know what they're looking for."

"We are very concerned that they may have met with a bad end. There are predators out there, and few of us are used to venturing out very far from the protection of our village. And well, you see now there are rats in this area brought by the humans. They threaten our colony."

Walter remained focused on Teek. "Then they could be almost anywhere," he concluded.

"There is really no way to know," replied the elder squirrel. "Their mission is very important to our colony, Walter Prudy. Unfortunately,many, including me, are starting to suspect that they may not return at all. We thought you might be of some help to Teek, but then you left suddenly."

Walter offered no excuse; he simply continued. "Which direction did they go?"

"Downriver, I believe. They'd be on this side of the canyon. There is no place to cross to the other side that I know of," Seek replied.

Sofia had been sitting quietly, staring intently at the talking squirrel. Although she was an unassuming young person who maintained a cool head and an open mind, she struggled to accept her sudden new reality.

Finally, she managed to gather her thoughts. "We will go find them!"

"Sofia!" her grandpa objected. "We need to get you back on time!"

"C'mon, Grandpa, let's go help them."

Walter turned back to Seek. "I'm afraid that my exuberant granddaughter needs to think this through."

"No, she doesn't," said Sofia.

Seek looked again at Sofia and then returned his attention to Walter.

"Let's go," she went on. "I want to help. C'mon, Grandpa! We've come this far. I never dreamed I'd be able to talk with a squirrel, and they need our help!"

"Sofia, it's almost noon. I'm not even sure where to begin to look. We don't want to get lost. Does your mother even know where you are?" Walter tried to think of every possible way to keep her out of trouble.

"I have the tapping stick. I assume they know the sound?" she said.

"Oh, they may or may not. It was a long time ago," said Walter.

"I did recognize that sound, so I think that Teek also would," Seek pointed out.

Sofia continued, "If we don't find them in a couple of hours, we'll come back and try again tomorrow. Grandpa, we have to help!"

Grandpa Prudy drew a great big sigh and wondered if it was a good idea to have introduced his granddaughter to the tapping stick, the language of nature, and all the things that may now complicate their lives and get them both in trouble.

"I suspect," said Seek, "that by now they are either on their way back or sadly... gone for good. There are a lot of real dangers out there."

"That's why we have to help them!" insisted Sofia.

Seek put his paw on Walter's boot. "Being an elder, I do know how impetuous young ones are. This is what got us in this situation to begin with. So, you do what you think you should do, Walter Prudy. We can take care of our own. We know death. It is part of our life."

Seek began making his way back up the hill to the colony. He had one ear pointed back and trained on the two humans.

Walter spoke. "Two hours, that's it... for today! You tap along the way. If nothing happens in an hour or so, we start heading back."

Seek couldn't help but smile with relief; he had made a wise move. His words and his actions had worked. The humans were back and ready to help, as he had hoped.

The second Sofia heard her grandpa's verdict, she launched herself off the rock where she had been seated.

"Now look, if you go too fast, we might miss something. What's worse, you might trip and fall. Then you won't be much help to anybody." A warm smile came over Grandpa Prudy's face after he barked his warnings.

The most important thing was that he realized that he and his granddaughter shared a very important quality. They both cared deeply about the lives of other creatures.

Seek rounded the corner to the entrance of the long passage to Rimrock, and there was Eechius.

"Well, was it the human that Teek knows?"

"It was! Walter Prudy is his name," replied Seek.

"And?"

"He is headed downriver to look for them."

"Wonderful! Nicely done!" exclaimed Eechius.

"But only for a short while, and then they will be back in a short cycle."

"They?" asked Eechius.

"Yes, they. Her name is Sofia. She is his young offspring, and she is very much like him. In fact, I awakened her."

"What? So now she knows about us? She knows that we can understand what humans are saying? She knows of our colony?"

"Yes, it was actually easy, she is much like Walter Prudy. She shares his sensibilities. She cares about us. She *wants* to help."

25

TRAILS AND TALES

Teek attached the travois to his back, and the rest of the team collected their satchels for the next leg of the journey. It was dawn on a cold and frozen morning as they departed. Teek outlined to the others what he expected next.

"We will travel at the top of the rimrock until we draw nearer to our colony."

"Would you like me to pull the travois for a while, Teek?"

It was Cheeks who, upon hearing the words 'nearer to our colony,' had begun rallying with renewed spirit. "I can stick close to you. Maybe I can help, and I, well, you see, I... I want to thank you for saving my life."

"I should not have sent you out alone. It was my mistake. We almost lost you," said Teek.

Glancing at Cicci, he added, "And yes, thank you. I would be most happy if you carried this load for a while. You stay close now. In fact, we should make sure we all stay together."

He said the last few words in a louder voice so that everyone could hear, adding, "I think if we simply follow the cliff line as long as we can, we will keep moving in the right direction."

Cicci and Peeps looked around and nodded.

As the sun began to peek over the top of the juniper trees, they stopped briefly to lift their noses and breathe in the usual sweet spicy flavor of the canyon carried by the morning breeze.

As it happened, the entire canyon had become aware of the small band of ground squirrels. The common knowledge was that the squirrels either had been looking for something valuable for their colony or had already found it and were possibly now carrying it back.

Birdcalls of every variety were following their movements. Rustling, twig breaking, squirrel chatter, and even some growling and howling could be heard. Unknown creatures were moving through the thick brush, and large birds of prey were circling overhead.

Out of the corner of their eyes, they caught glimpses of creatures scurrying from cover to cover. Some came quite close to them but then ducked back into cover before the squirrels could identify them. Teek noticed this, and so he warned the others.

"It seems that the closer we are, the more danger may lurk. So, keep a lookout and be ready to ditch."

They rounded a corner in the trail that hugged the edge of the rimrock. Teek stopped suddenly and chirped out, "Listen! I hear humans!"

Peering around a boulder, they could just see them through the trees. They discovered two male humans sitting at a campfire.

"Do you smell that?" asked Cheeks. "It smells like a biscuit!" Cheeks announced, "I think I could recognize that smell anywhere."

"Hold it, Cheeks. Let me think about this," Teek said as he looked to Cicci for her assessment.

Noticing that he needed her opinion on the matter, she began, "Well, the good thing about these two is that there are probably no predators to look out for while they are around. The bad thing is, we do not know whether these humans are going to be good or bad," she reasoned.

"Yes, very true," Teek agreed. "One of us will have to scramble out there so that we get their attention, and then we can see how they react," said Teek.

"I can do it," volunteered Cheeks.

Peeps rolled his eyes saying, "Such bravery for a biscuit crumb, very impressive."

"Do you always have to dig into me?" asked Cheeks.

"I am just trying to understand whether you are really brave or just really hungry," Peeps replied.

"Are you feeling up to it, Cheeks?" added Cicci.

"Take it just a few steps at a time, Cheeks," added Teek.

"Shall I go ahead and start then?" Cheeks asked.

"Let's get a bit closer," Teek answered, "then you can venture out. We will be just behind the nearest rock."

The squirrels approached the two humans. A local rancher, Harvey Badgett, and his hired hand, Long Jim Rowley, out of Durango Colorado, and their horses, Rusty, and Cisco, had been camped overnight.

They had roused a little late, having had a few sips of what they called camp coffee the night before. They were now sitting at a small fire, heating up the morning coffee and eating biscuits and bacon.

As Cheeks grew closer, he began to hear their conversation.

"Boy, I'll tell ya, ol' Billy sure handled that bronc yesterday, didn't he?"

"I s'pose so. I just love the way that announcer called out his age as thirty-five. Heck, he's forty if he's a day."

"You kiddin' me? He's forty-three!"

"Is that a fact?" There was a pause. "Hey, look at that, Harvey! You got yourself a friend."

"Yup, sure do. Somethin' usually shows up in the morning, hopin' fer a few crumbs of a biscuit. Don't see 'em as much anymore with all 'em new folks a comin' in. I sorta like 'em little fellas, though. Kinda cute and smarter than you'd think. Toss him a crumb, see if he comes closer."

Long Jim lobbed a crumb just in front of Cheeks.

Cheeks quickly stuffed the large wad in his mouth and scurried back behind the boulder where the others were waiting. When Cheeks returned, he was still out of breath from all the excitement.

"I... I think... I think those humans are safe folks," he puffed. "They were not scary at all. They just sat there. They appeared to know what I wanted."

"So where is the rest of it?" asked Peeps. "We did not think *that* part through, did we?" he added.

There was a hint of jealousy in Peeps' voice this time. He had gotten quite accustomed to being the go-to member of the group.

"Do you want to go out there *now*, Peeps?" asked Teek. Peeps kept silent.

"Heck, I ain't finishin' the rest of my biscuit, anyway," said Long Jim. "Might as well see if there are any more of 'em." Long Jim got up and set the rest of his biscuit on a flat rock just out in front of where he had seen Cheeks disappear and then sat back down.

The two cowboys sat quietly for a while, long enough for the four squirrels to venture back out from behind the rock. Teek made sure that the two men were far enough away so that they could have enough time to ditch, if need be. H

e was taking no chances at this point in their journey. In fact, it was very difficult for him to feel comfortable about leaving the Illumination Stone on the other side of the rock.

As the four squirrels sat nibbling the biscuit, the two humans continued their conversation. They spoke of places far beyond the canyon and beyond the squirrel's ability to understand. They spoke of a much larger world around them, of other humans and places that the squirrels could never have imagined.

"This *is* beautiful country, Harvey."

"Yup, it is. I'm lucky to 'ave growed up here."

"Where'd all this lava come from, anyway?"

"Oh, the whole place is volcanic, and I hear that most of it came from a big volcano just south o' here—*Newberry* I think it's called. From what I heard, there's a lotta small volcanoes called cinder cones. They made some pretty big lava flows out there. There also a lotta caves too, called lava tubes."

"Is that a fact? All that was south o' here?"

"Well, yeah... and north. There are other places, like one just north o' here called Crooked River. A friend o' mine has a spread up in there around Smith Rocks. That's just one part of another big volcano... they call 'em calderas."

"Like Yellowstone?"

"Yeah, I 'spose. No longer active, though. Also, the river itself is kinda strange."

"This one?"

"Yup, the Deschutes."

"Whaddya mean?"

"Oh, I guess it's pretty dangerous in some places. In some stretches, there's a river flowin' under the one that you see."

"How'd they figure that out?"

"Oh, some people study natural history, geology 'n' such. Anyway, the lava just flowed right over the top. They say that there are places down there that have never seen the light of day, least wise, not for hundreds of thousands of years or more. But like lots of things in this world, this place is changing."

"Yeah? How so?"

"Well, the West Coast is not like Montana or Wyoming, y'see. Lots o' people have moved here, and are still movin' here, lots of people. Heck, we all might just love this place to death someday."

"How do ye do that?" asked Long Jim.

Harvey took a long slow sip of his coffee. "I don't know. It's just that... well, a real long time ago there was just the original people here... sorta like your neck o' the woods, and everything was a goin' just fine."

"Tribes?"

"Yeah, you know, oh, let's see, uh, well, the Molalla was here, the Modoc (a little farther south), the Paiute, uh... There was some Cayuse, the Chinook from along the Columbia up north), uh, the Shoshone, of course, but most of 'em were in the Ochocos and Blue Mountains. Then there was them Sahaptin tribes: the Nes Perce, Umatilla, Tenino and the Yakama...oh, and the Wasco, too." He sighed. "And others. Early on they fought the Spanish, and then they had to fight what they called 'the Americans' (from the east), mainly because of the discovery of gold. The Americans wanted to take their land. A lot of tribes died either by warring or because of the diseases brought by the newcomers. The rest of the original people were mostly sent to reservations."

"You sure know a lot about it," said Long Jim. His eyes were sad.

"Yup, I do a little reading, I like history," replied Harvey.

"Well, everything seems all right now, don't it?"

"Well, I guess that all depends on what you think is 'all right,'" he said, a hard edge in his voice. "Long Jim, it's not a good thing, what we done. No sir! We didn't treat any of 'em fair at all. The original people loved this land. They worshiped this land. It was their home. It was everything to them. We just came in and took it. You can't own a place like this—nobody should. The sooner you learn that Long Jim, the wiser you'll be, and you'll be a better person for it."

Long Jim looked a bit puzzled. "Well, it all looks pretty nice to me right now. What'd we all do wrong?" he asked.

"Oh, no one thing, I s'pose, but lots o' things over a long period of time. Heck, I guess after all that time, you'd think we'd a learnt somethin'. Time is a strange thing, Long Jim, maybe the strangest thing. It's sorta what keeps us all here, I guess. I do wonder if *time* even exists elsewheres. Oh, occasionally time gives us somethin', but then sometimes it takes it away. It's a teacher *and* a thief! Heh. Strange, ain't it? It turns terrible things in history into, well, more interesting things sometimes. You could even say that sometimes destruction, after time goes by, can end up looking sorta, well, constructive. Sorta like this land. Change *is* hard to notice as it goes by. Nothing looks like it is changing, but it is. I guess that ye have to look back to notice what has changed."

"Ain't that the truth," replied Long Jim. "So how did this place get settled?"

"Oh, first, this territory was filled with French-Canadian fur trappers. Around 1834 or so, some say the first explorers started showin' up pretty much just to go after beaver. And them pioneers really looked forward to arrivin' in these parts. They would look for the buttes as a sign that they was a gettin' close. Back in those days, there was about three hundred or so settlers. Let's see, then statehood was in... 1859, but these parts was already settled for the most part. Then I think it was in 1916 or so that the governor at the time decided to call this area Deschutes County (after the river). Then the railroads came.

Then the logging started. Them mills were the largest timber mills of the day in the world! Then the gold miners came, and then the stockmen brought their cattle, like my great grandpa. The cattle sure liked the meadows in that Upper Deschutes area. Most of the settlers grew wheat and potato. Then from, oh, bout I'd say 1917 to 'bout maybe 1920, the settlers grew from about five thousand to over nine thousand or more. Well, it has just continued to shoot up from there. And whenever people moved in, they plowed everything up so that they could build their homesteads and own everything around 'em. The rest is, as they say—"

"Beggin' pardon, Harvey."

"Yeah? Oh, did I miss somethin'?"

"Well, I woulda asked sooner, but I couldn't figure out when to interrupt!"

"So, you tired a' listnin'?"

"Nah. Just that, what about your family ownin' that spread you got?"

"Yup, yup, been in my family nearly three generations. Not sayin' we weren't part of the problem. Just sayin' the whole thing is somethin' ta think about, ya know?"

"Hey, look at 'em, Harvey, starin' at ye like they'se a list'nin'! Ha! Well, boy, howdy!"

"Yeah, well, I don't seem to be boring *them* none, do I, Long Jim? This spot's probably their home. Once we're outa here, they'll be runnin' all over again."

Harvey threw his last cup of coffee on the fire and kicked dirt over it. "Well, best head back," he said.

The two cowboys saddled up Rusty and Cisco, mounted up, and headed out. Their voices trailed off as they rode away.

"I think there must be a couple more strays up this way."

The two horses snorted, expressing their reluctance to get back on the trail. Their heavy hoof clops reverberated through the ground as the enormous beasts climbed over the exposed lava rock.

The squirrels grabbed what was left of the biscuit and hauled it back behind the rock. The Illumination Stone was thankfully still there. Cheeks volunteered to keep the rest of the biscuit in his satchel.

"Well, that was interesting," commented Cicci. "I wonder what a railroad is?"

"Must be like that long flat black surface that they use when sitting in those fast-moving things," answered Cheeks.

"Yes, maybe so," she replied.

Teek directed the group. "The bright light of day is higher in the sky, so we need to try to make some progress while we can. Remember, you must try not to be seen. Moving from one hiding place to another is the only way we should travel at this point. I have a feeling that there are creatures searching for us, maybe even a band of rats. For all I know, we could be foolishly leading them in the direction of our colony."

The canyon was still alive with activity as they set off. Teek resumed carrying the Illumination Stone without a word from the others. They made their way back to the edge of the cliff and began following a deer trail upriver.

"Did you hear that?" Teek said presently.

"Well, I hear a lot of birdcalls," replied Cicci. "What did you hear?"

"Not sure yet. There it is again!"

"Croak–kkkkk–croaw."

"Could it be...? It is!"

Whoop–whoop–whoop. A very large and very familiar black bird landed in front of them.

"Great juniper berries!" exclaimed Peeps. "He scares me every time."

"KKKKK! Well, little ones! All accounted for, I see."

"Kanti!" shouted Teek.

"Teek!" Kanti croaked in return. "I smelled the meat cooking, saw the humans, then I spotted you," he explained.

"We are so glad to see you," said Teek with a smile.

"I wish I had better news for you," Kanti continued. "I have been flying over, and there is a lot of movement along the trail. From what I can tell, it looks like a band of those rats are following you."

The squirrels looked at one another.

"I had a feeling that might be happening," said Teek.

"They may not care about your stone," Kanti went on, "but you know how they do want to find out where your colony is. You should either get way ahead of them or take another route. So that is the stone, eh? Let me look at it."

Teek stepped in front of it, putting himself between Kanti and his precious cargo. "This is one shiny object you may not have," Teek declared.

"Easy, little fella. No need to get your fur all roughed up. I just want to look."

Kanti hopped to one side and looked around at the stone. "Where did you find it?"

"Well, we didn't, actually. It was at the bottom of the river. Fisk the otter found it," Peeps confessed.

"Haw-haw! I guess that *is* how things go! Fisk, eh? Makes sense! Well, I figured it was in the river, or I might have seen it myself. It sure is a beauty, to be sure. Must mean a great deal to you, little ones. You are risking a lot."

"Where *is* the band of rats, Kanti?" Cicci asked.

"Right now? Hmm, they might be back on the other side of where those two humans were camped, but be aware, they *are* up here atop the cliffs, and I am quite sure that they *are* moving again. I spotted two of them, and so I flew ahead to look for you. I thought that you might be up here somewhere. So, *do* be on the lookout and keep moving."

"Can you find any of the, uh, muhas (red hawks) to help, you know, grab some of them?" asked Cicci.

Kanti scanned the skies. "I'll be flying around and keep an eye out.

They are sort of a lofty lot, hard to talk to. They do not like me much, being predatory raptors, probably because I do not care much for catching and eating... well, you know. But if I tip them off to some easy pickens, they just might show up. I will look around to see if any of them are flying around. They are no good in the trees, but if we can get the rats out in the open, well then, it's feeding time," Kanti said. "Maybe I could let some of the other creatures know also."

Cheeks grimaced. He perceived the world outside of Rimrock as dangerous and violent. He wanted little, if anything more, to do with it.

"Oh, one other thing," added Kanti. "I found that family of rabbits you were talking about, but they were pretty scared of me. I was not able to get them to come out just yet, but I will go back and try again. There is a little brushy meadow farther downriver below the falls. I think they would be better off if they moved down there."

"Thank you, Kanti. If I were not on this journey, I would go back and help them too."

"Well, I will see what I can do," Kanti added as he launched himself from the cliff top and flew south up the river.

The squirrels watched him fly away. The canyon seemed quiet as the group of squirrels watched Kanti become smaller and smaller in the bright blue sky.

GRACIOUS VISITORS

Walter followed his granddaughter downstream. They walked as quietly as humans are able down the path, waist-deep in bunch grass, dogwood, and sagebrush. They slipped through thickets of willow, alder, sedges, and rushes.

Surrounded by the sounds and smells of the riverbank, they treated each step with a respect and politeness that would be shown by a gracious guest. The songs of chickadees, cedar waxwings, and thrushes filled their ears.

"Seep, seep, ree, ree, ree, ree. See seer, see seer, see seer. Seee, seee, seee, seee. Heeee, heeee, weeee, wrrrrrr."

Walter noticed a change in his granddaughter. Was this who she had been all these years, or had Seek awakened something in her that had been hidden all this time? As he observed her immersing herself in the discovery of this hidden world, he felt great pride in his granddaughter's reverence for the wilderness and her deep respect for the living things around her.

She didn't march down the trail with the loud and careless arrogance of a typical human. She was consciously aware of the fragility and sacredness of everything she approached. She made herself a part of the environment around her.

Walter stopped to observe her peer over the rushes into a pool. He was just wondering whether certain personality traits in their family might skip generations when he noticed Sofia's hand shooting up for attention.

She lifted her finger to her mouth to let Grandpa Prudy know not to make a noise, and then she pointed toward the water. Walter joined her and looked in the direction she was pointing.

A dark shape was moving upstream and across the pool. It created a wake that spread out behind it.

"A beaver," she whispered.

Walter peered over the rushes into the pool. The beaver spotted them and, in an instant, executed a surface dive.

As it submerged, its entire body whipped quickly, ending with its flat leathery tail slapping the water with a loud *whop-cabloosh!* Its tail caused a sound that stopped all the birds from singing. The two stood in silence looking at the bubbles and ripples on the surface of the water.

"Well, we just 'rang the doorbell.' Everyone knows about us now," Walter concluded.

"That may be a good thing. The sound of the beaver's warning splash carries a lot farther than tapping on a rock," replied Sofia.

"Sofia, unfortunately we have to head back now. If we don't, we'll be late, and I want to make sure I get you back on time. We need to build some trust so that your mom feels comfortable letting you go places with me."

"We can't quit now! We just started searching for them!" she contested.

"Remember, Sofia, we have to get back up the hill. When we get back to the truck, there'll be just enough time to get you home."

"But, Grandpa, we can't just abandon the search! We must help them. Tomorrow is Sunday and I'm coming back!"

"Okay, I'll pick you up in the morning. What time?"

"I'll be ready to go at 6:00 am."

"Can we make it 7:00 am?"

"I suppose," she replied. "But no later."

On their hike back, Grandpa Prudy began to gather the information he needed from Sofia to assess the state of family affairs.

"Did you happen to mention to your mom where we were spending our time together this weekend? Or did she assume that we were simply going out for breakfast? The only thing she mentioned to me was to make sure I brought you back before dark. Frankly I'm a little surprised that she hasn't been monitoring you much more closely."

Sofia paused for quite some time before speaking, and then she delivered the news in a low, understated tone.

"She's dating again."

The words cut through the air and right to the point, as Sofia leveled her gaze at Grandpa Prudy.

"Really!" he said. He then waited in silence for the rest of the story.

"So, her attention has pretty much been redirected," added Sofia.

"Are you saying that she is dating one person and that she considers this person to be... important?" he asked.

"Yeah, I guess. He is all she seems to think about lately—that and how to try to stay looking young," she continued.

"I see. And what do you think of all that?" he asked, trying to encourage her to share more.

"Well, it doesn't seem to me that she's able to think of more than one thing in her life at a time! Anyway, that's fine with me. I want to spend tomorrow doing exactly this, and if her attention is somewhere else, it just makes it all the easier," reasoned Sofia.

"Well, I'm sure she still loves you very much. You're her little girl." There was love and reassurance in Grandpa Prudy's voice.

"This is just part of growing up, and this is giving you a chance to see that your mom is human with all the things that go along with being human. She's probably happy that we can spend this time together. So, like you said, it just means that it will be easier to pick up our search tomorrow right where we left off!"

Sofia replied with, "Let's go then."

"Well, you certainly have had a very transformative day," announced Walter. "How many people are there in the world like you who can say that they've had a conversation with a squirrel?"

"Nobody, remember? This is just between us! I'm not saying anything to anybody!" corrected Sofia.

"You are absolutely right!" Walter replied.

Few other words were spoken all the way back up to the top. They climbed into Grandpa Prudy's pickup.

As he drove her home, he just wanted his granddaughter to let all the things that happened that day percolate for a while. They would talk again in the morning.

HISS AND CHATTER

Teek addressed his group in a quiet tone. "Peeps, can you take the rear of our group as we go and keep your eyes and ears open for anything that might be sneaking up behind us?"

"Yes, Teek, I will," Peeps replied.

Teek continued, "The rest of you stay focused and stay wary. We all need to be looking out. We should figure out how close the rats are. The worst thing we could do is to lead them right to Rimrock!"

"Teek?"

"Yes, Cicci."

"Something just occurred to me."

"Yes?"

"Well, I was thinking now that we seem to be over halfway home, I am starting to wonder... if there *are* rats following us, well..." she thought out loud.

"Continue," he encouraged.

"Well, maybe we do not keep heading for the colony just yet. Maybe we find some sort of vantage point to hide in. Maybe we make sure that they are not still following us. As it is, we just keep leading them to our colony."

"They will just not go away! They do not give up," added Cheeks.

Teek responded, "We need to know where they are to gain the kind of advantage that you are thinking of Cicci. To start with, let's get off this main pathway."

Since they were already up above the rimrock cliff, they decided to move farther up the hill. They found a rocky outcrop just below the top, and before the beginning of the burned area. It afforded a clear view of the deer path they had been traveling on and a good place to hide.

They stayed hidden and quiet for what seemed to be a long while. Then they noticed some activity in the clearing. Large numbers of different creatures were now all using the path.

To the group's complete surprise, the pathway they had been traveling on was heavily used by many of the creatures of the canyon.

First, three mule deer walked cautiously by, sniffing the air and flapping their ears, and then a rather sizable bobcat crept through the clearing. They all ducked down out of sight upon its appearance.

Teek could just see through a crack in the rock. The bobcat sniffed the ground where Teek and his group had previously assembled and, immediately upon picking up the scent, turned its head in the direction the squirrels had just traveled. It changed course and headed right for them.

"I think we may be in trouble," Teek reported.

Just then, a loud "Craow-crooa-kkk!" rang out from off the edge of the cliff.

The bobcat spun around in time to see a large black bird swoop down just out of reach yet close enough to cause the cat to leap toward it. *Whoop-whoop-whoop.* The large black bird circled and headed back downriver.

The bobcat landed at the edge of the cliff and watched the bird fly away. Its attention now directed downriver, it seemed to pick up a different scent and so continued down the path along the edge of the cliffs.

"Was that Kanti?" Peeps asked.

"I think so," replied Teek. "It was hard to tell through the trees, but who else would it be? That bird might have just saved us from a terrible fate."

"Well then, it probably was. He *did* say he would keep an eye out," added Cicci.

"Good old Kanti!" declared Cheeks, a note of relief in his voice.

Their reprieve didn't last long. Soon a coyote moved swiftly by, but it was clearly on its way somewhere. Everything seemed headed in the same direction, downriver.

"Well, this certainly is a major pathway. It looks like we got off just in time," said Peeps. "I wonder what they are looking for," he continued. "It looks as though they might all be after the same thing."

The clearing in the path that lay before them was now empty of visitors, but they were not ready to test their luck by resuming their journey just yet.

And so, they waited. They waited for quite some time. Peeps was curled up taking a nap, and Cheeks was sorting through his satchel. Teek and Cicci were huddled together at one end of the outcrop of rock, where they rested against the back of the ledge with a good view of the trail below.

They whispered to each other about where they had been, where they were headed, what it meant to them both, and what they meant to each other.

To anyone or anything passing by, there was no sight, no sound, and no sign of their presence. They were undetectable.

Teek just happened to have looked toward the path below in time to notice movement in a small bush at the base of a boulder. He lifted a paw to silently let Cicci know that something had caught his attention. Teek and Cicci peered over the ledge, focusing their attention on the rustling bitterbrush.

Two whiskered noses emerged from under the leaves, and then eyes and ears could be seen sniffing and looking around.

"Rats!" announced Teek. "The rats are here! Stay low and stay quiet!"

At this point, he had gotten the attention of Cheeks, who then roused Peeps. The two were crouched behind Teek and Cicci, out of sight and silent.

The thought of an approaching pack of rats was the worst possible turn of events. Although Teek and the others had hoped that they could avoid another encounter with a marauding pack, the possibility had always been on their minds.

And now the rats had arrived and were about to swarm into the clearing before them. The squirrels felt that their fear was beginning to build to overwhelming levels when they realized that there were only two rats emerging from the bush.

"There are only two of them. Look how small they are!" whispered Cicci.

The two small rats, unaware that they were being watched, gathered enough courage to crawl out from under their cover into the clearing of the trail. Their noses sniffed the air to try to identify the slightest sign of any others nearby.

"They look so young. They do not look as though they are searching for us, Teek. They look confused. Do you think they may be lost?" Cicci asked.

"Rats always look 'sorta lost,'" replied Teek. "Don't move everyone."

"Are there any more of them?" asked Peeps.

No one answered him. The two rats ventured farther into the clearing, and so the squirrels were able to get the first good look at them.

"Well, they *are* young... and small, I can see that," said Teek.

"How do we know that they are not scouts?" asked Cheeks.

"Good question. We should wait a bit and see what happens next," replied Teek.

Once the two rats had moved farther out into the clearing, to the squirrel's surprise, they both lifted their noses and squeaked. "Do you think that they are alerting the others, Teek?" asked Cicci.

"There is no way to know just yet." Teek's eyes stayed fixed on the two rats that were nose-to-nose and appeared to be comforting each other. Teek finally agreed with Cicci's suspicion.

"They do seem lost and, well, they seem... scared too, I guess."

"Shall we make a noise and see what happens?" asked Cicci.

Teek looked at Cicci and then turned back to face the two rats. "When I squeak," he said, "be ready to ditch."

Everyone looked around to find a spot to hide. Teek then let out a squeak! The squirrels all ducked down and waited. Nothing. Not a sound. No sound of marauding rats. Just silence.

Finally, all four squirrels rose up slowly and peered over the edge. There were the two rats standing in the middle of the clearing, staring up at them.

"We're lost," they called.

The squirrels quickly ducked back down behind the rock ledge in alarm. After waiting anxiously, turning to glance at each other's shocked faces, they slowly rose back up and all peered back over the ledge into the clearing.

"We're lost," the two rats called out again.

Teek and Cicci looked at each other, surprised at the outcome. Teek turned to Cicci and said, "I think that they are alone."

And so Teek screeched out to them, "Stop right there!"

The two young rats, startled by his command, jumped a bit, then collected themselves, and stood back up to face the squirrels, whiskers twitching. Teek and the others climbed down off the ledge and approached them.

"What are you doing here? Where are the rest of the rats? Speak!" ordered Teek.

The two young rats were shaking with fright. Still, one of them managed to utter a little high-pitched squeak in reply. The little voice wavered and quivered, just barely able to offer an explanation.

"We... we are lost. We want no trouble," one of them said.

"Then explain yourselves! Where are the others?" barked Teek.

"There are no others," said the other rat.

So, the squirrels continued to approach the two rats across the clearing and stood in a row in front of them. The two young rats quickly and anxiously shared their tale of sadness and horror.

They said that they were the first to be born in the encampment right there above the river. They knew no other place. They had been forced by the old alpha male rat, Sleg, to join a pack of rats that were hunting for ground squirrels. The two knew nearly nothing about why they were hunting for them and held no hatred, resentment, or any other attitude toward Teek and his group.

"Do you have names?" Teek asked.

"We are Hiss and Chatter," one said.

"So, which one of you is which?" asked Teek.

The two young rats looked at each other. One of them said, "We are Hiss."

This was very confusing to Teek. He hadn't yet realized that the rats in this colony had a very limited understanding of individuality. Although they all had names, there was apparently never any other self-awareness or concept of themselves as individuals. This sort of social structure allowed Sleg, the alpha male, and a few other rats closely associated with Sleg to control the other rats more easily in their displaced pack.

"So, you are Hiss, and this is Chatter?"

"Yes, we are," said the other.

The squirrels once again looked at each other with confusion, not understanding the rat's reply.

"What happened? Where are the others?" asked Teek.

"Our hunting pack was attacked. Some of us were killed. The rest fled back to the encampment."

"What attacked you?" asked Cicci.

"Many large creatures showed up suddenly. Some looked a little like dogs, others looked like large cats, and then there were some that flew in and grabbed us with sharp claws. We scattered in all directions. We ran and did not stop. Now we are lost."

"Do you think that Kanti had something to do with that?" asked Peeps.

"You mean that he led all those animals to attack the pack of rats?" asked Cheeks.

"It sounds like something he would do," Peeps added. "It would not surprise me even a little to learn that he had."

"Who?" asked the rat named Chatter.

"Tell you what," Teek said, addressing Peeps and Cheeks, "Cicci and I can take it from here."

"Do you want us to leave?"

"No, just... just let us do the talking," said Teek.

"We are hungry. We are always hungry. We hear about human food but never see any. We think we are supposed to live back over the mountains where there are many more humans, not out here. There is nothing here for us."

"Well, just wait. There will be more people," said Peeps.

"There is plenty of food out here if you know what to look for," said Cheeks.

Teek turned to Cheeks. "Maybe you two should stand over there, Cheeks. Peeps, you and Cheeks position yourself so you can keep an eye on the trail."

"Couldn't keep quiet, could you, Cheeks?" said Peeps.

"Me? You were talking too!" Cheeks replied.

Cicci leaned over and whispered in Teek's ear. "We need to feed them," Cicci concluded.

"Feed them?" Teek was surprised by this idea.

"Yes, do you see?" Cicci continued. "We give them the entire half a biscuit in Cheek's satchel. We make a couple of friends, and we tell them that they are to tell the other rats to go a different direction. Listen, they do not even know why they are out here, Teek."

Turning back to where Cheeks and Peeps were watching, Teek called out, "Hey Cheeks, bring me your satchel."

"What? Why?"

"Just do it!" said Peeps.

Cheeks begrudgingly obeyed the order.

Teek turned back to the two young rats. "I have a large piece of biscuit that I will give you."

The two rats squealed for joy. The one named Chatter rolled over and began crawling submissively toward Teek.

"But...," Teek continued, "if I give this to you, you have to do something for us."

"Yes, yes, we will!" said the one named Hiss.

"Well, let me tell you what it is first," Teek directed.

"Yes!" They were still quite anxious.

So, Teek explained how they were to return to the remainder of their hunting party or their colony and lead them in another direction.

"But we are running away, we are trying to escape the rats from our encampment," said the one named Chatter. "We are not planning on going back."

Teek looked at Cicci. Cicci kept her eyes on the two rats. "Where will you be going?" she asked.

"We do not really know. We just know that we do not want to return to the encampment."

"Well, I cannot blame you," she replied.

"We thought we would start one of our own little colonies somewhere."

They looked at each other fondly. Cicci and Teek looked at each other knowingly.

"Take this."

Teek handed the remains of the biscuit to them. They took it eagerly and began eating like they hadn't eaten for quite some time.

"So, if you see any of your, uh, fellow, uh..."

"It is all right we know you do not want us around."

"Oh no, not you, specifically. It is just that—"

"No, really, you can say that. We do not like them either. That is why we are looking for another place to live. But if we *do* encounter any of them, and we hope that does not happen, we will do everything we can to send them in another direction. After what we just went through, we think it is more likely that they are not following you now. The attack was so fierce, and there were so many predators, well, many of the rats in the hunting party were taken. And those that were left scattered, we believe that it is most likely that they ran back to the encampment to face the wrath of Sleg."

Teek's tone changed; he pitied the two rats.

"We wish good things for you both. Be very careful and look out. There are many things that you will need to stay hidden from out here. Many of the most dangerous predators are birds. We have a word we frequently use that you may find useful. The word is *ditch*. When any of *us* hear *ditch* called out, we scramble to hide in something like a rock or, well, anything we can find quickly...a hole or burrow. If either of you sense any danger, just shout the word, and know that both of you need to dive for cover as fast as you can. Food is everywhere, but you need to learn how to recognize it. It does not come from people."

Teek and Cicci told them what to forage for and then directed the two rats to the tower rock by the river where the squirrels had spent the night just after being captured by the rats, the same location where Fisk had recovered the Illumination Stone. It was defensible.

Hiss and Chatter departed, surprised to learn about the good nature of ground squirrels, which was not at all what they had been told, and grateful for the help that Teek and Cicci had provided.

Teek spoke. "Well, this is quite good news, and it means that Kanti is convincing other creatures that they are rewarded whenever they look out for us, or at least when they attack rats."

"I only hope that Hiss and Chatter find a safe place," Cicci replied.

Teek, Cicci, Peeps, and Cheeks stood side by side watching the two rats head back north downriver.

Cicci's plan had worked. She had successfully initiated a change in the way rats and squirrels regarded each other.

IMPORTANT LESSONS

Sofia heard the tires of Grandpa Prudy's truck crunching on the driveway at ten minutes after seven that next morning. She was waiting on the front porch, dressed for the mission.

Her long chestnut hair was tied up in pigtails so tight that they could have been used for rope. She was clad in her favorite pair of overalls, work shirt, high-topped boots, and a jacket.

Her mother, Helen, had come home late the night before, well after Sofia had already gone to bed. Although she had instructed Walter to have Sofia home before dark, she wasn't around to notice. And so, Sofia knew that her mother wouldn't be up and around to notice her getting an early start.

She hopped into Grandpa Prudy's pickup and blurted out a hurried "Let's go."

"Does your mom know you're leaving?" asked her grandfather.

"I left her a note. She's still in bed. She got home late after I was already asleep."

"Lovely," he replied. "She's not going to appreciate me taking you away without you letting her know where you're going and when you'll be back," he added.

Sofia responded, "Grandpa, she already said that she was happy that we would be able to spend the whole weekend together!"

"She said that?"

"Yes! And my note says that we wanted to get an early start and that we'd be back before dark... and..."

"What? And what?" Walter insisted.

"Well, I said that we were going fishing," replied Sofia.

Walter just kept driving without saying a word. Finally, he spoke. "You know, I don't want to see you get used to lying, Sofia. You'll start out thinking that lying is easier than the truth, but it's not. You'll have to lie to cover a lie, and that's how it starts. I've always been painfully honest and I'm proud of that. Sure, telling the truth sometimes makes people uncomfortable, or even angry. Sometimes people don't want to hear the truth, but at least *I* know it's the truth. That gives me a good feeling about myself, a feeling of peace. If you only speak the truth, you don't have to remember what you said. It's a lot easier. And I'll tell you something else, to stay tuned in to these critters, you must maintain a pure heart. Do you understand, Sofia?"

"I do, I'll be honest and try not to lie, Grandpa."

They drove in silence for a few moments. Sofia had a chance to think about the story she had chosen to tell her mother.

"You have to admit, fishing is a pretty good excuse for leaving the house at 7:00 am, and I figured that you probably didn't want me to tell her that we had to leave early to hike down into the Deschutes Canyon and search for a ground squirrel friend of yours so that you could help him bring a magic gemstone back to his colony, enabling a ground squirrel village—complete with little cottages, mind you—to continue to meet in a great hall and listen to elder squirrels recount stories of their history, did you? Well? Did you, Grandpa? Or would you have preferred that I tell her that story?"

Grandpa Prudy turned to look at Sofia with the same look that would have crossed his face whenever he realized that he had just lost a court case.

"Hmm?" she added with a little smile.

"You're dangerous!" he said. "Just remember what I said. It is okay to be clever, but never get used to lying."

"Well, I don't remember the clever part, but I do understand, Grandpa."

Grandpa Prudy returned his attention to the road ahead, muttering, "You'd make a good lawyer."

Then finally turning back to her, he concluded, "Well, okay, agreed. A fishing trip, it is. I suppose that, in a way, we *are* fishing."

Sofia shifted her attention to the task ahead. "I have a good feeling about today, Grandpa."

"You do?"

"Yes. I had a dream last night."

Sofia let that comment hang in the air for a few moments, waiting for her grandpa to show some interest.

"Well? What was it about?"

Sofia needed no further encouragement. "Well, I dreamed that I was on the edge of the cliffs looking down into the canyon and, um, but then I looked over, and there they were."

"There *who* were?"

The sound of tires ground into the gravel as Walter pulled off the road and stopped in a turnout. He put the pickup in park and sat staring intently at Sofia.

"What? What is it, Grandpa?" Sofia asked in a coy manner.

"Tell me all about your dream!"

"It was just a dream, Grandpa!"

"Sofia, it may not have been *just* a dream," he began. "At least, it's very possible that it wasn't."

"Well, if it wasn't a dream, what was it?" she asked.

"Okay, it *was* a dream," he continued, "but you see, sometimes dreams are about things that are not just created by our imagination. Sometimes, well, some dreams are more than that. I think that sometimes we go places," he explained.

"I didn't leave my bed, and I don't sleepwalk, and even if I did sleepwalk, I definitely wouldn't go *that* far," she reasoned.

"No, not physically. Our minds are more powerful than most imagine. And always remember, you made a connection on the riverbank with the squirrel Seek, and *that* is powerful stuff, especially if you already have abilities for such things. You are very special, Sofia. Your dream could very well provide us with some useful information. From now on, you need to pay close attention to anything that you feel, sense, or..."

"Or dream?" she added.

"Yes," he confirmed. "Pay especially close attention to a dream! Any hunches you get you need to listen to them. Trust them. Remember them. This is an important moment in your life, Sofia. Don't just assume it means nothing, like everyone else. These are the things that will make you extra special. So, tell me about the dream."

"I will if you start driving and get us there," she replied.

Without another word, the wheels were spinning and grinding on the gravel once again. They were back on the road. The sweet cool morning breeze whipped through the cab of the pickup, giving them a preview of the fresh, wondrous beauty that awaited them.

They passed fields with large circular bales of alfalfa that cast long cool morning shadows, and one of them hid a couple of mule deer grazing on the extra alfalfa littering the ground.

The morning sun shone through the window of the pickup, illuminating Sofia's still sleepy face in a warm glow. Her eyes lit up as she began to relate the events of her dream.

"Okay, so I dreamed I was on the edge of the cliffs looking down into the canyon," she began. "So then, I looked over and this group of squirrels, they were ground squirrels, were walking right past me. They didn't notice me. One of them was dragging some sticks, and it had some sorta bright orange thing on it. I couldn't really make it out. It was probably the stone that they're bringing back. Anyway, they were in a big hurry because there was this bunch of rats that was kind of trailing them."

"Not good," said Grandpa Prudy. "Then what happened?"

"Then I woke up," she said.

"That's it? That was your dream?"

"Well, yeah, I think Mom had just come home, and she was slamming the cupboards, so that woke me up." As Sofia finished revealing her dream, she watched Grandpa Prudy turn his head toward his window, slowly shaking it in frustration.

They arrived and parked the truck in the gravel parking area at the trailhead.

"Sofia, make sure that you watch me carefully while we hike down," said Grandpa Prudy. "I'll try not to be in a hurry."

"I'll go down first. You stay right behind me, Grandpa. We'll make sure that we get you down there," she assured him.

They headed down into the canyon, and Sofia helped her grandpa navigate the narrow and steep switchbacks.

"I hear a lot of activity in the canyon this morning. Listen to all the birds! Let's stop and listen for a moment, Grandpa," she said.

Grandpa Prudy stopped, but his attention was not as much on the chirping birds as it was on watching his granddaughter notice and understand the sounds and activity of creatures in the canyon. Sofia possessed a very special ability. She had a sensibility about her that had become increasingly rare in modern humans.

No matter how careful most humans tried to be while in natural places, there was something they had lost over thousands of years. They had lost an acute and intuitive perception of the natural world, a special sensory perception that had been developed from the need to use all their senses at once.

A long time ago, humans lived in harmony with the earth, alongside the other creatures. Over thousands of years, humans had separated themselves from the natural environment and from the other creatures.

Many humans even now are born to a greater or lesser degree with a close enough connection to the earth that this sensibility is part of who they are. Trying to remove this connection is like trying to change their personality.

Separating a child who has this tendency from the natural world is like trying to change a left-handed person into a right-handed one simply because the parent believes that it is the correct thing to do. To reconnect a human, they need to be awakened from that state of separation by a creature that is still living *in* the natural world.

And this is what happened to Sofia. She was born with this natural sensibility, which was then awakened by Seek. Walter knew this. He could see it in her, as could the creatures of the canyon.

So, it was particularly important at this stage in her life for her to benefit from the guidance of Grandpa Prudy. He would help her continue to develop and use the precious gift that she had been given.

They both came to realize just how lucky they were. Walter felt blessed that his granddaughter had been gifted with this ancient and valuable ability, and Sofia felt quite lucky that her grandpa was there to notice it, to nurture it, and to help her develop it.

"Hey, you're running into me, Grandpa, careful!" Walter's attention had abruptly returned from thoughts of Sofia's special abilities as he collided with her.

They had reached the river and were now headed down its banks through the high undergrowth. Sofia was clearly a girl on a mission. She silently raised her hand to stop his movement.

Their attention turned to snapping and rustling sounds as a small family of deer moved through some dense undercover into an area of lush grasses.

"Well, I might as well let them know we're here."

Sofia purposely picked up a small branch and snapped it in half. One of the adults instantly raised its head, ears pointed in their direction. Their white tails stood straight up and waved back and forth as they hurriedly trotted and bounded back around the bend and farther downriver.

"You wanted them to know you were here, didn't you, sweetie?" asked Grandpa Walter.

"Yes," replied Sofia.

He continued, "Even though you know that you could have gotten a lot closer to them?"

"Yes," she replied. "Even though I could have gotten closer. I don't want them to feel comfortable being near humans."

Walter beamed with pride. "It would put them in greater danger, wouldn't it? Befriending them would be a selfish act. Good for you!" he said. "We should never use our abilities to prove anything to ourselves or others, or to entertain ourselves," he added.

"All right, but what about the squirrels?" Sofia asked. "They need our help."

"Yes, but they made that clear to us, didn't they? Most of the time, they won't need us."

Sofia stared at her grandpa. This thinking presented a new perspective. She was realizing just how privileged she was to have such a special ability—an ability that so few others had.

With it came responsibility. She had a new and special relationship with the creatures in the canyon, and that was something to be proud of, and yet it was something that couldn't be shared with anyone.

She could also see how her grandpa was revealing to her a valuable lesson. He was letting her know how much he deeply cared for and respected the lives of these creatures. As they watched the deer bound away, Sofia shared her thoughts with her grandpa.

"They don't need or want us to care for them, do they? They just need us to let them live their lives in the special places that they need to live. We hurt them because we try to live where they live."

"Yes," he replied. "It's okay to visit them, but only if you do so with respect and care. With your ability comes great responsibility. It may not seem to you to be as much fun, but it is far better for them. You understand this?"

"I do, Grandpa. Grandpa, maybe understanding this is what it should mean to be a human?"

"Yes, Sofia, that is exactly right. You *do* understand. I am so proud of you. You have been awakened."

THE SMELL OF A MEMORY

Teek retrieved the travois, gathered his group, and continued upriver. This time they traveled parallel to, but not on, the trail so that they could stay hidden.

"I have been thinking," Cicci began.

"Again?" inserted Peeps.

"Shut up, Peeps!" everyone squeaked in unison.

She continued her thought to Teek, staring at the now sheepish Peeps.

"It seems as though, while actually being away from our colony, we have done quite a lot *for* our colony. Our village has been hidden from the rest of the canyon for so long. Well, I was just wondering... we seem to now have friends that we never would have had. We know creatures that we never would have known if we had not ventured away from the village. And as we have discovered, we were not all that much safer staying *in* our village than we have been out here."

Cheeks caught some of what Cicci was saying and contributed his perspective.

"To be honest," he commented, "I would still feel safer if I were back in our village. I sure have learned a lot, though."

"We appreciate your honesty, Cheeks, but I think Cicci is right. We are no safer hiding from others than we are going out to meet them. In fact, we may now be safer," Teek replied.

"For nuts' sakes, Teek, you still insist on being the one burdened with the stone! Can you please let me help?" Peeps implored.

"All right, Master Peeps, give it a try. Just remember, it is a heavy load, and we need to keep moving. Help me drag it over to that large flat rock on the edge of the cliff. That one lit by the bright light of day, it might be warmer. That spot will be a good place to rest in," answered Teek.

Once they reached the flat rock ledge with the travois, Peeps helped Teek remove his heavy burden. They then all turned to face the beautiful view of the river and warmed in the bright light of day.

"Teek, what is it? What is wrong?" asked Cicci.

"I am not sure," he replied. "There is a strange smell on this rock, sort of sweet but not a good sweet. It is sort of putrid and musky."

"I smell it, too," reported Cheeks.

"How very odd," Teek continued. "I believe that I have smelled this before somewhere. Where have I smelled this?" He thought back through all the places he knew, all the places he had been.

Strangely enough, out of all the places they had been, the one that stood out the most in his mind was the Great Hall back in Rimrock. The sense of smell is said to be responsible for more memory triggering than any of the other senses.

For squirrels, this had always been especially true. Stories told by the story elders often included how something smelled. It is a very important way to remember the details of an event. "

The Great Hall! Yes, that was where I smelled this before," Teek declared aloud to Cicci. "Why the Great Hall? The hall never smelled like this, except maybe one time, I remember being called to the hall by Eechius and Seek. That was the day that they discovered that the Illumination Stone had gone missing. The day we figured out how it had happened. I remember now this is what it smelled like after..."

He stopped sorting through his memory quite suddenly in the middle of his words. His eyes grew wide.

"Do not turn around," he whispered. "Just ditch right now... Ditch!"

Without another word, Peeps and Cheeks shot out in either direction. Cicci did not move from Teek's side.

"I said ditch!"

"No, not without you!" she insisted.

They both turned around to behold an unexpected and terrifying sight. The enormous gopher snake, Ish, had returned to his favorite warming rock and was now coiled for a strike.

"Well, well, well, ssssso look what we have here. What a ssssur-prisssse and ssssso convenient. No doubt you did not exxxxpect to ssssssee me."

Teek and Cicci stood frozen in fear. Teek held onto the two main poles of the travois. Cicci crouched behind Teek.

"Ssssso you found your sssssstone, did you? I must sssssay, I managed to find and feed on many of you young sssssquirrelsssss. I have managed to get sssome ratsssss, too, but they have a funny tassssste." His strange sweet musky smell was stronger and thicker in the air than ever as he prepared to strike. "You mussst have traveled a long way, only to end it all like thisssss... pity."

With the speed of a lightning bolt, he struck with a gaping open maw showing rows of needle-like teeth. Teek lifted the travois up just in time to block Ish's strike. The stone served as a shield.

Ish's jaws rammed into it so hard that with two squeaks, Teek and Cicci, along with the travois carrying the stone, were knocked backward and over the side of the cliff with Cicci still clutching Teek tightly. The two of them were propelled over the side, plunging down to a long drop.

As they continued to fall, everything around them seemed to slow down. Maybe their thoughts had sped up.

For whatever reason, Teek was just able to glance back up to the top of the ledge of the rimrock. In an instant, he thought he caught a glimpse of a muha, a red-tailed hawk, swooping by.

While the squirrels had been on the ledge, Kanti had been soaring up above, keeping an eye out. He had alerted one hawk named Apita about the whereabouts of Ish. Apita was the young hawk that had attempted to catch the snake before. The hawks were in a perfect position for a bird's-eye view of the developing scene below. Apita, the youngest of the hawks, was more open to the idea of allowing Kanti to approach where they were soaring, and so he heard him call out to them and listened to what he wanted to tell them.

The other older hawks had decided to maintain a rather lofty and detached viewpoint. They had chosen not to associate with ravens, and so they ascended even higher to avoid him. But Apita listened to Kanti and so soared down and timed his attack just as Ish had lunged toward the two squirrels.

As the snake lunged, Apita struck, making a perfect grab. He sank his talons into the back of the snake, this time right behind the snake's head so to avoided Ish's bite. The size of the snake weighted down Apita's flight to the point where he had to flap for all he was worth to gain altitude. The full length of the snake's powerful coils writhed and wrapped around Apita's legs.

Ish struggled with all his strength, turning his head one way and then the other in the attempt to bite Apita. He knew that if he did, the bird would drop him, as he had before. But it was not to be this time.

Apita was brave and determined. This was not just an opportunity for a meal; he was providing a valuable service. It was his time to show that he was now strong and powerful. He was a raptor to be reckoned with!

The struggle was too great for Apita to fight *and* fly at the same time, so he landed on a ledge at the top of the rimrock on the other side of the river.

Ish thrashed and hissed, wrapping himself around Apita, trying to get a grip so that he could squeeze the life out of him. His maw was open wide, ready to clamp down, but Apita's mighty talons held fast.

With a lightning quick strike, Apita's powerful beak severed the snake's head, allowing him to regain his hold of the still writhing serpent.

The snake finally became limp and lifeless. That was the end of Ish, the gopher snake.

Apita, lifting his head, screeched a mighty rapturous screech of victory and flew off with his prize. He knew he had proven himself to the other hawks with a victory over the most dangerous of foes. He knew that he had just played a vital role in the canyon community and had greatly helped the other creatures.

With that event, Apita became a big part of local legend and folklore. He had just written a new chapter for the lives of his fellow creatures. His heroic battle would be a tale told in the Great Hall and throughout the canyon for many great cycles to come.

DESTINIES MERGE

Teek and Cicci fell for what seemed to be a frighteningly long time. The longer they fell, the more terrified they became. The horror of a long fall seems most acute when one becomes aware that they are still falling.

Halfway down, they turned to each other and screeched in helpless panic, having had time to fully grasp the gravity of their situation. Down they fell and then—*Foop!* What had happened? How could this be?

They were not hurt. All was quiet and completely dark.

"Did you catch them?"

Teek heard a muffled yet familiar voice. An opening appeared above their heads.

As it opened wider, in front of them were two human faces, almost silhouetted but still discernible. Teek looked up. He did not recognize Sofia, but next to her was Walter Prudy's smiling face.

"Walter?" Teek chirped. "Is that you, Walter?"

"Walter Prudy, two names," came the reply.

"Walter Prudy! You *did* come to save us! I could not be happier to see you!" Teek chirped again.

Walter immediately introduced his granddaughter. "This is Sofia."

"Hello, are you Teek?" she asked warmly.

"Yes," he replied. "I am."

"Grandpa has told me all about you," she continued. "I am so glad that we were here to catch you! You are unharmed?"

"Yes! Well done!" answered Teek.

Sofia explained, "I met Seek, you see. He awakened me so that I could understand you. Do you understand me?" As she said this, she set Teek and Cicci down gently, opened her jacket, and stepped back.

Teek and Cicci crawled out. "Oh, yes, I can," Teek replied. "We understand *every* human, but what must now be different is that, thanks to Seek, you understand *us*. And you saved us! I thought we were done for."

"So, we meet again. Look who's falling now," said Walter.

"Yes, and here you are! I didn't think I would ever see you again. How...?"

"You have Sofia here to thank," Walter said with a smile. "She was definitely in the right place at the right time."

"Sofia, are you Walter Prudy's offspring?"

"I am the daughter of his daughter. I'm his granddaughter," she answered.

"You say that Seek awakened you? You have met Seek?"

"Yes, I have," she replied.

Walter then filled Teek in on the series of events, adding, "Fortunately, Sofia doesn't miss a thing. She noticed a red-tailed hawk circling and then spotted you on the top of the cliff. She just happened to be at the base of it below you. Then she watched your other two squirrel companions scamper away in opposite directions from the snake. One went one way, and one went the other."

"What happened to the snake?" asked Teek.

"The hawk swooped down, grabbed the snake, and carried it away," Sofia answered.

She and her grandpa would come to find out that they had, in fact, witnessed the final demise of Ish.

Teek stood by Cicci, who was still dazed and recovering from the traumatic fall.

"Your timing was, well, it was... you caught us!" he managed to say with a gulp.

The timing of Walter and Sofia was so uncanny that Teek paused to add the event to a series of events that, to him, could not have been anything less than destiny. He was, in fact, still puzzled by Fisk finding the stone in the first place and then how the travois mysteriously appeared behind him when he was leaving the burial chamber, and now he wondered what the likelihood was that Walter and Sofia just happened to be directly below them the moment that he and Cicci had fallen from the cliff.

"So, who is this with you, Teek?" asked Walter. Cicci, still trying to recover from the shock of the fall, the strange landing, and the humans, was a bit overwhelmed.

Nevertheless, she managed to gather herself enough to step forward and introduce herself. "I am Cicci."

Whereupon Teek added, "Without whom, we would never have made it this far."

Cicci had never been this close to humans and, like Teek, was still visibly shaken from the fall.

Sofia knelt to her knees, sensing that Cicci had just been through a lot. She sat silently and reverently and hoped that by kneeling she would become less threatening to Cicci. She understood that Cicci and all the squirrels needed a quiet moment to recover from all that they had been through.

Sofia spoke ever so softly. "Cicci, don't worry, you are safe now. We will take you back to your colony. It's not far at all. You have made it. Everything is going to be all right now."

Teek's recollection of the moments before they fell off the cliff started returning to him. He looked around. "We need to find Peeps and Cheeks. Did you see them?" he asked the humans.

"I did see two squirrels dash off in either direction up there just before you fell,,"said Sofia.

"Good, they must be around somewhere. I will go search for them," said Teek.

He didn't have far to go. The two had come down from the top of the Rimrock to search for Teek and Cicci.

At the bottom of the cliff, they had located the travois with the Illumination Stone still attached. But Peeps and Cheeks weren't prepared to see the humans, and so they scampered under a bush as soon as they noticed Walter and Sofia.

Teek looked back at Cicci. "I found them. I will go, let them know that we are here and safe."

"Peeps! Cheeks! This is Teek. Are you in there?"

"Yes, we are in here!" came a voice from within a thicket. "Why did you not ditch? Who are the humans?" Peeps asked.

"Do you remember the human who fell down the hill? You came out of the village to see him? The one who was hearing and understanding me? That was Walter Prudy. He is here to help us, and he is with his offspring, Sofia—"

"Granddaughter," repeated Walter.

"She is just like Walter. Seek awakened her," Teek went on. There was a long silence, so long, in fact, that Teek called out again. "Did you hear me?"

There was more silence, and then he heard a faint "Yes."

"Well, come on out then!"

More silence then. "Cheeks is not ready to move."

Teek called out again, "Cheeks... Cheeks!"

"Yes," Cheeks replied.

"We are almost home, Cheeks. Just a little more," Teek continued.

"We have the stone, and we are almost home. C'mon, Cheeks," Peeps prodded, and then reporting back to Teek, he added, "I think he just needs a little time."

Teek turned to head back to Cicci, Walter, and Sofia, saying "Maybe he can just come out a little way and see them from a distance."

"Yes, I think he is getting close," Peeps called after him.

Cicci positioned herself uphill on a rock behind Teek. She spoke to Sofia. "Seek awakened you?"

"He did," replied Sofia, "but Grandpa Prudy was the one who truly awakened me. He told me about you, and he helped me understand what sort of person I really am."

She turned to her grandpa and directed her words to him. "A lot has happened since you came to visit, Grandpa. A lot has changed in me. I am grateful for what you have done for me, for what you have awakened in me. And I... I love you, Grandpa."

Walter had never received better news. "Well, I love you, too, sweetie."

"I want to make sure that Teek and Cicci know that you have more going on in you than I ever did. You are still young, yet you have maturity beyond your years. Teek, Cicci, Sofia knows how to get you home."

Walter and Sofia sat quietly on a log and waited for Teek and the others to fully recover and gather themselves after their ordeal. They had been through a lot. They had endured hardships the likes of which none of them had ever experienced, or ever even imagined, before.

"Teek," said Walter, "maybe it would be a good time for all of you to just rest here for a while. Allow yourselves a few moments of peace. Let's take a short break and just make sure that everyone is all right. Sometimes doing nothing is the best thing to do. It's the most constructive thing to do. We'll make sure you get the rest of the way home."

"Yes, I think you are right. Thank you," said Teek. "We will sit now and rest for a little while."

"We certainly needed your help."

"Yes, Sofia was there for you."

Walter paused and looked at Sofia.

"Do you want to take the responsibility to check in on our friends in this canyon when they need you? Can you check up on them every so often? Are you willing to make this decision, Sofia?"

"Yes, I am," she said without hesitating.

Grandpa Prudy's gaze turned toward the slope on the opposite bank as he reflected. "Looking back now, I don't think that I made all the right decisions in my life. I didn't always do what was best, but I think that you will."

Sofia looked up from her focus on the squirrels.

"Grandpa? What do you mean?"

"Yes, Walter, what are you saying?" asked Teek.

"What I am saying is that my life is changing now."

"Again?" Teek inserted.

"There is much to be done if I am to move here from Portland.

Heck, even after I do, at my age, it's no longer easy for me to hike down into this canyon, especially alone. Sofia? Is this something that you would be willing to include in your life?"

"Would I ever!" she said. Then she checked her excitement, not wanting to alarm the squirrels.

"That's good because you will be in a better position to help now, much better than I will be. And besides, Teek, you may not need us very often. The best thing for humans to do is to let you live your lives, right?"

"Where is this place called Portland?" Teek asked.

"Portland is north and over the mountains, far away from here," answered Walter. "There are more humans there than you can imagine. I'll save that story for some other day."

Sofia pulled out the tapping stick. Holding it in both hands, she looked it over carefully and then raised her gaze to her grandpa.

"I'll do my very best," she promised.

Walter spoke softly and directly to his granddaughter. "Sofia dear, I know that this is a lot to process and understand. I also suspect that life's instruction manual can be pretty hard to read. The plan for each of our lives is far more sophisticated and elegant than most people realize. Most of the time we don't understand what that plan *is* until we look back on it. You just make your best choice at the time. But be sure to make the choice with your heart. Do you think this is something that you actually feel you want for your life?"

"I think it's more than that, Grandpa. I think that it may be who I am." she said.

"Well, you have all of the sensitivity that I ever had and much more. I will be here to help you whenever you need me. I gave you my best tapping stick. I did that because, well, I guess it is part of my legacy. But you'll make better use of them than I ever could. You can sort of look at this as a way for me to 'pass you the baton.' So, take it and run with it! When I move out here, you may have all of my tapping sticks."

"Grandpa, if you retire and move close by, you'll have more time to spend here with me. You *love* it here," she replied.

"Oh, you're so right, and I will. You don't have to worry about that," he said.

Walter looked at Sofia, who looked at Teek. Teek's attention was drawn back to the thicket where Peeps and Cheeks had been hiding. They had emerged and were headed toward the group with the Illumination Stone.

Teek went to meet them to reassure them and to reassume responsibility for the possession of the stone. Peeps and Cheeks joined Cicci over by Sofia.

Walter and Sofia sat and listened to Teek and Cicci tell them of their adventures. Peeps and Cheeks made sure that they added the usual humorous and interesting details to the retelling.

"What did you learn about the stone, Teek?" asked Walter.

"I am still not sure. I will have to think more about it and speak with Eechius and Seek. Right now, I just know that it appears to contain some sort of energy or information from a cave that we have found. This cave holds an ancient human and many, many wondrous things! I think that this ancient human may be the one that I spoke to you about before. It might be that the Illumination Stone has the history of our canyon in it!"

Walter stared at Teek. "This is important information, but I must be careful. A treasure like this is oh so tempting for a human like me, any human for that matter. Sofia and I will discuss this development. Meantime, let us discuss your Illumination Stone."

Sofia looked at her grandpa. He knew she wanted to speak to them, that she had some ideas. And so, he nodded to her an encouraging nod, as if to say, go ahead.

Sofia began, "Hmm, you know, it may be that it focuses energy. Are you sure it is the source of the energy? This stone of yours, well, it may be the origin of your historical stories, but have you ever considered that it may just be a way for you to focus *your* energy? Or maybe focus the energy that is all around you. This object might take energy, or the stories from some source and then channel them or deliver those stories to you so that you can recall them." Sofia sorted through the possibilities.

Teek thought about Sofia's words, remembering his experience while in the chamber of the ancient one, how he was lifted above the land and floated over the canyon. Teek shared what he saw while staring into the many facets of the stone and the many reflections of his own face.

"You know you may be right, Sofia. But it was quite an experience, like nothing I have ever experienced before. I did get the impression that the historic stories were already all around me and contained *in* me, almost as if the ancient human was simply giving me some sort of ability to see them or hear them. That was the first time that I remember thinking or wondering if maybe the stone was simply a tool for delivering those stories, not so much the source of them."

He looked up at Sofia to see what her response might be. Sofia lowered herself closer and spoke very softly.

"I think that you may be the magical one, Teek. I think that you may already possess the power to tell the stories," she said.

Teek then looked at Walter, who said simply, "She's right. She dreams about your whereabouts and your well-being. I could not have helped you very much without Sofia."

Teek turned to look back at Sofia.

"Maybe we can help each other, Teek," Sofia added.

"Well, maybe we should get started. We might as well finish the trip. I have not eaten all day," added Cheeks.

Peeps responded quickly, "Yes, well, that *is* important. Maybe while we are doing that, we might as well return the Illumination Stone to the colony!"

"All right you two, we are almost there, we can finish this. We are almost home, then you can continue picking at each other all you want," said Teek.

Walter and Sofia made the case to Teek and Cicci that the best way to travel the rest of the way back to the colony would be on the shoulders of humans. This idea, however, was completely unnerving to Cheeks. It was as if he was being asked to hop on the back of an elephant.

"You *are* hungry, right Cheeks?" asked Peeps.

"Well, yes, I..." he began.

"Then hop up so we can get home!" Peeps chirped.

"All right, everyone, climb up!" said Sofia.

She had a small day pack on her back, so she tied the sleeves of her coat about her neck and over her pack to give the squirrels a secure place to ride.

They scampered up her sleeve and tucked themselves into the coat on her shoulders. Cheeks, of course, required a lot of coaxing.

"All set?" Walter called. "Is everyone ready? Hang on tight! Off we go!"

THE FINAL LEG

"Teek, let me carry the Illumination Stone for you," encouraged Walter. "Then when we get to the passage that leads to your village, we'll let you down and you can take it the rest of the way in."

"All right, Walter," Teek replied, "but follow us in. I want you and Sofia to be able to be there with us."

Walter walked over to Sofia's shoulder, where Teek was perched. "That is very kind. We would be honored to share that moment with you, my dear friend," he replied.

They headed back up along the river.

"The trail looks pretty good from up here," said Peeps. "What a strange sensation. Hold on, everyone, it is a long way down! I can feel the movement of Sofia's steps. They cover so much ground! They are so long... she is so big... she is massive!"

"Well, thank you for those observations, Peeps," Sofia answered.

"Oh no, uh, not massive for a human, mind you... by squirrel standards."

"Best to stop there, Peeps," said Teek.

Teek leaned over to Cicci. "I am enjoying this. I think that this journey just might end successfully for both of us... together." He spoke softly into Cicci's ear. "I think that we very well may finally be safe."

"I am so proud of you and very happy to be with you," she replied.

It was a beautiful afternoon and a triumphant day, the kind of day that makes you glad just to be alive. Every living thing in the canyon glowed, every color was vivid.

Teek looked all around as they walked along the path. He had never felt a stronger connection to the canyon, or a greater love for it. And he was becoming very fond of Cicci.

A cool afternoon breeze flowed by them and down the river. It flowed just over the surface of the deep gurgling water. The river was more than just flowing water to Teek; it was a source of life for the entire community in the canyon. It flowed through meadows, through forests, undercut banks, past tall reeds and grasses, and around massive boulders.

The geography and ecosystems would change as it rolled northward, but the river flowed through them all, nourishing the land, bringing life to a ribbon of plants and animals along its banks for 252 miles. The river was the very soul of the canyon.

"*Croaw-croak-hroaw!*"

Teek's attention turned to the sky. There, soaring just over their heads, was Kanti. Being of keen eye, Kanti had been well aware of the humans' precious cargo.

Cicci leaned against Teek. "Kanti is a true friend. We should always remember that," she said.

"He sure is a very important part of helping the creatures in this canyon," Teek added. He called to him. "Kanti!"

But Kanti had already banked his flight back across the river and up over the pines and junipers along the opposite side of the river.

"Sofia..."

"Yes, Teek..."

"Could you stop for just a moment at this pool up ahead?" Teek noticed an old familiar creature, rummaging and foraging at the edge of the water. "There is someone I need to say hello to."

"Certainly. Who is it?" she asked.

"A raccoon," he replied. "I do not know his name."

As the two humans approached the pool, the raccoon dropped a crayfish, spun around, and began to make a hasty retreat.

"Hey, you there," Teek called out.

The raccoon stopped in his tracks. The small squeaky voice was vaguely familiar to him. It couldn't be coming from a human! The raccoon turned to look in the direction of the voice.

Teek sat on Sofia's shoulder and peered down at the raccoon. The raccoon was confused and in the middle of trying to figure out whether he should scamper off when Teek asked, "How is the fishing?"

The raccoon was finally able to see Teek sitting on Sofia's shoulder.

"You!" he hissed. "I remember you. Are you the squirrel that all the creatures in the canyon are making such a fuss about? What are you doing on a human?"

"These two humans are not like any other humans. We are their friends," replied Teek. "They are taking us home, to our colony."

"Really? Hsssss, befriending humans? You must have rabies! Well, you and the other squirrels have become quite well known up and down the river, young fella."

Teek ignored his comments, asking instead, "Why are you still fishing? The light of day is high overhead. I thought you only fished at early light."

"I, uh, I did not mean, well, I guess I was in a hurry." As he spoke, he backed up and glanced back and forth, first to Walter and then to Sofia, still quite confused by the squirrels' use of humans as a means of travel.

"It is not easy," he continued. "It is harder and harder to find crayfish. They used to be everywhere. Now I have to fish much longer."

"Hmm. Maybe you should ask others for help?"

"Who?" The raccoon looked puzzled.

"Have you ever talked to an otter?" Teek asked.

"No!" the raccoon said with an indignant tone.

"Well, maybe if you were nice about it and offered to return a favor, you'd have more crayfish than you could eat. Anyway, we must keep moving. You should give that some thought. You never know, you might find that other creatures would help you... So, what is your name?"

"I am Azban," he answered.

"Well, Azban, I am Teek. Teek is my name."

"Hmm, all right, Teek, I will give that some thought," answered the raccoon. Teek turned to Sofia and nodded.

She nodded back and started off again. Teek looked straight ahead, as did Cicci, but Peeps and Cheeks stared at the raccoon as they passed by. They wanted to enjoy every moment of the amazed and bewildered look on the raccoon's face.

"I have to admit that felt good," Teek whispered to Cicci.

"Well, I think that it is safe to assume that this is something he has never seen before," she replied with a little chuckle.

Teek and Cicci were beginning to realize just how much their adventure and their actions had touched and helped the other creatures of the canyon.

By taking the risk of venturing out and representing their colony, they had positively affected the ecology of their region and the great cycle of life. When a single thing is created or destroyed, it affects everything around it. Teek and his friends had set in motion a series of events involving humans, ravens, crows, geese, rats, raptors, and one snake named Ish and, in the process, rejuvenated their colony. In fact, they had made quite an impact on the whole canyon.

"*Weeer wip a wee wee—weeer wip a wee wee.*"

A birdcall rang out just above their heads. A western wood pewee was perched on a dead branch, tipping its head repeatedly to glance down, announcing that the group was passing by.

"Spell that, Sofia," said Walter.

Sofia laughed. "Why don't *you* spell it and *I'll* read it?"

"I think I recognize our cliffs! Are they just up ahead?" asked Cheeks.

Sure enough, as they approached a bend in the river, they stood before a very familiar cliff face that towered over the canyon slope. Sofia's shoulders afforded them a whole new vantage point.

"Rimrock! Home at last!" Cheeks exclaimed.

"I have a feeling, Teek," said Cicci.

"What is it?" he asked.

She attempted to explain. "It is confusing. I am excited to be home. Looking at those cliffs is like, well, it is like seeing a close family member after being parted for a long time. And yet..."

"Yes?"

"And yet I will never be the same. There is so much to see out there. There is such a bigger life with all kinds of creatures to meet. I have changed. The way I think about my sheltered life inside of that cliff, well, that has changed too. It is so small and closed in. It was our entire world and now... Well, I am so very glad I went away. I understand more things, and feeling safe and secure is, well, not actually any safer than being completely exposed to the entire canyon. I feel... free. There is so much more to this."

Teek placed his paw on her shoulder and replied. "You have been pushed and pushed. You have guided us with your wisdom. And I have learned a lot as well, my dear Cicci. I feel the same way. Who knows, we may need to leave Rimrock again and learn more about the canyon... and the world around us one day soon."

Walter walked back over to Sofia's shoulder where Teek and the others were riding.

"Teek," he began, "When we get near your hidden passage, you will probably have to show us where it is. Sofia has never been there, and I won't be able to find the little trail through the dense thicket of brush. It is still upriver some distance and around the bend, so we still have some time before we need to head up hill. For now, I need to rest a little. What would you say about sitting for a little while? There's a meadow just up ahead and some boulders under a large willow tree."

"I like that idea," said Cheeks.

"Thought you might," said Peeps.

"Shut up, Peeps!" said Cheeks.

"Now listen," Teek commented, "you two have been through a lot together. Everyone is different, Peeps."

"Yeah," added Cheeks.

"And Cheeks, that goes for you too. I hope you have both learned that there are a lot of different creatures in the world, all with different interests. And you can bet that the things that they care about are different than what *you* care about. From now on, I hope that you both think about how we are all different and that you are more accepting of that! Peeps, instead of making fun of someone else, find out why they are the way they are. Cheeks, there is more to life than comfort and food. Even though you may not want to venture out to see it for *yourself,* maybe you will begin to appreciate it because of this experience."

Sofia and Walter arrived at a grassy meadow that sloped down to the edge of the river. They sat on some low flat boulders by the edge of the swirling water in the cool shade of a willow tree. The river was wide and shallow. It was near an old road where pioneers had forded across to the other side. Mayflies danced on the water in a small pool eddy next to the bank. The water made splashing and rippling sounds as it tumbled over the shallow gravelly riverbed.

The squirrels climbed down from Sofia's shoulders to rummage through the green grass at her feet. Sofia pulled a snack bar from her pocket, unwrapped it, and took a bite.

"What is that?" asked Cheeks.

"Yes, what is that?" asked Peeps.

"Oh, so now you are interested?" Cheeks responded.

"Well, I have not eaten either!" replied Peeps.

"This is a snack bar or trail bar or granola... Well, anyway, it has nuts, honey, and a berry filling."

"Um, I like all of those things," Cheeks exclaimed.

"All right, I think that squirrels can eat this," she continued, "but you shouldn't eat too much. I'll give all of you a piece."

She broke off chunks of the bar and handed a portion to each squirrel.

"I have never tasted anything so wonderful in all of my life," said Cheeks.

"Well, that usually means that it probably isn't something you should eat all the time, but it will give you all a good boost of energy," said Sofia, now very amused at how eagerly the squirrels nibbled at the chunks of energy bar, quickly turning their morsels over and over with their little front paws.

Walter sat on a stone closer to the bank. His attention was turned toward the river. His gaze started close to shore where an American dipper was perched on a rock.

"*Chirwee-chirwee-cheeep-chip-chip-chip*" was its call. It bobbed up and down and then it bobbed up and down again. Then it dove into the clear little pool just below the rock, looking for aquatic insects.

"Now *that* is a resourceful little bird," Walter said.

Teek was watching the same bird. "It is," he agreed. "I would love to be able to dive into the water for food, but we do not swim. I am quite afraid of slipping into the river. That is how my mother..." He stared at the ground and was unable to finish his words.

Walter shared his moment of silence. Then his attention quickly turned toward some movement that caught his eye across the river.

In a broken-down and very old wooden mine shaft entrance, a mule deer buck had taken up refuge in the shade, escaping the midday sun. The mine shaft was built into the sloping hill so that a somewhat disheveled window on one side of the structure was close enough to the ground to allow the buck to sit quietly and peer through it. Walter had noticed the movement of his large ears, which periodically flapped at the flies. Then lifting his eyes farther up the slope across the river, way up to the top of the Rimrock, he saw two men—one with his hands on his hips, the other was turned to him—talking and gesturing. Both men wore hard hats.

I wonder what sort of damage they're planning, Walter thought, and let out a heavy sigh. "There is less habitat for the natural world than ever," he said softly. "Humans will not stop coming, Teek. The land beyond your canyon is so vast, and there are ever-increasing numbers of humans all around. They will not stop coming. It would be difficult for you to understand this."

Teek stood waiting, staring at Walter, hoping to hear the rest, but Walter just shook his head.

"It is difficult to explain," he added. "It would be nearly impossible for you to understand."

"I did float high above the canyon, but I do not remember seeing any humans that I can recall."

Teek recounted his mystical experience while in the chamber of the ancient one, how he floated over the canyon and how he could see stretches of land leading to the eastern slopes of the Cascades and farther east toward the high desert plateaus.

"I saw these things as well," Walter said. "And I also saw how this world was formed! As important as it was for your vision to be revealed to you, you need to understand that the world is a much bigger place than you realize. There are more people than you can imagine. Maybe someday soon we'll talk about that. For now, it sounds as though you were shown just what that ancient human wanted you to see. Possibly the canyon holds some ancient spirit that wants to awaken the story of this canyon and the surrounding countryside. Maybe that means more than I realize."

Sofia had brought the squirrels some water in the cap of her small thermos. "You should probably take some water," she said. "The energy bar gets a bit dry if you don't wash it down."

The squirrels didn't seem to respond to this. Drinking liquid with every meal was not something they required.

Walter stood up slowly and stretched.

Sofia understood that it meant that it was time to move on. "All right, everyone, back up on my shoulders. It's time to get moving."

Up they all scampered, securing themselves to Sofia's shoulders. Walter and Sofia followed a narrow footpath along the river to approach the rimrock cliffs.

From an outcrop of boulders at the base of the cliff, they could all hear chirps, cheeps, and screeches.

"We have been spotted," said Cicci.

"Do you think they saw us or just Walter and Sofia?" asked Teek.

"The first calls I heard were alarm calls. I am not sure what I heard after that. I think there might be some confusion," she replied.

"There probably is," said Teek. "Seems to me that alarm calls only serve to let everyone know where the colony is," he added.

But Peeps and Cheeks were so excited they almost fell off Sofia's shoulders.

"Now just hold on," Teek said. "Calm down and be careful! I do not want anything happening to you now that you are this close to the end of this long journey."

Walter, walking next to Sofia's shoulders, spoke to Teek. "You'll have to start guiding us to the opening of the passage to your village now."

"I will. As for right now, stay on this path. I believe you will recognize the draw that leads back up to the top. You do not forget *that* fall, I am quite sure," replied Teek.

"Ah yes, I'm sure I will recognize that spot," Walter chuckled.

"Oh, Walter and Sofia," Teek added, "before we enter the village, and everything gets..."

"Exciting?" Walter inserted.

"Yes, exciting," Teek continued, "I would like to thank you again for your help. We could not have survived without you."

"You know, Teek, I can't help but wonder if all of us might have been part of something greater than anything we could have realized," said Sofia.

Teek looked at Walter.

"That's my granddaughter!" Walter stated with pride.

"I think you are right, Sofia. We have been through many events that cause me to believe that we have been guided," replied Teek.

"Speaking of guiding," added Peeps, "we have arrived at the place where we head up the hill. We should guide Sofia and Walter through the brush to the opening of the passage to Rimrock."

"Thank you, Peeps," Teek answered, gesturing up the hill with his front paw. They pushed their way through the brushy thicket until they found the little trail leading to the opening of the passage to Rimrock.

"Teek should go first and drag the travois, followed by Cicci, then Peeps and Cheeks," said Walter.

"You have this all figured out, don't you?" said Sofia.

Walter was quick to reply. "If I've learned anything over the years, it's how to make a good entrance."

Sofia set the squirrels down in the opening of the passage. Walter set the travois next to Teek. They all turned and looked ahead. There peeking around the first turn were two young squirrels. They immediately squeaked, turned, and scampered down the passage toward the village.

"We had better hurry," said Teek, "if we want to catch up with the excitement."

"Onward!" said Walter, ushering Sofia ahead of him. Sofia slid through the opening to the passage following the squirrels toward the village of Rimrock. The squirrels led the way through the massive basalt walls.

3 2

A TRIUMPHANT RETURN

Peeps breathed in deeply. "Do you smell that everyone?" he asked.

The passageway channeled a very familiar gust of cool air, pungent with the smell of lush growing things.

Sofia walked slowly past the gnarled roots of old pine trees, sagebrush and juniper, looking all around her as though she were in a dream. She could see that the cliff walls held all sorts of amazing forms of life. She passed by things that scampered, flittered, crawled, and grew.

"Unbelievable, isn't it, Sofia?" said Walter in a quiet voice.

"Yes, unbelievable," she replied. "How could this be?"

"Oh, just wait. You'll see that there are many things hidden from humans," added Walter. "Oh, stay away from that large dark opening up here in the wall of the passage."

"Why?" she asked.

"Well, it is... sort of... startling. You just need to stay clear of it, trust me!" he continued.

"Okay," she said, looking somewhat perplexed.

Sofia and Walter continued to follow the squirrels down the

passage. Sofia noticed that when the squirrels began to round the next corner, they suddenly stopped. Something was in front of them.

As they drew closer, they began to hear a multitude of cheeps. It sounded very much like a large flock of birds, but there were none flying overhead, and the multitude of cheeps were coming from around the corner of the passageway.

Walter and Sofia peered around the corner. The cheeping stopped suddenly, replaced with a collective gasp. The entire colony was standing at the opening to Rimrock. Every face was looking up at the humans, frozen in shock.

It seemed that no one had prepared the colony for seeing humans at the entrance to their village.

Seek and Eechius squeezed through the crowd of squirrels to reach Teek. Seek turned to address the colony of squirrels holding up both of his front paws.

"Everyone, please, there is no need for alarm! These humans saved Teek. They have been awakened and can understand us when we speak. This is Walter Prudy and his offspring, Sofia."

"Granddaughter," Walter inserted.

"Just go with it," said Peeps, staring out at the entire colony that had turned out to greet them.

Seek continued in his best ceremonial voice, "Teek and these other brave young squirrels have returned our Illumination Stone!"

As Seek finished his announcement, a high-pitched cheer went up, and they all scrambled over to surround Teek, the Illumination Stone, Cicci, Peeps, and Cheeks.

"I never doubted you for a minute." It was Eechius, placing his forepaw on Teek's shoulder.

"Eechius, it is so good to be home. There were moments when we thought we would never return," said Teek.

"Well, I may have worried a bit, but I stayed positive, and I happened to believe that somehow you were not alone."

He grabbed the sides of Teek's face and pulled him close, nose to nose. "You did it, dear boy, you did it! Well done!"

"Well, *we* did it. If it had not been for my friends..."

Eechius looked over at Cicci, who was standing by Teek's side, and then looked back at Teek.

"Oh, I see," he said. "Congratulations to both of you."

"And if it had not been for Walter and Sofia," Teek continued, "we never would have made it. We even made friends with a large raven named Kanti. But I can tell you all about that later."

Walter and Sofia were kneeling behind the squirrels, trying to appear smaller.

"We thank you for returning these fine young squirrels to us," Eechius offered in formal gratitude. "We are all grateful to you, Walter and Sofia. Your lives are so different than ours. We do not know what we could ever do for you, but if we can..."

"Oh no, your well-being and success are reward enough for us."

"I would invite you to my home," said Teek, "but I do not think that I could accommodate even a small part of you!"

Walter chuckled. "I thank you for the thought. Right now, we should go back up the hill and return to our world. We don't want anyone in our family to get worried. And I need to get back over the mountains to Portland so I can move myself closer to you. We'll be back to check in on you."

"Walter," Teek called out, holding up one of the obsidian spear-points from the entrance to the village. "Here, Walter, take this. This means that you are always welcome in our village. Keep this with you and you will find your way back to us. You and Sofia return as soon as you can."

Walter accepted the spearhead from Teek. Holding it in his hand, he realized what a precious and meaningful gift he had just been given.

"I am grateful for this, Teek, and I consider it to be an honor and the most valuable of all my possessions. I will keep this on my person always. It will be a constant reminder of where I'm now headed. This spear point will represent the singular focus of my effort and goal, to return and spend the rest of my life closer to my loved ones. Do not be concerned, Sofia and I will see you again very soon."

"Time to go for now, Sofia... Sofia?"

Sofia was overwhelmed by the entire scene before her. Looking beyond the gathered colony of squirrels, she noticed the village—a tiny landscape of doorways, porches, pathways, and groomed gardens. She was enchanted by a world that only two other humans had ever beheld. "Grandpa, it's a tiny village!"

"Yes, Sofia. This is Rimrock, but for now, we have to leave them to it."

"No look, it's a tiny village!"

"Yes Sofia, you'll see it again soon, and we will return. Let's go now."

Walter gently took the shocked Sofia by the shoulders and turned her around toward the passage. With that, they slipped back through the narrow split in the cliff. Walter spoke into Sofia's ear.

"You must remember never to reveal the Rimrock colony location, Sofia, or even the fact that it exists to any other living thing. You mustn't even mention it outside of these walls. This, above all else, is most important. You have been given a great gift of trust, and so you must honor it."

"I will, Grandpa. I will protect this secret. Forever," she promised.

And so, Walter and Sofia returned to the world of humans.

"Here, let me help you. This way, Teek!" Seek said as he guided them through the entire colony of Rimrock. It was a cheering, chirping, and squeaking crowd of enthusiastic and appreciative squirrels.

"We have prepared a special feast for all of you in the Great Hall. We can bring the Illumination Stone to its place in the center, and then after you have eaten, you can get settled in and rest from your journey. You will be pleased to know that in three cycles, the bright light of day will be aligned with the opening in the ceiling of the Great Hall, and that will be the perfect time for you to tell us of your adventure and how you found the Illumination Stone. This will be the greatest story-telling gathering this colony has had in, well, a very long time!"

"A feast sounds good, is that now?" asked Cheeks.

His mother, Teese, smothered him with kisses. His father, Pinion, patted him on the back, saying with great pride, "I knew you had it in you, Cheeks!"

As Teek made his way through the well-wishing crowd, one broad-shouldered squirrel named Digger squeezed through to greet him.

"Welcome home, Sir Teek. I stayed at Stonewood as we agreed. I did a little burrowing so we can add on a bit. I thought you needed more room."

Digger always thought that there was more to build. He was from a long line of burrow builders.

Teek's home, Stonewood Place, had been the furthest thing from Teek's mind for such a long time that at first Digger's words were puzzling.

"Uh, thank you, Digger," Teek replied hurriedly. "We will have a look."

"Peeps! Oh, Peeps, dear!"

Meep, Peeps' momma, had made her way through the crowd of squirrels.

"I am so proud of you! I have missed you. Let me look at you Peeps! You have grown! You look bigger and stronger!"

"Oh, Momma, I missed you too."

She squeezed Peeps with a big hug.

"All right, all right, Momma. There will be plenty of time for that."

Meep knew that Peeps had grown mentally and physically. She quickly noticed that Peeps now preferred to maintain the dignity of a returning hero, and so she let him continue with the others without a fuss.

Eechius looked over the Illumination Stone-laden travois from one end to the other.

"Teek, you remembered one of the ancient stories! This is most impressive! You have taken on a heavy burden and no doubt found a most ingenious solution."

"Cicci came up with this idea. She remembered one of your stories about how early humans carried their belongings," he explained.

Eechius motioned to a small group of young squirrels that then came scurrying up, ready to help.

"Take our Illumination Stone and follow us to the Great Hall!" he ordered.

Seek and Eechius led the procession up the hill to the large heavy double doors. They opened with a familiar welcoming groan. The two elders, Teek and his group, their family members, and the Illumination Stone made their way down the passageway to the large inner chamber.

Teek noticed that there was not even a dim light shining down from the ceiling, but he could still see inside. He stood underneath and peered up.

Seek explained, "We have closed it off. The ceiling can only be opened from the inside now. The double doors at the beginning of the passageway are also secured. There is no way to enter The Great Hall now, unless you have forepaws like a squirrel! That bright young builder squirrel, Digger, built these things for us. So now there is little chance of anything breaking in again, at least not in the same way, and it keeps the rain and snow out too!"

"It *was* a bit drafty in here," mentioned Teek.

"Oh, and we now have several pieces of reflective glass to send light into our hall from a small opening toward the front, like your home, Teek," Eechus added.

Teek complimented Seek and Eechius on the additions. The young squirrels returned the precious stone back to its place of honor in the center of the Great Hall directly below the opening in the ceiling. Seek clasped his paws at the sight.

Teek looked at Eechius and Seek, asking, "Is everyone still outside?"

"No, no," Seek answered. "They will return after you have rested. In three cycles, the bright light of day will be just right for our first storytelling gathering time in, well, two great cycles! And this time, you all get to share your adventures with us. Now we need to feed you!"

"That's a great idea!" said Cheeks.

"Well, I see that you have not lost your appetite," said his mother, Teese.

"Oh no, Cheeks' appetite was our constant companion!" commented Peeps.

"And I suppose your constant commentary was too?" asked Peeps' mother, Meep.

Teek and Cicci looked at each other knowingly and smiled.

The morning after their triumphant return, Teek and Cicci made their way down the path to the double doors of the Great Hall. Teek released the new latch, and they entered the hallway and headed toward the sanctuary.

Seek and Eechius were in a chamber just off to one side. Teek called out to them, and soon there came a reply through the passageway to the chamber.

"We're in here, come in."

Teek and Cicci entered the chamber.

"We were just starting our day. Here is a cup of water from the spring. Have you eaten?"

Seek handed them both bowls of berries. The story elders expressed their deep, heartfelt gratitude again to Teek and Cicci and then were most anxious to hear the story of their journey.

Teek was, as always, honored to receive praise from the two wise old story elders. They had both noticed a change in Teek.

Seek spoke first. "We have always known that you were a special squirrel, Teek. Now we are noticing something new. When Eechius first greeted you as you entered the village and placed his paw on your shoulder, he felt something. Something he has never felt from you before."

"Teek, I felt an energy field around you," Eechius continued. "I could tell at that moment that something had happened to you. You have experienced an event that has changed you. What happened, Teek?"

Teek told Seek and Eechius the story of the burial chamber and his experience with the ancient human.

"You saw him?" Eechius asked.

"Have you seen him too?" Teek asked in return, surprised.

"Only fleeting glimpses of his spirit, Teek. Both Seek and I were visited, and our fathers before us, and their fathers. Your father was also, Teek. He was supposed to become a story elder, but his time was cut short. We felt that you had been through so much that, well, we just didn't want to ask any more of you. But we have learned something from this experience. We now know that this is who you are. This is your path. We now know that you *can* be a colony story elder, and we suspect that you know this."

Teek spoke. "I learned that the stories of this canyon and of our colony exist in an energy field that is all around us. Our connection to the ancient humans now exists only in this field of energy. It is who we are, and so it is important that we are the keepers of these stories. Our colony needs them, like we need air or water. It must flow through us, like our beloved river."

Seek and Eechius stared at Teek in amazement. The words he spoke seemed to be coming from a place that was beyond the normal realm of the squirrels.

Seek turned to Cicci. "Cicci," he said, "Teek will need your wisdom and guidance. He is very fortunate that you are with him. Teek, Eechius and I both believe that it is time that we suggest that you become a story elder!"

The day for the gathering of the colony arrived, and Teek was presented to the colony as a story elder. There were many good things to eat, much laughter, and many wondrous tales to tell.

With the help of Cicci, Peeps, and Cheeks, Teek told of their journey to find the Illumination Stone. The colony was proud and grateful and, most importantly, united.

The colony was full of energy once again. Neighbors were exchanging pleasantries.

Squirrels were no longer inside hiding but out greeting their neighbors. It was again a place where "Hello friend," "Greetings to you," and "How are you this fine day?" were happily called from one to another.

Neighbors took an interest in each other's well-being. Teek and Cicci were a frequent topic of conversation, but they didn't mind. It was all well-meant.

And so, it can be for all who move through this world with the ability to see the important little things. They are quietly all around us. You may find yourself out in a special natural place, away from cities, subdivisions, and automobiles—a quiet place where creatures live. You may be approached and given a long look by one of those creatures.

Stop and be very still. Listen very carefully for a quiet voice.

You may think you're just imagining it. You're not.

Think about the life of that creature. Know that you are part of that creature's story and that they are a part of yours. Know that everything you do affects them and that everything they do affects you.

If you pay close attention, you may just find that they have awakened something in *you*. Something that you didn't realize was there, quietly waiting for you to notice.

You may even find that you have been given a precious extra

perception you didn't know you had—a special energy that humans used a long time ago to live in harmony with the other creatures of the earth.

The End...
of book one.

ACKNOWLEDGMENTS

Lois Oberdorf, my loving mother; Robert McGuire, a dear friend who is responsible for the printing of the first book, James Turner, a dear friend and patron; Karen Chambers, for developmental editing; Laurel and Fitz Neal, my spiritual guides, mentors, and beta readers; Andrew Zeamer, earliest adopter and beta reader; John W. Oberdorf Jr., my brother and beta reader, Susan McNeil, my sister and beta reader; Ken Miles, a friend and beta reader.

PETER SANDEL

Arriving in Central Oregon at age 5, Peter Sandel grew up inspired by the beauty and natural history of the Pacific Northwest. Walking to and from Bear Creek Elementary School, in Bend, he would notice the ground squirrels foraging through the ponderosa pinecones. Examining the cones, he discov-ered pine nuts and began to nibble on them. Finding them to be a tasty treat, he soon became drawn into the environment around him. So much so, that throughout his young life, the Deschutes River Canyon became his most sacred place.

The first scene of the story was inspired by a real experience Peter had at the top of Lava Butte in Central Oregon, where Peter met the first of two of Central Oregon's finest, Phil Brogan, author of "East of the Cascades," and later, near Fort Rock, Rube Long, co-author of "The Oregon Desert." These two men were "living Central Oregon history." Their words made a big impression on Peter Sandel at a very early age.

Peter would spend many a morning along the Deschutes River, breathing in the sweet-spicy air and watching the sun peak over the rimrock, as the creatures of the canyon began their day. These times along the river would become the most formative of his life.

The family would soon move over the mountains to Salem Oregon, where Peter graduated from Sprague High School and then Oregon State University. During summer months, before and during college, he fought forest fires for the Oregon State Department of Forestry.

After college, Peter spent the next 30 years making his living writing, designing and illustrating as an art director and creative director in locations from the San Francisco Bay Area, to Portland Oregon, and Montana. He has developed and produced everything from advertising campaigns, annual reports, and capability brochures, to SEO copy and other online content, winning several awards for this work.

Peter Sandel's tranquil times along the Deschutes River, hiking and fishing with his father and brother, provided him with insights that would influence him for the rest of his life. While sitting for hours among the local inhabitants of the canyon, he began to understand more about each of them, and the interactions between them. These were the stories and images that would inspire him to create the world of RIMROCK.

www.rimrockbooks.com

ALSO BY

RIMROCK

The Illumination Stone

The Cavern of Ahtūn

Book 3—To Be Announced